GODS AT ODDS

GODS AT ODDS
CASE FILES OF AN URBAN DRUID™ BOOK 7

AUBURN TEMPEST
MICHAEL ANDERLE

DISRUPTIVE IMAGINATION

DON'T MISS OUR NEW RELEASES

Join the LMBPN email list to be notified of new releases and special promotions (which happen often) by following this link:

http://lmbpn.com/email/

This book is a work of fiction. All of the characters, organizations, and events portrayed in this novel are either products of the author's imagination or are used fictitiously. Sometimes both.

Copyright © 2023 LMBPN Publishing
Cover by Fantasy Book Design
Cover copyright © LMBPN Publishing
A Michael Anderle Production

LMBPN Publishing supports the right to free expression and the value of copyright. The purpose of copyright is to encourage writers and artists to produce the creative works that enrich our culture.

The distribution of this book without permission is a theft of the author's intellectual property. If you would like permission to use material from the book (other than for review purposes), please contact support@lmbpn.com. Thank you for your support of the author's rights.

LMBPN Publishing
PMB 196, 2540 South Maryland Pkwy
Las Vegas, NV 89109

Version 1.00, July 2023
eBook ISBN: 979-8-88878-169-2
Print ISBN: 979-8-88878-170-8

THE GODS AT ODDS TEAM

Thanks to our JIT Team:

Dave Hicks
James Caplan
Christopher Gilliard
Kelly O'Donnell
John Ashmore
Diane L. Smith
Deb Mader
Dorothy Lloyd

Editor
SkyFyre Editing Team

THE USUAL SUSPECTS

<u>Clan Cumhaill</u>

Aiden – the oldest of Fi's brothers, druid tank, Toronto police officer, married to Kinu, and father of Jackson, Meg, Ireland, and Carragh.

Bodhmall – Fionn's paternal aunt who raised him and taught him how to be a druid.

Brendan – Fi's brother, second in the birth order, formerly deceased, given back to the family after the Culling and restricted to living on the mythical Celtic island Emhain Abhlach with Emmet.

Calum – Fi's brother, third in the birth order, druid archer, Toronto police officer, and married to Kevin. Together they are foster parents to Bizzy, an otterkie shifter.

Dillan – Fi's brother, fourth in the birth order, druid rogue, Toronto police officer, and in love with Evangeline, Angel of the Choir, formerly a reaper, and now a guardian angel.

Dionysus – God of Wine and Fertility, Light Weaver, Hunter-god, guardian of the mythical Celtic island Emhain Abhlach, and honorary Cumhaill.

Emmet – Fi's brother, fifth in the birth order, druid buffer, guardian and committed caretaker of the mythical Celtic island Emhain Abhlach.

Fiona – youngest of the six Cumhaill kids, chosen by Fionn to represent the Fianna Warriors in a new generation of urban druids, Hunter-god, Celtic shaman, guardian of the mythical Celtic island Emhain Abhlach, bonded companion to Bruin and Dart.

Fionn, a.k.a. Finn MacCool – Hunter-god, mythical warrior in Irish mythology, guardian of the mythical Celtic island Emhain Abhlach, ancestor of and mentor to Fi and her family.

Jonah – public relations specialist, Texas cowboy, and partner to Dionysus

Kevin – artist, high school sweetheart, and husband to Calum.

Lara – Fi's grandmother, nature druid, and the Snow White of the Druid Order.

Liam – one of Fi's best friends, now her stepbrother, operator/bartender for Shenanigans.

Lugh – Fi's grandfather, druid historian, Keeper of the Shrine, and Elder of the Druid Order.

Niall – Fi's father, retired Toronto police officer, married to Shannon and living in Ireland with his parents.

Nikon Tsambikos – ancient Greek immortal, Light Weaver, guardian of the mythical Celtic island Emhain Abhlach, and honorary Cumhaill.

Shannon – mother of Liam, became the pseudo-mother to the Cumhaill kids after her husband and their mother died when the kids were young. Her husband Mark was Niall's partner and died in the line of duty.

Sloan Mackenzie – Fi's soulmate, druid healer, Keeper of the Toronto Shrine, and guardian of the mythical Celtic island Emhain Abhlach. Union bonded to Saxa.

Wallace Mackenzie – Sloan's father, master druid healer,

Elder of the Druid Order, recently separated from Sloan's mother Janet Mackenzie.

Animal Companions
   Aurora – Tad's red-tailed kite.
   Bruinior the Brave (Bruin) a.k.a. Killer Clawbearer – Fiona's mythical battle bear and Bear of native myth and legend.
   Daisy – Calum's epileptic skunk companion.
   Dartamont (Dart) – Fiona's Western dragon, involved with Saxa, and oldest brother to twenty-two other dragons.
   Dax – Lara's badger.
   Doc Martin (Doc) – Emmet's pine marten followed him home from the Santa Claus Parade.
   Nyrora (Rory) – Dillan's Koinonos Dragon. Dark purple with gold webbing for her wings, she bonds with him at rest, creating a living tattoo on his skin.

More Greeks
   Alec Tsambikos – Nikon's cousin, ancient Greek immortal, has the power of time travel.
   Andromeda Tsambikos – Nikon's younger sister, ancient Greek immortal, Light Weaver, guardian of the mythical Celtic island Emhain Abhlach, and legal counsel for SITFO.
   Nikon Tsambikos Senior – Nikon's grandfather, ancient Greek immortal, Light Weaver, and guardian of the mythical Celtic island Emhain Abhlach.
   Politimi Tsambikos – Nikon's younger sister and ancient Greek immortal.

The Moon Called
   Anyx – lion shifter, Garnet's beta, and mate to Zuzanna.
   Garnet Grant – lion shifter, Alpha of the Toronto Moon Called, Grand Governor of the Lakeshore Guild of Empowered

Ones, Fi's friend, mentor, and boss at SITFO, mated to Myra and father of adopted bear shifter Imari.

Myra – ash nymph, Fae Historian, mated to Garnet, owner/operator of Myra's Mystical Emporium, mother of adopted bear shifter Imari.

Thaos – lion shifter, one of Garnet's valued pack enforcers, third in the pack hierarchy.

Zuzanna – lion shifter, mate to Anyx, works with SITFO as a member of the Toronto Special Investigations Unit.

The Vampires

Benjamin – vampire, companion to Laurel.

Xavier – vampire, King of the Toronto Seethes.

The Nine Families of the Druid Order

Lugh and Lara Cumhaill – parents of Niall, grandparents of Aiden, Brendan, Calum, Dillan, Emmet, and Fiona.

James and Caitrona Dempsey – parents of Brian and Reagan.

Evan and Iris Doyle – parents of Ciara.

Connor and Kate Flannigan – parents of Erik.

Wallace Mackenzie – father of Sloan, ex-husband to Janet.

Tad McNiff – recently took his place as a head of the Nine Families after his father, Riordan, gave himself over to Mingin in a quest for ultimate power.

Finley and Elaine O'Malley – parents of Lia.

Brian and Gwyneth Perry – parents of Jarrod, Darcy, and Davin.

Sean and Maude Scott – parents of Seamus.

Friends

Danika – witch from San Francisco, Nikon's ex-lover.

Laurel – ghost, companion to Benjamin, Fi's high school friend.

Merlin/Pan Dora/Emrys – druid and wizard of legend, owner of Queens on Queen drag club and the attached soup kitchen, union bonded to the champagne-colored Western dragon, Empress Cazzienth.

Patty – Man o' Green, union bonded to Cyteira the Queen of Wyrms, a.k.a. the Wyrm Dragon Queen.

Suede Silverbirch – elven representative on Toronto's Lakeshore Guild of Empowered Ones.

Zxata – ash nymph, Myra's brother, nymph representative on Toronto's Lakeshore Guild of Empowered Ones.

More Hunter-gods

Ahren – Hunter-god, shaman, navigates the astral plane as a golden eagle.

Samuel – Hunter-god, shaman, navigates the astral plane as an ebony wolf.

Quon Shen – Hunter-god, shaman, navigates the astral plane as a water dragon.

Team Trouble

Brody – wolf shifter/vampire hybrid, new member-in-training for Team Trouble.

Dantanion Jann (Dan the djinn) – djinn, member of Team Trouble.

Diesel Demarco – goliath, new member-in-training for Team Trouble.

Jenna – siren, new member-in-training for Team Trouble.

John Maxwell – Deputy Commissioner of the Royal Canadian Mounted Police, founder of SITFO, the Special Investigations Task Force for Ontario.

Iceland Dragons – Free Dragons of Tintagel

Bryvanay – black, majestic, and slightly smaller than Utiss.

Cazzienth Empress of the West (Cazzie) – glistening champagne-colored dragon with gold and burnt orange wings, and a strong tail that ends in a treacherous-looking ball-spike.

Saxa – a sunshine yellow dragon with dark gold wings and a blunt snout of the same color.

Utiss – a massive purple dragon and the dominant male of the Free Dragons of Tintagel.

Ireland Dragons

Drakes – Chua.

Westerns – Abeloth, Cadmus, Chezzo, Dart, Esym, Kaida, Scarlett, Torrim.

Wyrms – Scarlett, +6 we haven't met.

Wyverns – Neak, Azure, +5 we haven't met.

Pronunciations

adelphos – *adelfos* – Greek for "brother" or "my brother."

agapi mou – *ah-gah-pea moo* – Greek for "my love."

Cumhaill – *Cool* – Fiona and the family's last name (modern).

gliko mou – Greek for "my sweet."

mac Cumhaill – *MacCool* – Fiona and the family's last name (traditional).

mo chroi – *muh chree* – Irish for my heart/my love.

a ghra – *uh grawh* – Irish for my love (intimate).

a stór – *uh stohr* – Irish for a treasure.

paidi mou – *peth-ee moo* – Greek for "my child."

Slan! – *slawn* – health be with you.

Slainte mhath – *slawn cha va* – cheers, good health.

Irish Terms

Arragh – a guttural sound for when something bad happens.

Banjaxed – broken, ruined, completely obliterated.

Bogger – those who live in the boggy countryside.

Bollocks – a man's testicles.

Bollix – thrown into disorder, bungled, messed up.

Boyo – boy, lad.
Cock-crow – close enough that you can hear a cock crow.
Craic – gossip, fun, entertainment.
Culchie – those who live in the agricultural countryside.
Donkey's years – a long time.
Dosser – a layabout, lazy person.
Eejit – slightly less severe than idiot.
Fair whack away – far away.
Feck – an exclamation less severe than fuck.
Flute – a man's penis.
Gammie – injured, not working properly.
Hape – a heap.
Howeyah/Howaya/Howya – a greeting not necessarily requiring an answer.
Irish – traditional Irish language (commonly referred to as Irish Gaelic unless you're Irish).
Knackers – a man's testicles.
Mocker – a hex.
Och – used to express agreement or disagreement to something said.
Shite – less offensive than shit.
Gobshite – fool, acting in unwanted behavior.
Wee – small.

PRONUNCIATIONS

Pronunciations
Adelphos – *adelfos* – Greek for "brother" or "my brother."
agapi mou – *ah-gah-pea moo* – Greek for "my love."
Cumhaill – *Cool* – Fiona and the family's last name (modern).
gliko mou – Greek for "my sweet."
mac Cumhaill – *MacCool* – Fiona and the family's last name (traditional).
Mo chroi – *muh chree* – Irish for my heart/my love.
a ghra – *uh grawh* – Irish for my love (intimate).
a stór – *uh stohr* – Irish for a treasure.
paidi mou – *peth-ee moo* – Greek for "my child."
Slan! – *slawn* – health be with you.
Slainte mhath – *slawn cha va* – cheers, good health.

Irish Terms
Arragh – a guttural sound for when something bad happened.
Banjaxed – broken, ruined, completely obliterated.
Bogger – those who live in the boggy countryside.
Bollocks – a man's testicles.

Bollix – thrown into disorder, bungled, messed up.
Boyo – boy, lad.
Cock-crow – close enough that you can hear a cock crow.
Craic – gossip, fun, entertainment.
Culchie – those who live in the agricultural countryside.
Donkey's years – a long time.
Dosser – a layabout, lazy person.
Eejit – slightly less severe than idiot.
Fair whack away – far away.
Feck – an exclamation less severe than fuck.
Flute – a man's penis.
Gammie – injured, not working properly.
Hape – a heap.
Howeyah/Howaya/Howya – a greeting not necessarily requiring an answer.
Irish – traditional Irish language (commonly referred to as Irish Gaelic unless you're Irish).
Knackers – a man's testicles.
Mocker – a hex.
Och – used to express agreement or disagreement to something said.
Shite – less offensive than shit
Gobshite – fool, acting in unwanted behavior.
Wee – small.

CHAPTER ONE

"Once upon a time, there was an amazing baby boy who lived in an amazing pink house on an amazing secret, magical island. He had two amazing parents. His daddy was a brave and strong druid who protected the people of both the fae and human worlds, and his mommy was a guardian angel who was fierce, funny, and one of the loveliest people in all the realms. But as perfect as they were for one another, things got even more amazing with the arrival of their baby boy."

Sloan chuckles. "This is an *amazing* story."

"It is." I brush a gentle finger over Haniel's ultra-soft wing and smile as he coos. "The rest of the little angel's family was just as amazing. They had humans, druids, immortals, shifters, and gods, but the best part was the way they loved one another. You see, that was their secret weapon…love."

Sloan leans forward and brushes a kiss over Haniel's cheek. "Aye, little one. Yer auntie speaks the truth."

Stretched out on our sides on either side of the baby, the two of us are enjoying an afternoon in the backyard with my nephew—the newest member of Clan Cumhaill—Haniel.

It's heaven.

And not only because he's a sweet baby angel.

"Do you think it's possible our babies will be as well-behaved and easy as this one?" I ask.

Sloan chuckles. "Given that Haniel is a celestial gift given to us by the heavens and delivered by the stork, I'm going to say likely not."

"Yeah, I didn't think so either. You could've at least tried to dilute that a bit for me."

His smile grows. "Since when would Fiona Cumhaill Mackenzie want somethin' whitewashed to be more palatable?"

"Since never."

"I didn't think so."

I close my eyes, absorbing the revitalizing energy that fills this magical city in abundance. It's no surprise to me that for centuries, this pocket oasis has stood as a refuge for the magically displaced citizens of all realms. "It doesn't get any better than this, does it?"

Sloan draws a deep breath, his mint green eyes dancing with happiness. "It doesn't. I can't say that there's a thing I would change about our lives."

"Me either."

As if the universe is giving us a middle-finger salute, a notification *pings* on my phone.

"Don't answer it," Sloan advises. "Let the world take care of itself fer a bit while we take care of wee Han."

Wee Han. Man, he's the cutest little guy.

"I know that look." Emmet chuckles as he saunters across the backyard of our little stone castle. "Is Irish wearing you down, sista? Are the drums of motherhood beating out their rhythms in your womb?"

I blanch. "Ew, please never reference my womb. It is evermore stricken from the words you may speak."

He laughs. "Gotcha. How about your girl bits? Baby machinery? Lady business?"

"Nope. You're banned all around."

"Touchy. You can reference my swimmers or my junk if it makes you feel better."

"Nope. Not even a little."

He laughs. "My comment stands. The two of you look extra content snuggling Han. Are you making plans?"

"If you're asking if I want babies, the answer is yes. That's not a secret. But I want to have the time and attention to focus on raising them and not be pulled a dozen different directions by the world's chaos."

Emmet makes a face. "There will always be chaos in the world, Fi. If you're waiting for that to die down, you'll miss your window for kids."

He's both right and wrong. "The current chaos is worse than usual. With the veil down between the realms and the existence of magical races exposed, things are more chaotic than ever."

"True. But what if that's the new normal? Don't put your life decisions on hold because of an obligation to the world around you."

Raising a hand, I wriggle my fingers and invite Emmet to help me off the lounger gracefully so I don't wake the baby. He knows the drill. A moment later I'm upright, and the baby is still lying there snoring with the gentle breeze blowing his fluffy white feathers.

He's cuter than should be legal.

"Trust me, Em. I'm aware of the state of the world and have no illusions of it ever being a campfire sing-along. I also know that Merlin is close to getting the veil up. With that, a lot of the current tensions and hostilities will finally be over."

"How close is he?" Emmet asks.

Sloan rises to his feet without the help of anyone and doesn't ruffle one of the baby's little wings. "Last we spoke, Merlin was confident he was weeks away at most, likely closer to days."

I love the sound of that. "When that's taken care of and the world settles down, I'll think about Sloan and I expanding the family. There's no rush. We've both got dragon longevity and have decades, if not centuries, to look forward to."

Sloan winks at me. "Good things come to those who wait, *a ghra.*"

Yes, they do. I read the subtext in his comment and smile. When I first learned of my druid powers, I wanted nothing to do with dating or complicating my already complicated life. Sloan is a persistent guy. He waited me out, all the while confident that we would happen.

Thank the goddess he did.

I wink at him, letting him know I know exactly what he meant when he said that. "Besides, we have enough little people here. If we need a kid fix, we can get it anytime we want."

Emmet nods. "All right. Consider me told. You'll have babies when you're good and ready. I get it. Just keep in mind that if you wait too long, they won't have the opportunity to experience Gran and Granda or Da and Shannon."

That thought hadn't occurred to me. He sees how the thought of losing them shakes my foundation and lifts a shoulder. "I don't want to upset you. Just make sure you've thought it all the way through."

I hug my brother. "Yeah, okay. I hear you."

Sloan is frowning at his phone, and I have a bad feeling our time relaxing on the enchanted island is over. "What's wrong, hotness?"

"Merlin asked us to meet him at the Batcave. He and Garnet have things to discuss and request our presence at our earliest convenience."

I sigh and look at sweet little Haniel sleeping on the lounger. "Poop, and everything was so perfect, too."

"I've got baby Han," Emmet says. "You guys go do what you need to do."

"Thanks, Em." I lean in to kiss his cheek. "Want me to bring you back anything from Toronto?"

"How about a busty brunette with a wicked sense of humor?" He waggles his eyebrows at me.

"I'll keep an eye out and see what I can find."

"You're the best." He goes over to look at the books Sloan and I were reading through while spending our time out here with Haniel. He picks up the doorstop Sloan was reading, makes a face, and discards it for the one I was reading. "Steampunk pirate romance?"

I shrug. "When fantasy is your reality, and action and crime are your everyday life, it's tough to find something that seems like an escape."

"Fair enough. Steampunk pirate romance it is." Emmet sits on the chair of our backyard furniture set and puts his feet up. "Safe home. Love you."

"Love you too."

Sloan and I change out of our shorts and into our fatigues and T-shirts, then portal to the golden palace—better known as the golden dildo. One of the best decisions we ever made was spelling a portal door at the palace that takes us into the kitchen pantry of our home in Toronto.

Now it's the work of a moment for us to leave our enchanted city home and be back in the thick of things in the human realm within minutes.

It doesn't cost Sloan his wayfarer energy.

It doesn't require a god to transport us.

And it doesn't work for anyone other than a Cumhaill or someone escorted by one of us.

It's made all the difference to me lately. I didn't know how badly I struggled with being separated from my family until we moved onto the Celtic island of Emhain Abhlach. Now I see them every day, get to play with my nieces and nephews, and Liam is running Shenanigans—island edition—so all is right in the world.

"Home sweet home," I remark as we step out of our kitchen pantry and into our restored Victorian home in Cabbagetown, Toronto. I run a hand over the polished stone countertop of the breakfast bar and island. "Did you miss us, old girl?"

"I'm sure the house missed us as much as any house could." Sloan sounds much too logical.

I open the freezer and pull out two ice cream sandwiches. "Oh, I've been looking forward to this."

Sloan chuckles and accepts the one I give him. "Ye realize ye can bring them with ye to the island, aye?"

"I could, but they're addictive, and I would eat the entire box. By leaving them here, I curb the impulse to binge."

"Yer strategy fer self-control is to leave yer treat in another part of the world?"

I peel the paper wrapper back and use it to keep my fingers from getting mucky cookie on them. "Exactly. It's ingenious, right?"

"Yer ridiculous."

I shrug and take my first bite of cookie and ice cream bliss. "Not everyone has the willpower of a saint. It's a proven fact that women get addicted to chocolate."

"Is it now?"

I groan and take another bite. "Yeah. It's a hormone thing. It's nature versus nurture, man. I can't fight it. I can only rig the system."

"I see." He wraps his hand around my elbow and *poofs* us to the elevator area of the Team Trouble headquarters. On the tenth floor of the Acropolis building Nikon bought us, the Batcave is where all the crime-fighting magic happens.

With the combination of the security pendant none of us ever take off and Sloan's hand on the biometric scanner, the door unlocks, and we step into the office to see what Merlin and Garnet need from us.

"Fiona! Long time, girlfriend."

I stride over to hug Andromeda as she emerges from her office. Nikon's sister is the quintessential triple threat. She's a smart, high-powered attorney. She's as beautiful as any Greek goddess. And she's a genuinely lovely person and a caring friend.

I love her to bits.

"It has been a while...I think it was at the baby shower for Haniel."

Her face lights up. "OMG, have you ever seen a cuter baby?"

"Nope. I love all my nieces and nephews, and they're all adorable, but those wings push the cuteness factor off the freaking charts."

She nods with a grin. "Absolutely."

"I was babysitting him until I got the summons to come here." I pop the last of my ice cream sandwich in my mouth and hand Sloan my gooey wrapper. After wiping my fingers on my pants, I pull out my phone. "I might have taken a few pictures."

Or maybe a few dozen.

"Will there be an end to this gushing soon?" Garnet asks from the conference table. "You *do* still work for me, don't you?"

I laugh and roll my eyes so only Andromeda can see. "I'll send you a few of these later."

She lights up. "Do that. I'm making a scrapbook for Eva and would love more pictures."

I turn on my heels and go over to hug Merlin and give Garnet my full attention. The lion isn't much of a hugger. I've gotten away with it a few times over the years, but I pick my moments.

"If the money being dumped into my account every month is any sign, yes, I still work for you." I can still taste the chocolate and ice creamy deliciousness. I glance at Sloan and realize he hasn't opened his. "Are you going to eat that?"

He chuckles and offers it to me. "I know better. Please, be my guest."

"Man, you get me."

"I like to think so."

I unwrap the second ice cream sandwich. Because it's been out of the freezer for five minutes, it's soft and super gooey.

The craziest thing about them is that even when I've gotten sidetracked and left one on the table for half an hour, it never truly melts. It's a little unnerving, but I try not to think too much about it because why ruin yumminess by trying to understand it?

Let it be one of life's mysteries.

"Are you listening?" Garnet tilts his head into my line of vision. "Or are you completely consumed with your snack?"

I blink at him. "Of course, I heard every word."

Garnet arches an ebony brow. "All right, Lady Druid. I call your bluff. What were we talking about?"

"The progress of raising the veil," I guess. It's a decent guess, given that Merlin's here, but as I read the faces of the three men, I know I guessed wrong. "Yeah no, I'm totally busted. I got lost in the creamy dreaminess of ice cream sandwiches. Take it from the top. I promise I'm paying attention."

Merlin chuckles. "Before we get to the issue of raising the veil, we were talking about the trouble yesterday in the financial district."

"Oh? What's going on?"

"A group of rogue pixies were wreaking havoc and vandalizing buildings along King Street. Diesel and Brody rounded up the troublemakers, and Dan put a memory charm on the most irate humans affected, but the division between races is growing wider. We need to de-escalate the tensions soon or we'll have a war in our streets."

I frown and meet Garnet's gaze. "Pixies don't usually incite violence. Any idea why they lashed out?"

"No idea. Pixies are usually harmless tricksters, not vandals. Something must have provoked them."

"What about the concern that the prana in this realm is tainting? Do you think that could affect fae beings?"

"It absolutely could, but I'm not sure that's what happened with the pixies."

Dionysus appears in the center of the room and strides over to hug me. "Have you considered the anti-magic factions? The hate propaganda has been growing bolder. Jonah's been tracking incidents, and he's not liking what he's found."

I ease back from his hug, troubled by the suggestion. The fanatics who make up the anti-magic factions have become thorns in our sides, but until now, the open aggression has been on the human side, not fae.

"Hopefully, it was an isolated incident and not a sign of worse things to come," I remark.

Merlin nods. "Hopefully."

Garnet doesn't look convinced. "Let's not wait to find out. It's yet another reason we need to get the veil reinstated as soon as possible."

"So, where are we on that?" I ask.

Merlin gestures at the conference table. "I'm glad you ask. I'm also glad you're here, Dionysus. I need your opinion, too."

Dionysus waggles his eyebrows and sits beside me. "I have lots of opinions and am more than happy to share them. I'm ready. Shoot."

CHAPTER TWO

The five of us sit. As we get ready for Merlin's debrief, it feels strange yet comfortingly familiar. Over the past couple of months, I've spent more and more time on the island with my family and less time actively working.

Garnet's been amazing about me needing time since Raven cursed me and left me comatose for three months. I wonder if that's because of our relationship or his fear of getting backlash from Myra.

Both are entirely possible.

Sloan pours a glass of water from the jug in the center of the table and slides it to me before filling a second for himself.

Merlin sits back in his chair and sighs. "It's been one hell of a problem, I'll tell you. At first I believed, like everyone did, that the veil coming down was a catastrophic tactic of the dark fae trying to gain power and wreak havoc on humanity during the Culling."

I sit straighter and set my water down. "You don't think so now?"

"No. I don't. In the initial days of trying to right this ship, I could affect the veil between realms with the help of Isilon."

Garnet frowns. "The Hidden City was helping you?"

Merlin nods. "The consciousness of the Hidden City is ancient and incredibly knowledgeable."

True story. "Yeah, he and I have had several mind-bendy conversations."

Garnet grunts. "The only experience I have with that side of your city is when we were all held prisoner at your wedding reception."

"Right, but now that he understands we're not all going to abandon him and send him into dormancy, he's much more reasonable."

Garnet arches a brow. "You realize you're talking about reasoning with a city, right?"

"Life is funny, isn't it?"

"If you say so."

I do. At least I think it is.

"You and Isilon were working on affecting the veil." I bring us back to the point.

"Yes, and during the times we tried to initiate the reinstatement of the veil between realms, we'd get some traction. Then everything would go back to the way it's been for the past year."

"That makes you think the veil falling *wasn't* intentional?"

Merlin tips his head from side to side, his long, dark waves brushing his shoulders. "It took me a while to get there, but yes. If it was Death, Mingin, Melanippe, or any of the other major players, we negated their influence over a year ago. The work I've been doing should've countered their intentions and the veil should've been reinstated."

"But it wasn't," Sloan confirms.

"No. Which is when I wondered if perhaps it was an unintentional by-product or a natural side effect that occurred during the Time of the Colliding Realms."

"You no longer believe that?" I ask.

"I don't, because when I changed my approach to account for

a naturally occurring event, I still couldn't get the damned thing to take hold."

"Where does that leave us?" Dionysus asks.

"Well, if it wasn't part of the Culling and it wasn't a naturally occurring event, I can only surmise that it's the result of intention. Whoever or whatever caused the veil to fall, that influence is still in play because everything I'm doing is being actively undone just as quickly."

"You think there's someone actively keeping the veil down?" I try to imagine who would do that and why, but I've got nothing. "For what purpose?"

He shrugs and leans back in his chair. "I don't suppose we'll know until we figure out who's behind it."

"Who has that kind of juice?" Garnet asks.

"Gods would." Merlin glances at Dionysus. "Or maybe some of the greater fae or greater demons. Or maybe if a group of empowered created a coalition to do it, they might amass the power."

"But yer confident it's an active and ongoing intention." Sloan frowns.

Merlin nods. "It's the only thing that makes sense. No sooner do I get things moving in the right direction than something shuts my efforts down and everything reverts to the way it's been the past year."

"Who benefits from the veil being down?" I ask.

Merlin shrugs. "That's what we need to figure out."

"That's why you're glad I'm here," Dionysus observes. "You think it's a god from one of the pantheons?"

"Not necessarily, but if it is, you're our best source of figuring it out."

"Because you're amazeballs." I grin at him. "And you know all the playahs."

Dionysus laughs. "Because I *am* a playah."

"Yeah, you are." I hold up a fist to knuckle-bump. Then we get serious. "How could a god, a fae, or a group of empowered benefit from the veil being down?"

"There have been fae factions who wanted the exposure of their existence since the beginning," Garnet reminds us. "Whether it's to feel like part of the community or to laud themselves over the measly humans, they've wanted to be seen."

"I wonder if those people still feel that way," Sloan muses.

I doubt it. "Have there been any fae factions that gained power or traction since the fall of the veil?"

Garnet shakes his head. "A few criminal elements have gained power because they can intimidate the humans they're threatening with their magic, but nothing on a global scale. Certainly no one that has the power it would take to take the veil down and thwart Merlin to keep it down."

I giggle. "I love the fact that you use words like thwart, bossman."

Garnet rolls his eyes at me.

Man, how broody tough guys feed my soul. "So, let's talk about greater demons."

Sloan nods. "Greater demons would love the chaos and division of the past year. The suffering of the individuals and the families of those who experienced awakenings would be bonus amusement."

"Would the veil being down offer them any greater reach into our realm or give them any better chance to escape purgatory or the hell realm?" I ask.

Sloan, Dionysus, and Garnet all shake their heads.

"So, other than shits and giggles, why would demons be behind it?"

"They wouldn't," Garnet states. "If a greater demon was behind it, he or she would've made some kind of play before now, and we would be well aware of why."

"True story," Dionysus agrees. "Hellspawn don't play a long game. They are more of a play, flay, and slay crowd."

"That leaves gods or a collective of empowered," Sloan sums up.

"Or a collective of gods," I add.

Dionysus shakes his head. "Unlikely. Gods don't generally play well with others, and they don't care enough about anything to stick it to all of humanity."

"Maybe revenge?" I suggest, remembering how Loki stalked and tormented Dionysus. That was a long game plan to wreak havoc.

"Maybe. Even so, gods generally don't care a fraction as much about others as they do about themselves. Taking the veil down and keeping it down against Merlin's efforts suggests an ongoing commitment."

"You're leaning toward a cabal of empowered assholes?" Garnet asks.

Dionysus nods. "It seems the likeliest answer."

I sip my water and swallow. "Well, if the horse has stripes, it's most likely a zebra."

Garnet frowns. "One would think."

"Occam's razor." I emphasize my point.

Garnet grunts. "I'm aware of the principle of parsimony, Lady Druid."

Oh, fancy. "The question remains—who benefits from the veil being down and staying down?"

"Aye, it would be good to know that, luv," Sloan agrees. "I think the more important question is how do we counter their efforts if we don't know who they are and they're actively working to keep the veil down?"

Yeah, there's that too.

With the meeting adjourned, I hook arms with Dionysus, and he flashes Sloan and me upstairs to catch up with what's been happening in my city while I took a mental health break. He and Jonah have taken up the hometown mantle and have been making a go of it as a couple for...wow, *six* months.

"Hey there, good-looking." I hug Jonah and let him sweep me over to the couch. Dionysus' cowboy is a clean-cut blond with broad shoulders, narrow hips, and nothing but lovely sculpted ridges in between. He's also one of the sweetest down South boys I've ever met. "How's Toronto life going? How's the new job?"

Dionysus scoffs. "And just like that, I'm a second-class citizen abandoned by the female of my heart."

I laugh and blow him a kiss. "You know I love you huge in a special place in my heart only for you."

His grin breaks brightly across his beautiful face. "Yeah, I do." Dionysus flops on the couch and pats the seat cushion.

"Life is good." Jonah joins him. "We're settling in, and I think we're on track for greatness."

Dionysus pushes his chest out and stretches his arm across the back of the sofa. "You here that, Fi? Greatness."

"I'm glad, sweetie. I want nothing but the biggest dose of love and acceptance the universe can offer you."

"Me too," he agrees. "I've been taking everything I've learned about love from Clan Cumhaill and putting it to good use."

Jonah narrows his gaze at him. "What's this about?"

Dionysus swings his leg up and pivots on the couch to face him. "I once had the love of a goddess. I thought we were great the way we were, but I found out a year or two ago I hadn't been paying attention and I really hurt her."

True story. That was Loki's daughter Hel.

While Hel moved on, Loki didn't forgive or forget. Instead, he targeted Dionysus and sought revenge on behalf of his daughter.

"So, this time, I'm paying attention. I've been noting all your likes and dislikes and learning about what makes you happiest."

Jonah frowns. "I don't want you twisted up, tryin' to keep me happy."

Dionysus leans forward for a quick kiss. "No. Not at all. I'm talking about paying attention to the little things, so I get it right."

"Like what?"

"Like that, you like action movies and cheesy rom-coms more than when I watch reality TV. So I watch those when you're asleep, and I'm bored."

Jonah laughs. "You could always sleep more."

Dionysus waves that away. "I'm a god. I don't need sleep like you do."

"Fair enough. What else?"

"I know how you hate it when I leave toast crumbs in the butter."

Jonah nods. "Well, you got me there. I do hate that."

Dionysus nods. "Whether the toilet seat is up or down doesn't seem to be an issue, but in the morning, you like to lie awake and think for a bit before I talk and break your sleepy spell."

Amazing. "Good for you, sweetie. You're really paying attention."

Dionysus leans toward me and draws a deep breath. "I really want this one to work."

Jonah pats his leg. "Don't try so hard. We *both* want it to work, and I don't want either of us stressed over every itty-bitty thing."

Dionysus grins and winks at me. "How cute is it he says things like itty-bitty?"

"Adorable," I agree. "Back to my original question. How's the new job?"

Jonah smiles. "To work for Garnet is an adventure every day."

"I know that firsthand."

"With the state of the realm the way it is, there's plenty for me to do in the way of spinning the optics of empowered issues."

I bet there is. "I guess making people look good follows the same principles in any realm."

"It does."

"What about the outreach fer orphans and adoptions?" Sloan

asks. "Calum and Kevin mentioned ye've been doin' a fair bit of work fer them, too."

Jonah smiles. "I think that's been my favorite assignment. I've faced the world on my own for years. To bring folks together and make families fills the well inside me somehow."

I love that. "After seeing firsthand what Bizzy has brought into the lives of my brother and Kev, and Imari into the lives of Garnet and Myra, I'm with you. It's magical to be part of that."

Jonah leans sideways, snuggling into Dionysus' side. "It might be the only magic I'll ever possess, but it'll do."

Dionysus winks. "Not the only magic. There's that thing you do with your tongue when you—"

"And on that note." I stand and pull Sloan up beside me. "We're headed to the bookstore. Do you want to join?"

Dionysus looks at Jonah to give him the first right of refusal. "It's the magical bookstore Fi used to work at with Garnet's mate, Myra. I don't think I've ever taken you there."

Jonah shrugs and gets to his feet. "Y'all had me at a magical bookstore. Who says no to that?"

"No one worth knowing." I take Sloan's hand. "Certainly no one in our circle."

Often compared to New York City's Soho, Queen Street is recognized as the place to go for trendy dining and nightlife, cutting-edge fashion, art galleries, and magic shops. Whether they are warded for secrecy or accessible to humans, whatever you need, you can find it here.

Crystals, books, tarot and psychic readings, herbs, and apothecaries. It's all here. Of all the boutiques and shops, none rivals Myra's Emporium.

Of course, I might be biased.

The four of us materialize below the old-fashioned sign

swinging on an iron rod. As always, my gift tingles to the fore, and I trace the lettering of the lit sign in the green-tinted window.

Myra's Mystical Emporium
Augury, Alchemy, Astrology,
And all Implications of Same

"This is amazing." Jonah grins as we escort him inside and toward the back of the main store. "I swear I've walked by a dozen times and never noticed this store. How could I have missed it?"

"Because it's spelled not to be seen unless you're an empowered person who has needs to be fulfilled," Myra answers, rounding the antique pine table at the back she uses for a checkout counter.

"That says it all." Dionysus beams. "I assure you, my guy has no unfulfilled needs. He's fully filled."

Myra winks and hugs us each in turn. "I have no doubt that's true. Now, to what do I owe the pleasure?"

"Auntie Fi!" Imari races in from the store's back section, and I bend to hug her. "Hey, little bear. How's life treating you?"

"Good. Even better now that you're here. Can Bruin come out and play?"

I chuckle as I release my bonded battle bear. He might be a mythical god and an infamous slayer of foes, but he also kills it with the kids.

Bruin bursts from my chest and fills the air with a surge of magic and a gusty breeze that follows him as he circles me and materializes in the space near the opening to the other half of the store. "Come, little one. I'll meet ye under the canopy of yer mama's tree."

He ghosts out, and Imari is gone like a shot.

Myra swipes a loose piece of electric blue hair from in front of her wicked cool, vertically slit eyes and sighs. "I've missed you, girlfriend."

"I've missed you, too…and this place."

The boys disperse and move off to the other side of the store. I'm not sure if they're giving me time to catch up with Myra or if they're curious to hunt through the stacks.

In Sloan's case, there's no question. "Merlin's looking for a way to counter an unknown magical player from enforcing an unknown spell to keep the veil down despite his efforts."

"Oh, is that all?" She chuckles. "He was in here grumbling the other night. I find it's best to let him do his thing when he's that deep into things. The man knows more about magic than most covens or magical sects."

A tingle of awareness twists behind my navel, and I wander to the gemstones. My shield is calm, but my instincts kick in as I run my fingers over the new arrivals. "I suppose if you live centuries as one of the magical marvels of our world, you pick up a few things."

She grins. "That's one way to look at it."

The pull I feel takes me past the gemstones and crystals and over to the enchanted objects display case. Raising my hand, I glide it over the glass window, letting the energy prickling over my skin guide me in a game of Hot and Cold.

"What is it?" Myra asks me.

"I'm not sure. Something is calling to me."

She leans in and frowns at the collection of brooches, pendants, pocket watches, lockets, and daggers. "I don't think we got any new arrivals since the last time you were here. Actually, I don't think we have anything you haven't passed a few hundred times."

I shrug and point at a silver amulet. "It's that one."

Myra takes out her keys, opens the case, and plucks the amulet off the velvety display cushion. "Well, we both know better than to ignore magic when it wants to be heard. What's it telling you?"

I turn the crescent-shaped amulet over in my hand. "It's insisting it needs to come with me, so I guess I'm taking it."

Myra chuckles. "Easiest sale I ever made."

I laugh. "Maybe you should enchant all your wares to seduce your customers into taking them home."

"Genius. Why didn't I think of that?"

Holding the silver crescent in my hand, I finger through the chains until I find a thick, woven one that will look good. Once I lace the chain through the loop to wear it, I set it against my chest. "How does it look?"

"Like it belongs there," Myra replies.

I hand her the little ticket for the chain, and she takes it and the price sticker I peeled off the amulet. "Do you want me to charge you or take it off your pay?"

I laugh. "You better charge me. I haven't been working enough to earn a tab."

The two of us head to the desk as I admire my new necklace. "Does this piece have any provenance paperwork?"

Myra sets the two price tags on the counter and pulls open a drawer in the floor-to-ceiling hutch behind her. She pulls out her brown leather ledger and flips through some of its oversized pages.

Turning it sideways, she points at an entry and reads aloud. "The Blind Moon Crescent. Forged from pure silver, it represents the moon's power and influence over the mystical realm. When worn during rituals, especially moon rituals, the amulet enhances the wearer's ability to channel lunar energies to strengthen the veil."

I blink at her. "Well, that can't be a coincidence."

She shakes her head. "I wouldn't think so, no."

CHAPTER THREE

With my new pendant resting happily around my neck, Sloan and I say our goodbyes to our friends and return to Isilon. I find the calling of the amulet energizing and look at it as a sign that something might work for us. Sloan is less impressed.

"Maybe it's a nudge from the fae powers," I suggest.

"Or someone is manipulatin' us."

"You think so?"

"I think if someone is actively workin' to counter Merlin's efforts, that same someone might have the power to set us on a false course."

I close my eyes and let my instincts weigh in. "My shield would warn me if there was ill-intent in play. I've got nothing. I think it's the real deal."

"So, why now? Myra said the amulet has been sittin' there fer months. Why did it signal to ye now if we've been tryin' to bring the veil up fer the past year?"

I shrug. "Timing is everything, right? Maybe it's time for us to pay attention."

"How so, *a ghra?*"

"Well, its provenance says when it's worn in a ritual, especially a moon ritual, it enhances the wearer's ability to channel lunar energies to strengthen the veil."

"And the message ye took from the universe is?"

I shrug. "To search for rituals that might help Merlin counter whoever is keeping the veil down. It sort of gives us a direction to focus on, don't you think?"

He opens the door of the room we portal into and steps back to allow me to exit before him. "I suppose that's true."

"I think so. Because before this afternoon, we could've been searching for any number of solutions and now I'm pretty sure we're supposed to start with rituals."

With a hand on my lower back, he leads us to one of the major libraries in the palace where Emmet and Brendan live. I go to the wooden table in the middle of the room and hop up to sit.

Sloan scans the hundreds of leather-bound spines and sighs. "The hint of 'look for a ritual' doesn't narrow things down by much, I'm afraid."

"Maybe not, but I truly believe this amulet seeking me out is a good sign."

He nods. "Yer instincts are incredibly intuitive in these things. I'll never argue with that."

Still, he doesn't sound all that pleased.

I grip the table's edge beside my thighs and swing my legs. "What about moon rituals specifically? Surely that narrows the search, doesn't it?"

He steps sideways, drawing his fingers along the shelves. "It might. If only there was a directory of spells, and we could look it up."

"Well, there sort of is." I pull the folded paper from my pocket. "Myra's a Fae Historian, after all. She made me a list of a few books that might have the rituals we need."

He scowls at me. "And yer just bringin' that up now?"

"Oops. Sorry. I didn't think of it until it came up in conversation. I was distracted by my purdy new magical amulet."

He extends his hand toward me. "Aye, all right. Let me see what books she suggested, and we'll see if we have any of them here on the island."

I snort. "How will you know? There must be thousands of titles between the palace and the libraries in this city. Ninety-five percent of the city is still vacant, and half of the people who used to live here had rare magical belongings from their sects."

He waggles his brows at me and chuckles. "If only we knew a bit of magic that could make searchin' fer things a wee bit easier."

"Oh, right. You're going to scry for the titles?"

He taps his finger on the tip of my nose. "It'll be a damned sight easier than searchin' through every book in every home, aye?"

I wrinkle my nose at him. "I guess there are still times when I forget to think like a druid."

"Aye, but many fewer, thankfully."

He takes a bronze bowl off one shelf, sets it on the table beside me, and pulls his pendulum out of his pocket. "Would ye like the honors?"

I wave that away. "No. You go ahead. It was your idea, and you have a much stronger intention of seeking books and knowledge than I do."

His pendulum falls free and dangles above the bowl when he unfolds his clenched fingers. After placing Myra's list of books into the bowl's body, he closes his eyes, and his lips move.

There's something incredibly attractive about my guy speaking Irish and the cadence that his spells take as he casts. Maybe I'm still in the honeymoon swoon, but I think he's incredible.

I listen to his spell and understand about every other word. *Yay me.*

When he falls silent, the folded paper bursts into flame, and smoke swirls up in purple tendrils. The colored wisps wind around the bulbous body of his pendulum and tug the point toward the bookshelf.

"What are you guys—" Brenny stops mid-sentence and holds up his palms. "Sorry."

"You're good, B." I wave my brother in as Sloan strides toward the bookshelves. "We're looking for books about magical moon rituals."

"Oh, is that all?" He backs against the table beside me and hops up to sit next to me. "I guess the magical world doesn't index their libraries, eh?"

"Nope."

Sloan selects a book from a high shelf and hands it back, dangling it in the air. I take the hint and jog over to grab it. The moment he surrenders it, his pendulum pulls him toward the next book.

It goes like that, and the three of us finish in the palace with four books. Then we pick up another two by winding through the streets of Isilon, and we end up at the Light Weavers' temple.

"I guess this makes sense." I enter the public section of the temple. "The Light Weavers have their super-secret sanctum. I bet they have a few spell books tucked away."

Sloan calls faery fire to his palms and reaches toward a small trough high on the wall. Like the first time, the trough ignites when the fiery blue flame gets close, and flames race along the ceiling line.

The fire illuminates the entrance wall in both directions, turns the corners, burns along the sidewalls, and goes across the back.

"That never gets old." I grin.

"I doubt it will, luv." Sloan's focus is still locked on the pendulum pulling out in front of him like a divining rod bringing him to water.

Together, the three of us stride across the open floor where the Light Weavers' followers likely worshipped their protectors. The stone walls shimmer with magic and come to life as the image of five oddly tall women pushes out from the flat surface.

All around us, the same shimmering energy illuminates the ancient runes and carvings. It highlights the three-story walls with symbols recording their accomplishments.

The first time we were here, we had to search for the panel for the hidden door to the inner sanctum. Since then, Sloan has been here many times and doesn't hesitate to open our way and get us inside.

As the wall slides to the side, we enter the private space of the Light Weavers. This area is as stunning as the public area is impressive. The space reaches high above and is as breathtaking as the temple itself.

What makes it ethereal is how the sunlight streams through the windows high above and fractures through the myriad of crystals strung above our heads.

The effect is one of being surrounded by a prism explosion.

Sloan heads to the mystical library of the ancients, letting the tip of his pendulum guide his journey.

"Will that spell wear off?" Brendan asks. "Or will he be stuck doing this until he's claimed every ritual book on the island?"

"I'm not sure what spell he used, so I can't say."

Brenny chuckles. "Are you claiming 'Not my circus, not my monkeys,' Fi?"

I laugh. "I guess I am."

The two of us mill around, checking out the dazzling light show glistening off the walls as the afternoon sun streams in through the vaulted glass ceiling above. The space's architecture is quite spectacular.

Sloan takes another two books off the shelves, and his pendulum dangles lifelessly toward the floor, its work complete.

"All righty then, do you want help to go through these?" I

gesture at the stack of tomes piled on the table in the center of the room.

Sloan smiles at me and winks. "As much as I appreciate the offer, luv, if ye don't mind, I'd like to dive into these pages myself and have a complete understandin' of what they offer."

I step closer and kiss his cheek. "I don't mind at all. Enjoy your bookworming, hotness. I think I'll hang out at the pub for a while and check in with Liam."

"Aye, that's a fine idea. Given the situation, if I've not caught up with ye by dinner, don't wait on me."

"You do you. And have fun."

His smile is brilliant as he sets out the books to examine them all at a glance. "Och, ye know I will."

Laughing, I link my arm through Brendan's and lead him out of the Light Weavers' sanctum. When we hit the city streets of Isilon, we hang a right and head toward Shenanigans.

The two of us are enjoying a silent sibling stroll until we round the corner. Then Brendan cracks and stops to look at me. "He was serious, wasn't he?"

"What are we talking about?"

"Sloan. He was setting out that stack of doorstops and practically vibrating with excitement about spending the next hours and days reading through every one of them himself."

I laugh. "Oh, yeah. That's his jam for shizzle. There's nothing he loves more than diving into massive texts and novels and devouring them."

Brendan shakes his head. "Then there's you."

I smack his arm. "What's that supposed to mean?"

"Other than high school book reports, how many books had you read before you met him?"

I wave at Binx and Jackson chasing one another down the street as we round the last corner toward the pub. "Rude."

He laughs. "I didn't say anything rude or judgy. I was merely pointing out that opposites attract. He's the bookish scholarly type, and you're a social butterfly. He's a designer clothes and fancy car kind of guy, and you grew up wearing your brothers' hand-me-downs and driving your beater Jetta. What was her name again?"

"Her name was Molly, and she died a violent and horrible death at the hands of the Barghest. Do not speak ill of her."

Brendan chuckles. "I'm sorry for your loss. My point is that the two of you seem very different, but I've never seen you happier."

I hug his arm and rest my head against his shoulder, pulling him back into motion. "I'm deliriously happy."

"It's sickening, actually."

I laugh. "I used to watch the way Mam and Da were with one another and wonder what made her eyes twinkle like they did or why he had a special crooked smile he only gave her."

Brendan pauses outside the inn's door and grins. "I know exactly the look you mean."

"While I know he and Shannon love one another, he hasn't had that special smile since Mam died."

Brenny shrugs. "You were only a little squirt then, Fi. I'm not sure you really understood how devastated Da was when she passed."

I step back and meet the sadness in his gaze. "Maybe not then, but I've almost lost Sloan twice now. Once when the witches hexed him and during the Culling when we didn't know if he'd come out of his coma."

Brenny brushes a finger down my cheek. "When did you get so grown up, Fi?"

"Likely in the years you were undercover."

He nods. "I'm sorry about that. In hindsight, I wish I'd spent those years coming home to my family and watching the monkeys grow."

"If you stayed dead, I'd agree with you, but since you came back to us, you get a second chance."

"Since you all moved here to the island to be with Emmet and me, that's possible. You do not know how much it means to the two of us that you, Calum, Dillon, Aiden, and Liam all moved here."

I wave that away. "It wasn't totally selfless. I wasn't functioning well without you all, and Sloan saw it. When I woke up from being hexed by Raven, he had things pretty much settled."

Brendan's smile falters. "Those were the worst three months ever, Fi. You gotta try never to let something like that happen again. We were all wrecked by it…especially Sloan."

I don't like the direction this conversation is taking, and I steer it back to happier thoughts. "Well, since we moved here, I've been much happier. Seeing one another every day grounds me."

He kisses the top of my head. "Yeah. Me too."

Shenanigans—the Isilon edition—is more tavern than pub and more cowboy rustic than Celtic dancehall, but it's fabulous just the same. Plus it's a place where I can spend time with Liam, my first and longtime bestie.

When we all moved to the island, he was the only member of the family still living our past lives back in Toronto. Then he agreed to help Brenny and Emmet by running the island tavern, giving the refugees of Isilon a social watering hole.

Anyone who knows anything about the social order of things understands establishing a place where people can share a pint and get to know one another is a must.

Shenanigans was that for us our entire lives. Now it can be that for others as well.

"Hello the house!" Brenny shouts as we pass through the double doors and head inside.

I wave at Liam working the long bar against the back wall,

and Brenny breaks off to stop and say hi to HaiLe and a table of locals who have come for her stew.

The woman is a wonder. She has five children to care for, is adjusting to her mate's death, and is still here, cooking and caring for the island's people every day.

"Hey, stranger. What's the craic?" Liam grins at me.

I pull out one of the stools at the bar and climb onto the seat. "Oh, plenty of craic today. Worlds to save. Rituals to find. Veils to raise."

Liam grabs a glass and fills it with ice. "High octane or regular?"

"A lemonade is good, thanks."

He's got his thumb on the dispensing gun when the door to the kitchen swings open, and Kady comes through carrying a tray of cut fruit for garnishes.

I'm not sure what the two see in my expression, but they both burst out laughing.

I jump off my stool and stop gawking. "You're here. Is this... what does this mean?"

Liam's smile says it all. "It means she missed me and decided to give this fantasy realm life a try so we can see if we can make it work."

I rush to the end of the bar with my arms open. "This is fantastic. Kady, I'm thrilled you didn't give up on us."

Liam tosses his bar rag at me. "This is about me, Fi, not you. She missed *me*."

I toss the rag back at him and laugh. "Okay, fine, but the result is the same. She's here, and you can stop moping around like a sad puppy."

Kady meets his gaze and arches a blonde brow. "See, you missed me more."

He lifts one shoulder and shrugs. "Maybe I was a little more heartbroken than I let on. I didn't want you to come here out of guilt. I wanted it to be your choice."

She rounds the end of the bar and meets him with a hug. "This is my choice. I'm right where I want to be."

I fist-pump and do a little happy dance. "Yay! I'm so happy for you two. When did this happen?"

Liam grins. "Nikon brought her last night. She helped me close up, and we went back to my place—our place—and talked it through."

I clap madly and hug them. "Congratulations."

Liam leans over and hugs me tighter. "Thanks, Fi."

I meet Kady's gaze. "It's going to be great. You'll see. With our family and friends, we can get you back to Toronto fast if ever you need to be there."

Kady nods. "That was a selling point that helped me decide. For now, we'll be taking the Nikon shuttle back and forth to monitor the other bar."

Liam looks at me and arches a brow. "I wondered if Nikon and Merlin might open a portal door between the bars. Or maybe from the bar here to our apartment upstairs at the bar there, if that's better for security?"

"It would be convenient, yeah. I'm not sure how many access points we should make between Toronto and this island."

"Maybe we move the portal door in the palace down here?" Brenny leans against the bar and joins us.

"Maybe. I'll talk to the brain trust and see what they think. I like the idea of moving it better than having two points of exposure."

"That's understandable," Liam agrees. "We don't want to cause trouble, but it would be great to have access to both businesses."

Yeah, that's important too.

Liam and Shannon arranged for several longtime managers to step up and take charge, but it would be good if they kept close tabs.

It means that Sloan and I would lose immediate access to our home…

It also means kitchen and living room sex would be back in play because my brothers couldn't arrive in my pantry at any moment.

Pros and cons, baby.

"The important thing right now is that the two of you are back together and making a go of it, despite the bizarre turn life has taken."

Liam steps behind Kady and pulls her against his chest. "Bizarre turn. That's one way to describe it."

Brendan reaches across the bar to shake Liam's hand. "Congrats, bro. I hope the two of you find the happiness you both deserve."

I hear the truth in Brendan's words but also read the sadness in his gaze. Man, I've gotta find someone who can love my brother like he deserves. Someone with longevity so he doesn't have to lose them, but who also accepts that he can't exist anywhere beyond this island.

Sadly, that eliminates all the feisty biker chick types he usually goes for.

Looking between the happiness of the reunited Kady and Liam, and the loneliness of my brother, I decide to make that a priority in the days and weeks to come.

Emmet too.

The Isilon Cumhaill boys need to find love. Since they can't go out and find it themselves, it's up to me.

Challenge accepted.

CHAPTER FOUR

"*Aghra*, wake up." I'm roused from a deep sleep, pulled from a lovely dream about private islands, sexy times, and the sun's warmth on my skin. "Luv, stop fighting me and wake up. I've got somethin' important to tell ye."

"Not more important than what we were doing on the pearl pink sands in my dream."

Sloan chuckles. "Are ye forgettin' yer rule about no sex on the sand? Ye said the invasion of grit to yer lady bits is a nonstarter."

"I make an exception for my dreams."

He arches a brow. "Noted, but that's neither here nor there. Right now, I need ye here in the awake world because ye'll want to shower and get dressed before the others arrive."

I scrub my hands over my face and draw a deep breath. "Okay, I'm awake. Who's arriving and why?" I sit up and swing my feet over the edge of the mattress to land on the fuzzy purple rug beside my bed.

With my head clearing, I look up at Sloan and his uncharacteristic state of wrinkled and disheveled strikes me. "Wait. Are you just getting home now?"

His grin is sheepish. "Time might have gotten away from me, but I assure ye, it was time well spent."

I shake off the last of my dreams and shuffle across our bedroom, stopping at my dresser to grab fresh clothes. "You don't need to apologize to me for your passions. I'm glad you had a good night. What did you find?"

Sloan grabs a fresh shirt from the walk-in closet between our bedroom and the ensuite bathroom and tugs it off its hanger. "A good many things, but in the context of restoring the veil, I found what I think could be a startin' point. It isn't exactly a ritual, but it might give us a bit of extra strength in our efforts."

"To get the veil back up or to thwart whoever is trying to keep the veil down?" I place my clothes on the gray marble countertop of our bathroom vanity.

He chuckles. "Are ye plannin' on usin' thwart now that Garnet got ye hooked?"

I giggle. "As much as possible, yes." I turn the handle for the faucet and start the water running to warm up.

"I figured as much." He shakes his head and chuckles. "What I found will not only be a startin' point to bring the veil up and help us thwart our foes, it'll also spark yer interest."

I step under the spray. "Spark my interest? Why is that?"

"Because it mentions a certain crescent amulet and its ability to enhance the focus of a druid's power while reinstating the veil."

I stop rinsing my hair and look at him. "Holy schmoly, I just got chills. Look."

I hold my bare arm toward the glass wall of the shower, and Sloan arches a brow. "Trust me, *a ghra*. When yer in the shower, I'm lookin'. Ye don't need to tell me to take notice."

I chuckle and go back to showering. "You know what that means, don't you?"

"That I'm a man in love with his wife?"

I roll my eyes. "Not the gawking. I was talking about the

mention of the crescent amulet."

"Oh, aye. I'm with ye now. What does it mean?"

"That the universe is pulling for us and the amulet reaching out to me wasn't our foes trying to thwart us and lead us astray."

"Possibly, but let's not get ahead of ourselves. I found a ritual that mentions the need fer a Blind Moon Crescent amulet—"

"Which I now have."

"Aye, ye do. Still, I want Merlin, Lugh, Dionysus, and Isilon to weigh in on that before we set ourselves on one course over another."

"Granda is coming too?" I shut off the water and crack open the shower door to hold my hand out and wriggle my fingers. There are few things I hate more than cold air hitting my wet flesh after a shower.

Sloan knows this, and being the indulgent rich guy and lover of shopping he is, he installed heated towel racks. I thought them over the top at first, but now I'm a spoiled little convert.

He hands me a towel so I can bring it into the shower stall to dry off. "Aye, I asked yer grandfather and asked Dionysus to fetch him on his way here."

I finish drying off and wrap the damp towel around my wet hair. This time, I open the shower door, and Sloan wraps a second towel around me, enveloping me in warm, plush coziness. "Thanks, hotness."

"Ye needn't thank me, luv. It truly is my pleasure."

I go on tiptoes to kiss his cheek. "Where are we meeting everyone, and when?"

"Up in the Great Room of the palace."

"Do we have time for breakfast before we go?"

He takes my towel while I get dressed and hangs it over the rail to dry. "No, but Dionysus said he'd take care of the spread."

My stomach growls in anticipation. "Perfect. Then give me two minutes to run a brush through my hair, and I'll be ready to roll."

"I'll run downstairs to get yer shoes and tell Bruin and Manx what we're up to. Back in two shakes."

The Great Room of the Isilon palace has been our family meeting place for all the important events since Emmet first became the island's caretaker. It's seen our holiday celebrations, strategy meetings when we were trapped here, and family announcements like when Dillan and Eva told us about baby Haniel.

It's a huge rectangular room with rough stone walls and polished stone floors. On the far long wall, two open archways let us step outside onto an oversized balcony looking over the city, the city gates, and the meadowlands beyond.

It's one of my favorite places on the island.

It also has a stunning, antique wooden sideboard and hutch that runs along the wall between the archways to the outside.

That's where Dionysus is famous for setting out his feasts—another of my favorite things on the island.

I'm in luck because although Dionysus has not arrived yet with Granda, our breakfast feast is here and waiting for me.

I head over, grab a plate, and dig in, heaping my selections into a glorious pile of breakfast casserole, Canadian bacon, and a few silver dollar pancakes.

Once I locate the syrup, all is right in the world.

Garnet walks in with Merlin at his side. "Lady Druid. Imagine finding you at the buffet table."

"I'm not sure if I should laugh or be offended by that comment." I blink.

"It wasn't meant as a criticism. It was simply an observation that you gravitate toward the table if there is food laid out in a room."

I blink again. "First, buffet tables are like the water coolers in an office. All the best conversations are held there. Second, it takes a lot of calories to fuel this crime-fighting bod, and I know better than to monitor what I eat. If there's no fuel in the furnace, I burn out at the worst possible moment."

"Exactly right, Fi," Merlin agrees. "No one wants you burning out because you're counting calories. Being healthy and strong is more important."

Garnet holds up his hands. "Relax, people. I appreciate seeing a woman eating her fill. I just meant that Fi always seems to mill at the—"

"Give it up, Lion." Isilon flickers into the human form of my grade eleven English teacher, Mr. Epima, and joins us. "There is a human saying Emmet tells me often. When you're in a hole, stop digging."

I chuckle and tap the end of my nose as I pass Garnet. Taking my plate over to the long meeting table in the center of the room, I claim a seat on the far end, away from where Sloan admires two leather-bound tomes sitting open in front of him.

They must be powerful because the tingle of ancient magic and the thick scent of parchment and power lace the air.

Sloan looks equally content flipping through the pages of the books as I am with my breakfast. That's not surprising. Information feeds his soul.

As I eat, I watch his gaze wander over the discolored pages. His pale green eyes shine with excitement as he takes in the passages.

I love watching him like this.

Honestly, I love watching anyone when they are blissfully consumed by their passions. There's something to be said about embracing what makes you thrive.

As we await Granda and Dionysus, I continue to eat my breakfast. Isilon ventures over to see what Sloan has selected to show us.

I'm finishing my casserole when the hair on my arms stands on end, and a golden mist bursts into the air.

Dionysus materializes with my grandfather and my father at his side. "Let's get this party started."

I set down my fork and hurry over to hug them. "Hey, you two. Thanks for coming."

Granda winks, gives me a quick hug, and passes me to my father. "Och, we'll always come when ye call. Ye know that."

I do. They've proven that repeatedly over the past three years since Fionn first marked me as his heir apparent and the leader of the Fianna Warriors.

"Hey, Da. I didn't know you were joining us. How are you, oul man?"

Da holds me for an extra squeeze and kisses the side of my head before easing back. "I'm still above the ground, so there's that to be thankful for."

I chuckle. "True enough. With a bar that low, everything else is a win."

"Right ye are, *mo chroi*. Right ye are."

With everyone assembled, Sloan clears his throat and addresses the room. "All right, everyone. Here's what we know fer sure. The veil wasn't brought down as a by-product of the Time of the Collidin' Realms last year. Instead, it was a deliberate act to destabilize one or both realms."

Da, Granda, and Isilon haven't heard this turn of events yet, and their surprise shows.

"Our theory is that we're up against a powerful individual or a group of individuals actively workin' against us to keep the veil down."

"A mystery saboteur," I add for dramatic effect.

Granda scoffs. "Fer what purpose?"

"Chaos, fuckery, or shits and giggles?" I suggest.

"More important than the *why* is the *who* in this scenario," Da points out.

Sloan nods. "We're hypothesizin' either a disgruntled god or a group of empowered who want magic to be outed to the world."

Da frowns. "Gods could certainly be selfish enough to cause this level of mayhem without care. No offense, son." He meets Dionysus' gaze.

Dionysus shrugs. "None taken. There's no one more aware of the selfishness of gods than I."

Sadly, I suppose that's true.

Zeus and the entire Greek pantheon have disregarded him and treated him like dog shit squished into the tread of their sandals since the beginning of time.

"How do we counter them?" Granda asks.

"That's the question." Sloan spins one of the open books on the table to face us. "Merlin and I have searched fer magical answers fer months, but yesterday I set out to study rituals—specifically moon rituals."

Da arches a brow. "How did ye narrow the focus so specifically?"

Sloan's mouth quirks up in a crooked smile. "Yer daughter had one of her moments."

Da and Granda both turn an assessing look on me. At first, they seem worried, but then their gazes narrow, and they look annoyed.

"What now, *mo chroi?*" Da asks.

"Why are you looking at me like I did something? I didn't. Myra and I were minding our own, chatting at the Emporium, when one of her enchanted objects demanded my attention."

Da lowers his chin. "Demanded yer attention how?"

I roll my eyes. "Seriously, it was nothing. Like I said, Myra and I were catching up on the latest tea, and I felt a magical pull toward the enchanted object display. This little guy insisted he come home with me."

I pull the chain around my neck until the amulet is free and hold it out to show them. "According to the provenance, the Blind Moon Crescent represents the moon's power and influence over the mystical realm. When worn during rituals, especially moon rituals, the amulet enhances the wearer's ability to channel lunar energies to strengthen the veil."

Da's brows arch. "It called to ye out of the blue?"

"Yep."

Da scowls at the amulet and curls his fingers toward himself. "Give it here. Let me have a look."

I do as I'm told and hand it over to be inspected by my father and my grandfather.

When they finish, Merlin steps up to be next in line. "Remarkable," Merlin murmurs, running his fingers over the amulet's smooth surface. "The power emanating from it is very similar in energy and frequency to the power of the veil itself."

"Let's hope that's a good sign," I comment.

Sloan picks up the spell book he was referencing and continues. "So, when Myra gave us a list of spell books that might contain a moon ritual to help us, I found this one in the Light Weavers' library."

"There is great wisdom secured in that chamber." Isilon's curiosity is piqued.

"Aye, it's incredible," Sloan agrees. "I found a moon ritual that holds potential, especially with the arrival of Fiona's new magical silver accessory."

Batting my eyes at him, I reclaim the amulet from Merlin. "Normally, I'm not a jewelry girl, but I seem to amass quite a few pendants."

"There's only one that really matters." Dionysus winks and taps the silver pendant with his likeness encircled by leaves, vines, and bunches of grapes around the outer edge.

I stroke a caressing finger over the oval pendant and my heart swells. He gave it to me in the grove of Nikon's family estate in ancient Greece. When we first met, Hecate was out to get me because of my relationship with Nikon, and he wanted to keep me safe.

Tarzan is good like that.

"Not that you're biased," I tease.

"Nope. Not at all."

"So, bringin' the focus back to the point at hand." Sloan ignores us. "Another of the components we need fer the ritual involves us findin' an ancient tree. It's said this mystical elder possesses roots so deeply entwined with the heart of the Earth that it forms a connection between both realms. Apparently, it will know what we need to do to raise the veil."

"Quite the arboricultural marvel," Dionysus quips, raising an eyebrow.

"Arboricultural is quite a mouthful," I respond.

"It is, but I sound very smart when I use words like that. And we both know how you like smart guys." He waggles his brows at me.

Sloan flashes the two of us a look, and I bite my lips together to keep from laughing and try to focus.

Behave, or we're going to get detention. I project my thoughts to Dionysus.

Good. I've gotta keep up my bad boy rep. Having a loving relationship with a sweet, Southern cowboy tarnishes a guy's cred as a manwhore troublemaker.

I'm sure that's true. Don't worry. The people who matter know you're a giant rebel and rabble-rouser.

Thanks, Jane. You say the nicest things.

Sloan is staring at me, waiting to start. I press my fingers to my lips, turn the imaginary key to lock things up, and toss the key over my shoulder.

He rolls his eyes and continues. "The tree we are searchin' fer is said to hold immense power, and only when someone worthy reaches its heart will they be given the knowledge sought."

A shiver runs down my spine. Trees have always held a special place in my heart, first as a kid growing up in the last house on the street next to the Don Valley River System, and more so now that I'm a druid and I magically connect to all living miracles of nature.

"There are several mystical trees of lore, lad," Granda interjects. "Can ye be more specific?"

"No. That's all it says."

"There can't be that many ancient trees of lore, can there?" I ask.

The men around me exchange glances, everyone lost in thought.

"Could be Yggdrasil, the World Tree from Norse mythology," Garnet suggests.

"Or the Tree of Souls from Celtic lore," Granda adds.

"What about Gaokerena, the life-giving tree from Zoroastrianism?" Dionysus chimes in.

"The Tree of Life?" Da suggests.

Try as I might, I can't think of any actual trees to add. All I've got are pop culture references like Treebeard, Groot, the Whomping Willow, and the Red Tree of Winterfell. None of those will be helpful.

"Aye, it's an impressive list," Granda acknowledges. "But consider the possibility that it's a tree unknown to us. Perhaps one hidden from history and legend."

I wince. "That would suck."

Dionysus nods. "No kidding. There's nothing like the world depending on you, and the key to salvation is something no one has any knowledge of."

I blink. "This has happened to you before?"

He waves my question away. "Don't even get me started on that fiasco. Let's just say Eros and I should never play Truth and Dare with our alcohol inhibitors removed."

"Sweetie, it's Truth *or* Dare."

He frowns. "Well, that would've saved us a lot of trouble if we knew that."

The men continue to discuss the possibilities but are adding to the list instead of narrowing things down.

"All right," I interject, pausing their brainstorming session. "Let's table the tree discussion for the moment. What's the third step of the quest?"

Sloan taps a finger against the page. "The third component is the staff of Hermes. If lore proves correct, Zeus had it turned on the lathe of Hephaestus, and it holds the power of inviolability."

"*Annnd* what does that mean?" I ask.

Sloan grins at me. "It means it is a weapon of the unassailable."

I shake my head. "Sorry. I've still got nothing."

Sloan tries again. "If something is not to be changed or challenged, the staff will ensure its purpose remains sound."

I blink and search the faces of the others. "Am I the only one not getting this?"

Dionysus meets my blank gaze and winks. "It's an 'Oh no, you don't. You can't fuck with that' magical stick."

I gesture at Dionysus as I catch up with the conversation. "Why didn't you just say that, hotness?"

"I thought I did."

I roll my eyes at my genius hubby and get back to the point. "So, we need the MC Hammer staff. Got it."

"MC Hammer?" Sloan repeats.

"*Can't Touch This.*" I do my best to dazzle them with a few flashy '80s dance moves, but only Dionysus appreciates my efforts.

I give up and turn toward Dionysus. "Sorry, sweetie. I'm not up on the family tree of ancient Greece. Who is Hermes to you and is he a giant dickwad like the rest of them, or do you think he'll help us?"

Dionysus shrugs. "They all rank in varying levels of dickdom, but Hermes is okay. He's a bit of a daddy's boy and likes to rub it in my face that while our father sent me away, Zeus appointed him as the official messenger of the gods."

"How does that put him in the range of okay, Tarzan? He sounds shitty."

Dionysus chuckles. "Being an arrogant git is so far down on the list of offenses perpetrated toward me that it isn't funny. He did nothing truly vile or hurtful, so he gets a pass in my book."

If I could raze the whole of Mount Olympus on his behalf, I would. Gods might be self-involved, but in Dionysus' case, their arrogance hurt someone sweet and kind who simply wanted to be loved.

I blink against the sting of tears, my emotions vacillating between hurt and fury.

Dionysus claims my clenched fist and brings my knuckles to his lips. "It is what it is, Jane. All gods are arrogant, and yeah, when our father gave him that staff, Hermes had every right to be cocky. Whenever gods or mortals see him holding the caduceus, they know he's about to deliver an official message from the gods of Mount Olympus."

"That's badass," Isilon claims.

I scowl at him. "You have been spending too much time with Emmet."

Dionysus chuckles. "No, he's right. It's a badass staff, and it commands a great deal of respect."

"Do you know where it is, Greek?" Merlin asks.

"Sure. Hermes hasn't gone anywhere without it since the day our father gave it to him. Wherever he is, his staff will be there, too."

"We know where two of the components are," Garnet sums up. "That's better than most of our adventures."

True story.

Sloan nods. "Next are a set of stones lost since time immemorial. Lore says they were stolen by a moon demon and imbued with the power to harness the magic of the lunar cycle."

"Handy during a moon ritual," I remark.

"Any idea where they are?" Da asks.

"Destroyed." Dionysus frowns. "Ages ago, that moon demon you mentioned took a run at Selene and tried to manipulate the tides. She confiscated the stones and to ensure they didn't fall into the wrong hands, she destroyed them."

I sigh. "Of course she did. What are the odds we can do this ritual without the stones?"

Sloan shakes his head. "Not good."

"Maybe those weren't the only stones, or maybe there is more than one moon demon that made magic stones?" Granda suggests.

"Or maybe she didn't destroy them," I muse. "What are the odds that she tucked them away for safekeeping?"

Dionysus chuckles. "A million to one, Jane. Deities don't generally hang onto our personal Kryptonite."

"Well, poop."

Da sighs. "Is that the last of it, son? The amulet, the tree, the staff, and the stones?"

Sloan shakes his head. "There's also a rare combination of dried herbs and essences to blend as an incense fer the cleansin' of the ritual."

"Lara and I can work on that or at least start the preliminary research," Granda offers.

Sloan nods. "Grand. That leaves the last component, findin' a celestial map that charts the constellations of the magical worlds." He turns the spell book to show us a page covered in symbols and drawings. "It says here the map will pinpoint the precise location to perform the moon ritual for the greatest chance to raise the veil between worlds."

"Well, is that all," Garnet snarks.

"Not it." I hold up my hands. "This girl is no good with maps. I can't navigate them, can't decipher them…hell, I can't even fold them."

Da chuckles. "True enough."

Merlin has moved close to Sloan's side and is studying the

symbols of the celestial map. "By what I see here, it looks like the alignment of the realms plays a large part in the ritual's success."

"Meaning what?" I ask.

"Meaning we need to light a fire under our asses so we can perform the ritual during the upcoming Vernal Equinox of Ostara."

I blink. "Exsqueeze me? That's a lot of questing to get done in a week."

"True, but if I'm reading this star chart correctly, we need to harness the power of the moon ritual when the veil is thinnest."

"Does it need to be thin if it's not in place?"

They consider that.

"I think so," Sloan finally replies. "Perhaps durin' the equinox, when the veil is thin, we'll have the best chance at restructurin' the fabric of the magical divide."

If I imagine the veil as a physical fabric, I see how that could work. Still, it doesn't give us much time. "So, we need to find a celestial map, a tree that might or might not be known, a staff that Hermes won't part with, and a substitution for the moonstones...unless Selene hid them instead of destroying them."

"Is that all?" Garnet asks.

Da raises a finger. "And a mixture of rare incense and herbs to cleanse the ritual area."

"Within the next week," Merlin adds.

"All righty." I throw my hands up. "What are we doing lazing about? We've got shit to do."

"Spoken like a genuine leader." Dionysus smirks, raising his glass in a toast. "To the quest!"

"To the quest!" I echo, my mind tumbling through the checklist of things that need to align to pull this off. "And hey, searching the globe and taking on gods to save the world, this is just another Thursday."

Isilon frowns. "But it's Monday."

CHAPTER FIVE

Over the course of the day, Dionysus and I update my brothers on our quest, Sloan goes back to the Light Weavers' library with Isilon to search for more information about legendary trees, and Da and Granda head over to Aiden's and Kinu's home to play with the kids.

"Where do you think we'll find the map?" I ask Dionysus as we lounge under the tree in my backyard.

Dionysus sips from his glass of wine and grins. "I hope it's on a pirate ship somewhere and we get to swashbuckle. That would tick off a fantasy of mine."

I chuckle. "You could totally pull off the ruffled shirt and those big boots with the tight pants. I'm not sure about you in braids, though."

He shrugs. "Johnny Depp went the dreads and beads route for Jack Sparrow. It worked for him."

"It certainly did." I extend my hand, and we clink glasses in a toast to Captain Jack.

Lost in the images of my favorite pirate, I miss when the mood changes and Dionysus goes quiet. When I look over, he's biting his bottom lip and looks anxious.

"What is it, sweetie?"

He glances at me and frowns. "One thing I love most about being a Cumhaill and working with Team Trouble is that I don't have to deal with pantheon bullshit. But this ritual…"

"It's got pantheon bullshit smeared all over it," I finish.

"Yep." He sits there for a moment, then chuckles. "Do you remember how gross it was when we went to the zoo, and the gorilla smeared his poop all over the glass of his exhibit?"

I love how Dionysus' mental trains can derail at any moment. "Yeah. Even more disgusting when he started licking it."

We both scrunch up our faces, ending that train of thought.

Dionysus swirls his wine and takes a long drink. "There are a few ancient libraries where a map like that might be held for safekeeping."

I grin. "Well, we can't go on library runs without Sloan. He'll be heartbroken if he misses that outing."

"It's weird how much he loves dusty old books."

I shrug. "It's less about the dust and more about the information they might hold. Books hold the answers to mysteries. Oh, and in that vein of thought, I wonder if Myra might have some intel on the map or the tree."

"Do you want to go?" He sits up, raising his wineglass to keep from spilling it. "I bet we'll be back before Sloan misses you."

I laugh. "Tarzan, there's a mystery afoot, and it demands research. Sloan won't look up for days unless he finds something interesting."

Dionysus grins. "I want a hobby that gives me that much pleasure."

"Drunken debauchery doesn't count?"

"Not anymore. I'm in a committed relationship and am mature now."

I tip my glass back and finish my drink. "Then sure, I'll text Sloan, and we'll take a toodle to the Emporium. Don't worry.

We'll work on finding you a hobby. How do you feel about knitting?"

He scrunches up his nose. "I don't do yarn."

"Cycling?"

"Working up a sweat solo? No thanks."

I laugh and take his hand. "We'll think of something."

After texting Sloan our plans and gathering Bruin from where he, Manx, Daisy, and Doc are playing with the kids in Calum's and Kevin's yard, Dionysus portals us back to Toronto.

The moment we materialize inside the Emporium, my shield flares to life and I step away from Dionysus. Tensed for trouble, I scan the quiet stacks. The fiery burn on my back isn't a heads-up...it's a full-blown warning. *Bruin, search the bookstore. Something is wrong.*

There's a stir in my chest before my battle bear releases and the air around me swirls up in a gust.

Tarzan? You feel it too, right? I ask, sending him my thoughts.

Rigid muscles and a deep scowl have replaced Dionysus' usual lackadaisical swagger. *Call your staff, Jane. Whoever or whatever is here, they've got power behind them because they're shielding from me.*

Securing Myra and Imari is our priority.

Agreed.

With a twisting knot in my gut, I flex my fingers and...

Birga doesn't come.

I frown at the spear tattoo on my inner arm and call her again. Nothing.

Someone's blocking Birga from manifesting.

Dionysus reaches toward me and offers a wicked rapier he calls to his hand. *It's not the same as a spear, but it's long, and it'll get the job done.*

That's what she said.

Yeah, she did. He waggles his brows at me, and the two of us advance.

Bruin? What's our sitch, buddy? I ask.

Two in the front and four in the reading area.

What about Myra and Imari?

Locked in the back storage room. Scared but fine.

Thank the goddess. I pull my Guild pendant out from under my shirt, press down on the centurion helmet, and hold. That will send an all-call to those of us in the realm—most importantly, Garnet.

If he finds out after the fact that someone was here endangering his girls, he'll lose his mind.

The moment I feel the air around me surge with magical energy, I release the pendant and get ready for the coming storm that is my alpha lion boss.

Garnet flashes in looking homicidal with Anyx, Zuzanna, and Thaos at his side.

"They locked your girls in the kitchen," I whisper.

Zuzanna nods and is gone a moment later.

"Who?" Garnet growls.

I shrug and signal two in this section of the store and four in the back area where Myra's home tree grows.

Garnet and his men flash out.

The *whoosh* of a breeze lifting my hair brings my battle bear back to me. *Zuzanna took Myra and Imari.*

Good. Now, where are the two in here, buddy?

One at the back counter. One near the doorway to the back room.

Cool. Garnet and his pack have the back room.

Any idea who they are?

They all look Greek to me.

Dionysus pegs me with a frown. *Look Greek? Do we have a look?*

When ye wear tablecloths and sandals, ye do.

If there were time, I'd laugh at the annoyance in Bruin's tone.

He doesn't like Dionysus being able to listen in on our private chats.

It doesn't bother me. It often saves me from repeating myself.

There's no time to get into that now.

A fight has broken out in the back of the store, and we've got two to deal with in the front.

With the alpha males in full offensive mode, if I'm not fast, there won't be anyone for me to take on. They won't leave anyone for me if I don't get my elbows up.

Greedy men.

I call my body armor forward—whatever is blocking Birga thankfully didn't negate that—and jog up the main corridor between the rows of books. The crash and clash of fighting in the back swallow my footsteps.

Sadly, the sound of fighting will also swallow the sound of—

My shield singes hot, and I duck a moment before a bolt of golden magic skims past my head. The power of it snaps in the air and raises the hair on my body.

It explodes against the bookshelf by my shoulder and sends sparks flying.

"Incoming," Dionysus shouts.

I get my sword up in time to slice the next bolt, but the magic doesn't dissipate so much as split and crawl up both sides of the blade and up my arm.

I stiffen as the magic takes hold. It's like an electrical field of power. It tingles over my flesh, and my body locks in place. The immobilization spell takes hold in an instant, and I'm frozen and rooted to the spot.

Dammit. I counter the spell and push out my intention. *Freedom to Move.*

The hold breaks as a woman in a red and gold peplos flies in to attack. I barely get my hands up before she pummels me with a magical assault. The impact knocks me off my feet, and I get air as I fly backward.

My head cracks hard against the shelving unit, and I topple over a row of books. It's not graceful, but my armor protects me from any actual damage.

"Impenetrable Sphere." I blink at the ceiling while the Tweety Birds circle over my head. Then I roll to my feet and reclaim the rapier.

"That was rude." I dust myself off.

Another barrage of magic comes at me but can't penetrate my sphere. It doesn't get me any closer to taking her down, but it gives me a chance to determine that she's a witch.

Crashing over the shelves tore the neck of my shirt, and my pendants swing in full view. The woman's gaze locks onto the silver crescent moon, and she shouts something in ancient Greek.

"Yeah no, sorry. I don't speak screaming bitch."

Seeing that her magic has no effect, she pulls a bejeweled dagger and comes at me physically. So, she fancies herself as a witch *and* a warrior—that's unusual.

The polished blade glints in the light as she jabs.

She's stabbing me—or at least, she's trying to.

The good news is that my sphere is keeping her at a distance. The bad news is that with every strike of that blade, the integrity of my bubble of protection is weakening. So, not a normal dagger then.

I curse, lift the rapier, and release the sphere when she's fully engaged and leaning forward. The moment the resistance of the sphere disappears, she stumbles forward, and I'm ready.

I swing hard and slice her hand, knocking the dagger away and severing a few fingers.

I don't feel bad. "Who are you? What do you want?"

The woman is cradling her bloody hand and casts me a ball-shriveling glare.

Not a talker then.

With a banshee scream, she rushes me, her entire body

bursting into a supernova of magical energy. With a couple of quick retreating steps, I get the rapier's tip up and meet her attack with mine.

The tip of the double-sided blade pierces the crimson fabric of her dress, and our opposing forward momentum has the blade sinking into her guts like a beef chunk on a barbecue skewer.

The two of us meet chest-to-chest, and I read the surprise and fury in her gaze.

Yeah, well, I can't help that. You started this, bitch.

"And you finished it." Dionysus grips the woman's shoulder and pulls her away from me to let her drop onto the floor.

I straighten and Dionysus frowns at my blood-soaked T-shirt. "Are you intact?"

"Perfectly. You?"

"Same."

The two of us leave the mess of books and blood to hurry to the other side of the store. The long, steady growl of Garnet's lion vibrates in my chest as we join the others.

Scanning the carnage, the first thing I notice is that the attackers are all women. The second is that they all wear traditional red and gold Greek gowns.

"Who are they?" I ask.

"Who *were* they?" Garnet snarls, his eyes glowing gold with the power of his lion.

"Carians," Dionysus informs us. "A cult of followers from Asia Minor dedicated to Hecate."

I glare at the woman dead on the floor. "Why are we dealing with Hecate's brand of crazy?"

Bruin lumbers over, and I scrub my fingers through the thick guard hairs of his long coat. No armor. No blood. He's not even breathing hard.

"Not much of a challenge for you, eh, Bear?"

He shakes his head. "An amuse-bouche with no entrée to follow."

I scrub his velvety ear and chuckle. "Maybe next time, buddy."

Garnet grunts. "Tell me where and when, Lady Druid. I want to know who thought they could come into my mate's safe place and threaten not only her but our cub as well."

Yeah, whoever thought that was a good idea didn't have all the facts. "We'll figure that out. Tarzan? Who are the Carians, and why would they be here?"

"They were looking for something." Anyx gestures at the smashed display cases.

Unlike Garnet's ebony hair and tanned skin, his pack beta and second in command, Anyx, possesses the golden skin, flaxen hair, and leonine features you'd expect from a Moon Called lion.

"Zuzanna got Myra and Imari home safe?"

Anyx nods. "They're at the compound now."

Good. That's good.

"So, what's with the Carians?" I ask again. "When you say followers dedicated to Hecate, what does that mean, exactly? Do they mindlessly worship her? Follow her teachings? Do her bidding?

"Yes. All the above."

"What does that have to do with Myra?" Garnet snaps.

"Not Myra," Dionysus says. "The one Jane was fighting shouted that she found it."

My fingers move to the silver amulet hanging against my chest. "They were after my pendant. Her eyes bugged wide when she caught sight of it."

Dionysus nods. "That's my guess, yes."

The brass bell over the front door jingles wildly, and a wave of warriors joins the party. Dan, Diesel, and Brody rush through the front and slow to a jog as they see the result of our battle.

"Sorry we're late," Brody says. "I've never been here and had a hell of a time finding the place."

I wave his worry away. "No harm done. But yeah, everyone

should know where this place is. If for no other reason than the cool stuff Myra sells."

Diesel wipes his hand over his skull and sighs. "Sorry. It looks like we missed all the fun. Is everyone all right?"

"Fine," I assure him. Glancing at those in attendance, I'm missing one of my favorite people. After handing Dionysus the bloody rapier, I wipe my hands on my shirt and pull out my phone.

Hey Greek, I pressed an all-call, and you didn't show. All is well on our end, but I'm wondering where you are. Check in. Something is happening, and Hecate is involved.

Dionysus is reading over my shoulder. "You don't think she's done something to Nikky again, do you?"

"I don't know, but he wasn't in Isilon, so he should've gotten the call."

"Unless he's in another time?" Dionysus suggests.

"But we just saw him, and he didn't mention any traveling with his cousin."

"Maybe he slipped through one of his portals to the fae realm," Garnet suggests.

"It's possible, but he would've said something. Nikon knows I worry, and he's good about things like that."

Dionysus frowns. "I'll go check Isilon just in case. Maybe Sarah knows where he is."

"Who's Sarah?" Brody asks.

"Sarah Connor," I tell him. "A white witch from Ireland. The two of them are dating. She was living in the Hidden City, but now that it has revived from its slumber, she spends most of her time back in Blarney."

"I'll check there too," Dionysus confirms before he's gone.

Garnet frowns. "Dionysus is the only one who knows who the Carians are. Can we get him back here?"

"I understand your frustration, bossman, but no. First, we make sure Nikon is okay. Then we worry about whatever Hecate is up to. If she's back on the scene, Nikon needs to know about it."

Diesel frowns. "Hecate as in the patron mother of Wicca?"

I nod. "Yes, but despite being the goddess of magic, she's also a spiteful, selfish ex-girlfriend who has an obsessive fixation on Nikon."

Brody makes a face. "That's a tough ex to have."

"You don't know the half of it." The next number I call up on my phone is Andromeda's.

It only rings once before she picks up. "Is everyone all right? The all-call went off, and Max and I are sitting here losing our minds."

"The situation at the bookshop is sorted, and no one was hurt. I'm calling because your brother didn't respond, and I don't know where he is. Can you track his pendant and give me a location?"

"Sure, hold on. I'm putting you on speaker." On the other end of the line, I hear Andy give Maxwell a quick update. Then she asks him to track Nikon's location using the GPS coordinates of his Guild pendant.

"Has he ever missed a call before?" Max asks.

"No," Andromeda and I both reply at once.

I wait with bated breath, hoping with every racing heartbeat that Max will break the tension and tell us where Nikon is.

He doesn't.

"Come on, Max. Tell me the good news," I say, prompting him.

"I'd love to, Fi, but I've got nothing. He's not showing up. I just finished a diagnostic on the system and can ping all the others—but not Nikon. The trackers in this realm are active. The ones your brothers wear read as out-of-realm. I've got nothing for Nikon."

I hit speaker so I don't have to catch up the others. "What does that mean? Could it be broken?"

"Unlikely. Merlin spelled them himself. More likely…"

"What?" I snap. "More likely what?"

"More likely, the magic hooking it to our system has been masked or destroyed, so we can't track him."

"It would take some real juice to out-magic Merlin," Brody remarks.

I curse. "Like maybe a witch-bitch goddess with an ax to grind?"

Garnet growls and holds out his hand to me. "We're coming in, Max. Track Nikon's last known whereabouts and put it on the monitor wall."

"Yep. Doing that now."

CHAPTER SIX

"Aw, *a ghra*, did ye get any sleep, luv?" Sloan strides into the kitchen, scanning me with an assessing gaze. The sun has barely dawned in Isilon, and the room is still more gray than gold.

"Not really." I set down my chamomile tea and offer him as much of a smile as I can muster. "Every time I closed my eyes, all I could see was Hecate taking out her revenge on Nikon. Torturing him. Threatening the people he cares about. Taunting him about what she can do to him."

Sloan pulls out the chair beside mine and turns it to face me. "Ye should've woken me, luv. I hate the idea of ye hurtin' and bein' down here all alone."

Patting his knee, I lean forward for a kiss. "I wasn't alone. Bruin stayed with me for most of the wee hours, and even if he hadn't, I still would've let you sleep. You were up the entire night before, researching rituals."

"Aye, but I would rather comfort my wife than sleep any day of the week."

I shift from my chair to sit on his lap and let him wrap me in his embrace. "You can do both."

We sit like that, quiet in our worries, for a long while.

With his arms around me and his fingers tracing a lazy circle along the outside of my hip and thigh, I must've dozed off because the next thing I'm aware of, Sloan's talking on the phone in the hall and I'm lying on the couch with a blanket tucked around me.

His voice is too quiet for me to hear what he's saying, but when he hangs up and comes back in, I see that it's my phone he has in his hand. "Who was that? Does Garnet have a lead on Nikon? Dionysus? Merlin?"

He hands me my phone and sits on the edge of the couch next to me. "Dionysus hasn't returned from Mount Olympus yet, and no one has any new information. That was Merlin. He has a few ideas about the ancient tree and wanted to know if we are proceedin' with the quest or focusing on Nikon?"

"With everything in me, I want to say Nikon, but Hecate has blocked every avenue we have to find him. Garnet, Dionysus, Max, and I tried all day and evening yesterday and got nowhere."

The worry in his expression deepens. "I'm sorry I wasn't there, luv. I feel terrible about that."

I wave away his concern. "This is a multi-faceted quest, and we've all got our part to play. I don't need you with me every moment to fix every problem. I just need you to love me and pick up my slack when I've got too much weighing me down."

He nods. "I can do that. Just remember to let me know if the weight of the world is too much to bear."

"Deal."

I run my fingers through my hair and shake off the last of my sleep. "What did you tell Merlin?"

"I said, ye'll likely want to move forward with the ritual components, but the moment there's news about Nikon, we'll switch gears. He is our priority."

I draw a deep breath and exhale. "Good answer."

"Now, why don't ye hop into the shower and get dressed? I'll make ye a breakfast sandwich, and ye can eat it on the go. Merlin has a bit of a lineup of locations fer us to check out, so the sooner we get there, the sooner we're home."

I fold the blanket and set it over the arm of the couch. "Sounds good. I won't be long."

The thick canopy of leaves overhead blocks most of the sunlight, shrouding the forest in an emerald gloom. Massive tree trunks twist into the sky, their gnarled branches intertwining to form a leafy ceiling. My boots *crunch* on the underbrush as we hike along a narrow, winding path.

Calum swats at a mosquito buzzing around his head. "There's got to be an easier way to do this."

Dillan scowls at the forest surrounding us. "It's probably un-druidy of me to say this, but all these trees look and feel the same."

They're not wrong. We're deep in an old forest with massive trees all around us, and it's impossible to tell which tree is the oldest or holds the most ancient power.

"And these bloody insects are driving me mad," Calum adds. "They're not responding to my magic. Do insects speak other languages? If so, I need a translator, or I'm going to start squashing mosquitos."

Dillan chuckles. "That is *very* un-druidy of you."

"Yeah, well, I'm done being nice."

It's not really about the trees or the insects. I know my brothers well enough to know their grumbling is about Nikon and them feeling useless when he's in trouble.

I know this because I'm as cranky for the same reason. "When we get him home, I think we should have a toga party. Oh, for my birthday."

Dillan grins. "That's a damn good idea."

Calum nods. "We'll invite a bunch of girls. Brenny and Emmet really need help on the female front."

"Agreed. I thought that the other day."

Sloan chuckles. "Isilon has begun to repopulate. Don't ye think they can find their own women in their own time?"

Dillan rolls his eyes. "Fi's Greek orgy idea is better."

I blink. "Hey, I said I should have a birthday toga party, not a Greek orgy."

Dillan and Calum exchange glances and grin.

"Okay, Fi. Sure. Just a toga party." When Dillan winks at me, I know this has become a losing battle.

I throw up my hands. "Fine, we'll have it in the Great Room in the palace. Then Sloan and I and Aiden and Kinu can excuse ourselves when the night gets out of hand."

"Deal." Dillan smacks Calum's arm and grins. "We'll see if Bizzy and Daisy can have a sleepover with Jackson and Megs. If not, I'll ask Mickey."

"Fuckin' A," Calum says. "I love this idea."

"Dionysus is going to lose his mind," Dillan adds.

Yeah, that's probably true. He might be adulting and working on having a stable relationship, but he's still the God of Feasts and Fertility.

"First we've got to get Nikon home," I remind them.

The guys all nod in agreement.

"We will, *a ghra*. We definitely will."

With Dionysus reaching out to the Fates to locate Nikon and Sloan not having the same freedom of distance and energy expenditure the Greeks have, dragon flight is our best mode of travel for the day.

Not that I'm complaining.

It's always amazing to fly with Dart, and now that Sloan and

Saxa have bonded too, it's even better. Dragon flight might not be as immediate as portaling, but it's much more exhilarating.

Seeing that it's Dart's first time in the Black Forest, I tell him and Saxa to stretch their wings and have fun while we tromp around searching for a magical tree.

Which isn't as easy as I had hoped.

It's not a needle-in-a-haystack scenario. It's a tree in a forest scenario, which is a million times more difficult.

The Black Forest has some of the oldest trees on Earth, and Merlin thinks the one we're looking for could be one mentioned in the fairy tales of old.

The five of us—me, Sloan, Bruin, Calum, and Dillan—traipse through the forest for ages, following Merlin's map, Calum's GPS coordinate calculations, and having Sloan *poof* us through the forest using line of sight.

We take over an hour to find the area where Merlin thinks we need to be. Even then, there's no straightforward way of figuring out which tree is older or more majestic than another.

I stare at the endless stretch of trees on one of our water breaks. "Think about how many classic children's stories have been anchored around this forest."

My brothers nod, but for once, Sloan looks blank.

"Hold the phone. Is this something we know about, but you don't?" I check with my brothers, who seem as surprised as I am.

Sloan arches a brow. "I'm sure there are a great many things the three of ye know about, which I don't. Why do you look so shocked?"

"I don't know. It feels monumental."

He laughs. "All right, luv. Enlighten me on the children's stories that focus on the Black Forest. I'd love to hear about it."

A comment like that would almost certainly be sarcasm if it were anyone else. With Sloan, it's not.

"All right. If I'm right, Cinderella, Little Red Riding Hood, Rapunzel, and Hansel and Gretel were all set in the Black Forest."

"Sleeping Beauty, too," Calum adds.

"What about some of the other Grimm fairy tales?" Dillan asks. "They were around here too, weren't they?"

Calum nods. "Yeah, still a forest in Germany, but a different one."

I'm not sure why knowing this when Sloan doesn't seems like such a win, but it does. It absolutely does.

Guaranteed, the moment we get back to civilization, and he has time to look things up, he'll download all the information on the forest fairy tales, but for now, we know things he didn't.

I bask in that triumph for a long while before I giggle and hold up a finger. "I have an idea."

"Look at you, happy clappy," Dillan says. "You're full of ideas today."

"She's full of something," Calum adds, giving me a sidelong look. "Why are you laughing? Does this idea involve humiliating one of us?"

"Possibly."

"Not it!" Dillan holds up his palms and takes a step backward. "Stamped it."

Calum curses. Dillan removed himself from what's coming next, and we all know it. "Fine. What's your idea?"

"I was thinking about spelling a divining rod to help us find the tree in question."

Calum rolls his eyes. "Tell me I'm not going to end up with poison ivy on my junk."

Now Dillan's laughing too. "Damn, that was one of the best Emmet moments evah!"

"Emmet might disagree," Sloan counters.

"All I can picture is him getting dragged over that log, getting air, and his shoe flying off into the trees."

Dillan shakes his head. "If only you had a GoPro on. We need that on a highlight real."

Calum nods. "It's definitely in the vault of classic Cumhaill moments."

It is. "So, what do you think? Divining rod, or no?"

Sloan nods. "Sure. What's the worst that could happen?"

Dillan groans. "Dude, bad form. Did you really just ask that? Have you learned nothing from three years with our sister?"

Sloan rolls his eyes. "I've learned yer all ridiculous."

"Says the man who just jinxed us." Calum sighs. "I vote Irish is the man holding the rod."

I blink. "Rude."

Calum laughs. "I didn't mean that to be rude, but yeah, good one. Point for me."

I laugh and start searching the underbrush. "We need a forked branch from an oak, ash, or a yew."

"Oaky doaky." Dillan searches the scrub. "I've got this."

"Yeah, yew do," Calum adds.

"Yew being an ash, brother?"

"Yew know it."

I'm laughing because I remember having a very similar conversation with Emmet three years ago when we were in the same situation.

We are all cut from the same cloth.

I spot a forked branch in the scrub and jog over to pick it up. After Sloan inspects it, he nods, holds the branch between his palms, and closes his eyes.

I've always loved watching him cast spells because, unlike my brothers and me, he casts in Irish.

There's something sexy and magical about that.

I don't catch the entire spell, but I understand the part about us seeking an ancient tree.

When Sloan opens his eyes, the forked stick in his hand points out in front of him, and he lets himself get pulled by the power of the spell.

Dillan, Calum, and I follow.

Where Emmet looked like a ragdoll getting bumped and banged off the forest floor, Sloan looks like a man completely in control.

It's impressive…but *waaay* less fun.

Still, we're making good time.

We dodge a patch of prickly scrub, hop a couple of downed trees, and search the forest around us as we go. "You're doing great, hotness. Love you."

Bruin is in his spirit form, riding the wind that encircles us as we run. He's no doubt monitoring the surroundings as we push through, ensuring we're not surprised by any unexpected evildoers.

My gaze sweeps through the surrounding forest, searching for anything out of the ordinary.

So far, nothing about these woods seems magical or mysterious. Well, other than the natural magnificence of the forest itself. But in the context of us finding the tree that will anchor the veil, nothing so far.

Then it happens.

We round a thick cluster of trees and stop in front of what has to be one of the biggest trees in the natural world.

It's massively wide and seems to reach up to the Choir of Angels. Ebony bark encases the beast's core in rough scales and makes it seem like it's been scorched by time itself.

While it's brutal-looking, it's also badass.

"We have a winner." Calum tilts his head back to stare up at its branches.

"Now what?" Dillan asks. "Find the tree, and if we're worthy, we'll find the answers at its core. What does that mean?"

No idea.

"Maybe ye need to connect with it," Bruin suggests, taking form beside me. "Yer druids, after all."

True story. "Okay, we'll try that."

The four of us step up to the tree, and each holds up our

palms. One by one we press our hands flat against the trunk's bark and wait to see if anything happens.

The tree is magical—there's no denying that—but while it holds power and wisdom, nothing suggests this is the tree of our quest.

We stand there, waiting…

My shield flares at the same moment as a surge of negative energy blasts through me. It is so powerful that it knocks me off my feet, flying backward.

CHAPTER SEVEN

Instinct more than intention calls my body armor forward. There's nothing to do to negate the blast and no time to defend against it. I don't have time to cast a cushioning spell before I'm plucked out of the air by a massive paw.

"Got ye, Red."

I blink at my bear and scrub his cheek. "Thanks for the save, buddy."

He's grinning at me. "My pleasure. Unfortunately, I can't be in four places at once."

His meaning becomes clear as a long string of colorful swearing echoes off the surrounding trees. All four of us got flung back at the same time.

I get my feet under me and glimpse Sloan straightening from a straight-up superhero pose.

Knee to the ground, fist to the earth, and a look of determination on his face. *Yeah, baby. That's my guy.*

Dillan wasn't quite so graceful. He's tangled in the roots of a fallen tree, and Calum is...

"Shit, Calum." I'm on my feet and running to where my

brother is lying face down in the dirt with a nasty gash open and bleeding on his forehead. "Sloan, I need you."

Sloan kneels beside me. "I'll stabilize his neck while you and Dillan gently roll him onto his back."

Dillan is with us too, his pissy mood temporarily postponed while Calum needs us. "You're okay, bro. We've got you."

When Sloan tells us to, we gently roll Calum onto his back and wait while the Mackenzie magical signature tingles over our skin.

Sloan's a good healer.

His father is a *great* healer.

I know that if Calum needs help, between my hubs and my father-in-law, Wallace, he'll be okay.

I've learned to trust in that.

There's a tense few minutes, then Sloan smiles. "Here he comes."

Calum's eyes flutter open, and he winces. "Who cracked my coconut?"

"It was the fucking tree." Dillan scowls at the ancient oak and raises both middle fingers. "Fuck you, tree. That was an asshole thing to do. You suck."

Calum's scowl softens. "Are you seriously flipping off a tree?"

"It's an asshole tree, but yes," he rants. "If it doesn't like to be touched, it could say so. That was uncalled for."

Sloan and I help Calum to his feet, and I wait to make sure he's steady before I let go. "Are you okay?"

"Yeah, I think so, but either we're not worthy, or this isn't our tree."

I sigh and step back. "Sadly, I was thinking the same thing. I say we portal back to the clearing where we left the dragons and take you home."

Calum shakes his head. "Nah. I'm good. We should move on to the next forest on Merlin's list."

I look him over, not sure that's a good idea, but Sloan doesn't seem bothered by it, so I give in. "Fine, but promise to tell us if you get dizzy or queasy."

"Yes, Mam," he agrees.

"You should text Dionysus our next location, too," Dillan suggests. "If he comes back and has something to tell us about Nikon, we all want to hear it ASAP."

Yeah, we do.

We hike for hours through dense forests, ducking under tangled branches and skirting massive tree roots. Merlin's list was as accurate as he could make it, but in the end, there are no blinking neon signs that point at a magical tree and say, "This one, right here."

Wouldn't that be nice?

By the fourth forest, the sun is dipping toward the horizon, and it's getting darker and darker beneath the canopy of leaves.

I'm tired. Frustrated. And my guts are knotted up so tightly about Nikon being in the clutches of Hecate that I'm about to bend over and hurl into the ground cover.

I'm scared for him.

I'm angry at her.

And I'm buried in a heap of guilt that I can't shake. Nikon being taken made me realize I haven't been making time with him lately.

I've been so caught up in getting back on my feet after being cursed, starting my life with Sloan, and spending time with my family, that I've neglected my friendship with him.

He's one of my best friends, and I can't remember the last time we took off together and spent some time.

I swipe the tears leaking onto my cheek and draw a heavy breath. My crying in the middle of a remote forest won't do him any good.

Red? Are ye all right?

I rub the ache in my chest and try to get a grip. *I'm scared for Nikon and don't think I've been a very good friend to him lately.*

Och, I don't know if I'd agree with that. Yer a damn good friend to everyone in yer circle.

I try to be, but Nikon is different. He's special.

Aye, and I think ye'd say that about each of yer friends if ye think about it.

Maybe that's true, but I think he tries to stick to the periphery of my life because of his feelings for me. I know he wants Sloan and me to be happy, but I want him to be happy too.

Love is a tricky thing.

I know. I just...I thought once he started dating again, he'd find someone and be happy. I want that for him.

Aye, and he knows that. Yer overcome with worry, and it's makin' ye feel things more keenly. Once we get the Greek home, ye'll feel better. Ye'll see.

I hope so.

I'm tromping along behind my brothers when Sloan holds a branch to keep it from snapping back to hit me. When he sees my expression, he stops. "Why are ye cryin', luv?"

At the mention of me crying, Calum and Dillan turn to see what's wrong. Nothing like all eyes on you when you feel like bursting into tears.

"I'm fine. I miss Nikon and am worried about him. It hurts my heart that I haven't spent much time with him lately and now he's being held somewhere by that bitch."

Sloan frowns. "First, none of this is yer fault, and second, we only suspect that Hecate is behind him bein' gone. Perhaps he took some time off-grid, and he's baskin' in the sun somewhere."

"I appreciate the effort, hotness, but we both know you're trying to cheer me up. Hecate has him. I feel it in my bones."

"If so, we'll get him back, luv. He's immortal, right? We've got that goin' for us."

I suppose that's true. If nothing else, he should be able to survive anything she puts him through. I'm about to say something to that effect when a surge of power zings over my skin.

The others must feel it too because we all straighten and look around.

"Did you feel that?" Dillan asks.

Calum scoffs. "You mean the weird magnetic pull drawing us all toward our impending doom? Nope. Didn't feel a thing."

I roll my eyes at Calum and draw a steadying breath. "Let's do this and get home. I want to be there when Dionysus gets back from Mount Olympus."

My brothers nod and lead the way. I follow them, and Sloan takes up the rear.

"We're close to the coordinates," Sloan murmurs, squeezing my hand.

I hope so. After playing this game all day, I want to find the right ancient tree, go home, and wait for word from Dionysus about how we're going to get Nikon back.

"Do you hear that?" Dillan straightens.

We all freeze, the four of us turning our heads to listen to the forest's cues. At first, there's only the usual scurrying and scampering of woodland life.

Then a faint, unearthly melody reaches my ears. It's like the ringing of tiny bells. The notes hang in the surrounding air, crystalline and pure.

Calum's eyebrows arch, his green eyes alight. "Does anyone know what that is?"

By the looks on our faces, that's a no.

Whatever it is, it's lovely. The cadence and the pitch are otherworldly, and as I ask my shield to weigh in, I get nothing back but warm, safe reassurance.

As the pull of the magical calling grows more intense, I pick up the pace. Jogging first, then breaking into a run, I succumb to the overwhelming need to close the distance between me and the tree.

Yeah...somehow, I know it's a tree.

In the back of my mind, somewhere, I hear the guys calling my name and telling me to slow down.

Heedless of the roots that threaten to trip me, I skim through the maze of trees. The song's magical melody grows louder until at last, I burst into a clearing and skid to a stop.

It's incredible.

An enormous tree towers before us, its gnarled branches seeming to reach all the way up to the fiery tangerine sky.

This is no ordinary tree. It glows with an inner light, and the melodic ringing undulates in the air as if being carried to us by unfelt waves.

Power radiates from its golden branches, resonating with my magic until I feel lit up from within.

Tears prick my eyes as I grasp the truth. This is the tree we've been searching for...the anchor that holds the veil between realms.

We finally found it.

I take a hesitant step forward, almost afraid to breathe for fear of shattering the illusion of the vision before us.

The tree isn't going anywhere. Its ancient magic is as vibrant and alive as mine.

I close my eyes and let the tree's song wash over me, reaching out in response with my druid magic. The massive oak senses my touch. Its melody shifts in welcome.

A vision of a massive, gnarled door set into the tree's trunk and sealed with potent magic blooms behind my eyelids.

My eyes fly open as the vision fades. "Did you see that?" I ask Sloan and the others.

Their expressions remain blank, Sloan's dark brow arching. "See what, luv?"

"It's hard to explain. The tree showed me something—a door. It's here, but not here."

I let the pull of the tree's call draw me closer, knowing with everything in me we are exactly where we need to be. With my palms up, I ready myself to touch the wide trunk.

"Carefully," Sloan warns.

"Yeah, no more tree concussions." Calum gently probes his forehead.

I shake my head. "This beautiful beast doesn't want to hurt me."

Dillan cracks his knuckles. A wicked grin stretches across his face. "Then there's nothing to worry about. Go ahead, Fi. Touch the tree."

Calum snorts. "You're half hoping she gets rejected and you can watch her get zapped, aren't you?"

Dillan's lips quirk up at the corners as he feigns a look of shock. "Who? Me?"

I laugh. "Rude."

He pulls out his phone and starts a video. "You've got your armor. It's not like you'll get hurt."

Yeah, yeah. I step forward and stick my tongue out at him while I press my palm to the wood. The moment I make contact, I sober and pay attention.

Power surges through me in a rush, carrying with it a single word. *Speak.*

Okey-dokey. "We are druids working to restore the veil between worlds. Our quest has been to search for the great oak with roots that span both realms. We're told finding the tree is part of the moon ritual we wish to perform to restore the magical balance."

For a long moment, all is silent, and I wonder if I said something wrong and blew our chance. Then a deep, rasping noise issues from the tree, and two glowing amber eyes blink open.

"Oh, geez." Dillan throws up his hands as he and Calum take a quick step back.

Sloan's hand finds mine, firm and steadying. Yeah, I agree. Holding our ground shows respect, and we're serious about what lies ahead.

Still, seeing an ancient tree blinking is uber creepy.

"I, uh…did we wake you?" I ask, not sure what to say.

The blinking continues, and the *crackle* and *snap* of bark bring a three-foot bark man pulling himself free of the trunk.

My mouth falls open, but I hold my ground.

The tree man is short and covered in bark, so he's bumpy all over. He looks a little like a crusty, older version of Groot.

"You think yourself up to uniting the realms, druids?"

I pull back my shoulders and meet the bark man's glowing gaze. "We're committed to the task and have powerful allies, so yes, I think we've got an excellent shot."

"Bold words. Can you back them up?"

I blink and look at my brothers. I've never been smart-mouthed by a tree before, and I'm not sure how to come at this. Do I give as good as I get or take the high road?

While I decide that, the little bark man rumbles, and the ground shakes beneath our feet. "Listen well, druids. Solve this riddle of old, and I'll consider your worth."

A riddle? Weird. Suddenly, I wish Nikon was here, and my heart aches again.

"Taller than trees,
Stronger than beasts,
But the wind overtakes me,
With the greatest of ease.
What am I?"

The four of us look at each other for a moment before Sloan's eyes light up. "A mountain."

There's a brief pause, and the bark guy grins. "Correct. Next one.

"In forests deep, I dance and sway,
A cloak of green in proud display.
Whisper my name, and you'll soon see,
I'm ground to dust and heal with glee.
Tell me, wise druid, what am I?"

I look at Sloan, my mental hamster cramping up on this one. "There are a lot of green growing things deep in the forest."

Calum shakes his head. "But it's something you grind and use in a healing spell. Whisper my name, and I'll heal with glee. It's an herb or a medicinal plant."

I look at the bark man. "Does medicinal plant work or do we have to guess until we narrow it down to which medicinal plant?"

The wee man chuckles. "I will accept it. There are many magical florae found in forests that provide healing properties used in druid remedies."

Yeah, there are. That's why I was afraid he would make us keep guessing.

"Next riddle." The bark man claps his wooden hands.

"Seriously?" Dillan sighs. "How long are you going to make us do this? Is this really serving any purpose?"

The bark man's amber eyes flare brighter, and his smile dissolves. "You are free to leave, druid. I was under the impression that you seek answers."

"We do." I hold up my hands. "Forgive my brother's impatience. He's tired and didn't mean to offend. Did you, Dillan?"

I shoot him a look, and he forces a smile. "My bad. Sorry. I didn't mean to be rude. Yeah, sure. Let's play the riddle game. Good times. Give us your next one."

It certainly wasn't his best apology, but it does the trick because the little bark man's smile returns, and he continues.

"Born of the sun and kissed by the breeze,
My layers bloom in vibrant seas.
I shimmer with colors, both bold and bright,
Guiding lost souls through day and night.

Oh, mystic druids, what am I?"

I look at Sloan and frown. "I want to say rainbow, but I don't understand the guiding lost souls part. Is there some reference in lore that says lost souls can find their way by following the arc of a rainbow?"

Sloan nods. "It could be interpreted that way, aye. There's a saying, 'When lost loved ones are near, rainbows appear.'"

That's good enough for me. I meet the bark guy's glowing gaze and nod. "I'm going with rainbows."

Bark guy grins. "Good one, Red. All right. Last one…

"Gentle and swift, through meadows I glide,

Where rivers meander and spirits reside.

Hidden from view, a secret unseen,

A conduit for whispers, the forest's own dream.

Dear druid, can you tell me what I am?"

I've got nothing. I look at Sloan and can tell by the look on his face that he's sussing out an answer. Remaining quiet, I give him the time and space to get his gray matter grooving. Glancing at Dillan and Calum, I read their expressions.

They've got nothing either.

"Yer the hidden pathways of nature spirits," Sloan answers. "The paths used as the conduits of dreams within the natural world."

I wonder at first if the bark guy is pleased or annoyed with Sloan's answer. After a tense moment, his uneven smile widens, and he claps. "Well done, Shrine Keeper. I always enjoy your deductions."

Sloan inclines his head as his gaze narrows. "Have we met before?"

He laughs and throws up his hands. "Some might say yes and others no."

My instincts say yes, and the familiarity niggling at me finally makes sense. "Discord? Is that you?"

The man made of bark who pulled himself out of the trunk of

the tree grins at me as the image of him morphs before us. My shield warms but doesn't flare and I take that as a good sign.

When Discord's transformation is complete, he takes the form of a red fox and appears as he did three years ago when we first met.

"Hello again, Red."

"Hello again, indeed. What are you doing here?"

He lifts his snout and chuckles. "That's for me to know and you to figure out."

Of course, it is.

He scans our group and frowns. "Where's the blond? The one who appreciates my riddles."

"We think Hecate took Nikon."

His lips curl up off his teeth. "And I liked him too."

The defeatist way he says that strikes a chord. "He's not lost to us. He's just missing."

"To you, he's missing. To her, he's found."

"I think we're gettin' off point," Sloan interjects. "Why are ye here playin' yer games, trickster?"

Discord shrugs. "I have to be somewhere, and games are fun. It's been a long time since I've played with Red. I like her."

I know from experience that's not a good thing.

Discord isn't exactly evil. He simply has no moral compass in any direction and is ambivalent about his actions, who's hurt by them, and what others want.

He's only in it for shits and giggles.

Thinking about him that way, here of all places, I look at the fox and the magical tree, and it clicks. "Maximum chaos and two realms turned upside down."

Sloan meets my gaze and frowns as he follows my train of thought. "Ye think?"

I do. "Discord, you took down the veil between realms, didn't you? And you're keeping it down to stir up maximum trouble."

The fox opens his mouth in what I can only describe as a smile. "I do love maximum trouble, but no. You have your first piece of the puzzle but have a long way to go until you put it all together."

Of course, we do, because what fun would it be if we figured it out before maximum chaos is reached?

In Discord's eyes—no fun at all.

"But it's not a coincidence that you're here."

Discord wiggles his ears at me and grins.

"And you're here because this is the tree we need to access to set things right."

"What is right? What is wrong?"

There aren't enough hours in the day to teach Discord morals and consequences. Instead, I appeal to his chaotic neutral personality.

"Forget right and wrong. How about a game?"

His amber eyes shine with excitement. "Yes! A game! What shall we play?"

I think about how to phrase this before I speak. With Discord, I have to work within his world, or I'll lose him. "My friends and I are working to reinstate the veil. Your friends are working to keep the veil down. It's like a tug of war with magic with lives in the balance."

Discord grins. "High stakes. Many surprises."

He didn't correct me about him working with "his friends," so I take that as another piece of this puzzle. I've dealt with Discord enough to know he holds no loyalties to those he conspires with. He wants to have fun causing trouble.

"I'm guessing you were sent to keep people from accessing this tree, but that's boring, amirite?"

"Very boring," Discord agrees.

"You've probably been sitting here for ages. Wouldn't you rather cause trouble?"

He flashes me a sly grin. "What kind of trouble?"

"You give us another riddle, and this time, if we get it right, you let us access the tree."

His smile falters. "You're not supposed to access the tree."

"But you love surprise twists. It'll be a twist in the plan for the group that wants to keep the veil down. It'll make them angry and drive them crazy."

His bushy tail swishes against the ground, and he nods. "All right. Another riddle. If you win, I allow you to access the tree. But *if* you win…I get to come with you. I'm tired of tree-sitting, and if you access the tree, I don't have to. I want to see the fallout."

Having Discord in our lives is the last thing I want, but maybe it's a case of keeping our enemies close. Besides, I might get more information about who he's teamed up with.

Taking a knee in front of him, I extend my hand and shake his paw. "Deal. Let's play."

I straighten from striking a deal with Discord, and magic erupts around us. My stomach roils as the forest swirls in a green blur and morphs into a long stone wall lined with six identical wooden doors.

Stepping over to Dillan, Calum, and Sloan, I study the pattern numbering the doors from left to right: 1, 11, 21, 1211, 111221.

"What is the number of the sixth door?" Discord asks.

At first, all I see are a lot of ones and twos.

"It's a logic puzzle," Dillan says.

"That lets us off," I razz my brother. "Logic has never been our strongest event."

Sloan presses a finger over his lips as he studies the number sequence.

Calum points and moves closer. "The first three are an add ten. One plus ten is eleven, plus ten is twenty-one…"

"But the next two don't track," Dillan says.

"No, I know."

Dillan, Calum, and I continue to talk among ourselves as

Sloan ponders. Honestly, watching his mind work could give me a complex.

"Do you give up?" Discord asks, disappointed.

I laugh. "Not in a million, dude. Cumhaills don't give up. We persevere. Or, in this case, we wait while our resident genius saves our butts."

Dillan shrugs and nods. "Irish. Irish. Irish."

Calum and I join in, and he sends us a dirty look. "Yer not helpin'."

The three of us sober and wait patiently. Taking another look at the numbers, I give it a shot. Trying to find a math sequence, I look for a pattern in the changing numbers.

1, 11, 21, 1211, 111221, *annnnd?*

I've got nothing.

"I've got it." Sloan nods. "The number for the next door is 312211."

Discord claps, beaming. "Very well done, Shrine Keeper. I thought I might stump you with this one."

"Aye, ye almost did."

The numbers Sloan recited appear on the sixth door: 312211. I try to see how he got there and give up. "Okay, one of you will have to explain this to me because I'm not seeing it."

Sloan winks. "It's not a math sequence. This is what's called a look-and-say sequence. Each number describes the previous number in a numerical manner in order as it appears with the words of how ye say it."

I blink but am no closer to understanding.

"Ye see, the first door has a one and there is only one of them, so on the next door, the number is one one—11. Then, the description of that fer the next door is—"

"Two one because there were two ones."

"Aye, that's right. On the next door, the description is one two and one one, so 1211."

"Then one one, one two, and two ones."

"Right, which becomes 111221."

Calum nods. "I get it, so the last door is three ones, two twos, and one one—312211."

I laugh and kiss Sloan's cheek. "Well done, hotness. That was amazing. You win the day. Five Oh Henry! bars for you."

Sloan grins. "More importantly, we passed the test."

Discord sweeps the black pads of his furry little paw through the air. The stone wall dissolves, and the world around us spins in a green blur until we're back in the forest where we began. "You proved yourselves worthy. You may approach the tree without interference."

The ancient tree before us is rooted so deeply into the earth that it connects the two realms. Powerful energy radiates off it, and I feel the call of magic even stronger now than I did as it guided me here.

Its gnarled branches claw toward the night sky, shadows dancing in the pale moonlight. Raising my palm toward the wide, rough trunk, I close my eyes and reach out with my druid powers.

CHAPTER EIGHT

I've spent many conversations—and more than a few bottles of Redbreast Whiskey—describing to Liam and Shannon how magic feels.

It's tangible, yet it's not.

It's sensory, but that's not it either.

Sloan's and Tad's wayfarer energy feels like you're *poofing* from one place to the next, while Nikon's gift feels more like you're snapping through space. Dionysus' energy is like a burst of mist, while Garnet and the Moon Called sort of flash you places.

The same goes for when you're touched by someone's magic, either through an attack or healing. We often comment on the "magical signature" of someone's powers when we come into contact.

It tells you a lot about a person...or in this case, a magical tree.

The moment my palm presses flat against the rough bark, magic thrums through the connection, vibrating in my bones. My shield remains calm—no traps or foul magic to warn me away—and I sink deeper into the sensation that I need to be fully present.

The gentle rumble of movement has my eyes flipping open

and my heart racing. A door has appeared where I have my hand on the trunk and I'm pushing it open.

Hesitating, I shift to the side to peer inside the tree.

Then Sloan's words come back to me. *"Only when someone worthy reaches its heart will they be given the knowledge sought."*

Well, if it's inviting me inside, I can hardly decline.

I draw a deep, steady breath and step across the threshold. *To the heart of the tree, I go.*

"A ghra, wait!"

Sloan's worried plea gets cut off as I'm sealed within the cylindrical tower of the ancient oak. It's bigger than I imagined… it's also brighter.

Phosphorescent growth bathes everything inside here in an eerie blue-green light. The rich scent of nature and earth envelops me, more potent than any incense. Power feeds my cells, and the influx of energy is wild, primal, and as old as nature itself.

The melodic song we heard while out in the forest hums softly in the background, and it's wondrous and terrifying all at once. I feel the tree's concern woven into the sharing of power. It believes the imbalance in the realms threatens us all.

"I agree. That's why we're here. We hope you will help us reinstate the veil between realms." I rest a hand on the trunk's ridged inner wall.

The tree rumbles deep in its roots, wordless but distressed. Images flash through my mind of foul, unnatural magic twisting together and shadowy figures shrouded in mystery. But no clues as to who is behind this mess.

I hoped for more than a magical movie.

The tree grumbles at last, its voice like the groan of branches in a storm. "The veil must be mended before the fabric of the division collapses entirely."

No pressure. Just the fate of two realms. The usual.

I rub my forehead, feeling the onset of a stress headache. "I would appreciate any guidance you can offer. Who is behind this? How do we stop them? Where do we start?"

There's a long moment of silence, and...

"Speak this incantation when all is prepared. Tie the four powers of nature to the darkness and to the light. Balance is the key. Only then can the veil be restored."

A burst of images and sensations floods my mind, the magic of the incantation searing itself into my memory. I stagger to the side and clutch the meaty inside of the trunk to remain standing.

When the bombardment ends, I catch my breath. "Thank you."

Pushing off the moist insides of the tree, I scan the glowing interior, unsure of how to exit this place. A surge of energy answers that question and power washes over me.

"Do you know who's behind this? It would help us to know who and what we're up against."

Another set of images flashes through my mind, and my cranium feels like a watermelon being hollowed out from the inside.

I clutch the sides of my head and drop to the ground, falling...falling...falling.

I come to with a start, senses instantly alert, and with the faces of Calum, Dillan, Sloan, and Bruin framed in my view. "Looking good, boys. Nice to see your faces."

Dillan rolls his eyes and exhales. "She's fine."

The familiar scents of moss and damp earth tell me I'm still in the forest, although the moon's position indicates a few hours have passed.

Sloan crouches beside me, frowning in concern. "Welcome back. How do you feel?"

I push into a sitting position, wincing at the throbbing in my head. "Like I went a few rounds with a troll whacking me with a fallen tree. What happened?"

"You disappeared into the tree," Calum answers. "A couple of hours passed, and you appeared here, unconscious."

I see the emotion swirling in Sloan's gaze. "Sorry. I didn't mean to worry everyone."

Sloan closes his eyes and shakes his head. "It's not yer fault, luv. Havin' ye disappear and blackin' out is part of the package of lovin' ye, I'm afraid."

"Which you knew before you married me," I point out. "You picked me."

He chuckles and grips my wrist, pulling me off the forest floor and onto my feet. "Aye, I did. I'd pick ye again a hundred times over. Still, I prefer our quiet days over adventures of the unknown."

I check that I'm steady and brush the moss, twigs, and leaves off my butt. "To each their own."

Calum winds his hand in the air expectantly. "Marital banter aside, did you find out anything?"

The memories flood back…the tree's dire warnings, the incantation searing into my mind…the faces of our foes…

I lurch toward him and lose my balance, tipping as the forest spins around me. "Dizzy…."

I don't come close to hitting the ground because steadying hands grab me from all sides.

Sloan's in my vision, assessing my pupil dilation, no doubt. He frowns and pulls me to his side. "We'll talk about what ye saw when yer at home, sittin' on the couch."

"Excellent." Discord bolts out of the shadows. "Home, we go."

I blink as my memory catches up with the deal I made with our annoying trickster. Right. He let me connect with the tree, so he gets to come with us to watch the fallout instead of tree-sitting.

Except, there's no way I'm taking him back to Isilon. That's where my family lives. It's a protected haven and not a place I want a morally ambiguous trickster god to be, let alone know about.

"Okay, yeah. Home to Toronto, everyone." I meet the gazes of Sloan and my brothers, and they were thinking the same thing.

"Aye. To the dragons and home to Toronto."

The moment we land in the backyard of our home in Toronto, Calum, Discord, and I jump down from Dart, and Sloan and Dillan dismount Saxa.

I explained to Dart over our bond why we were here instead of the Hidden City, and the two of them stretch their wings, bid us good night, and head into their den.

Our sacred grove here isn't what it used to be now that almost all our fae friends moved with us to our new grove in Isilon, but it still holds power and the dragons' lair is still here as their home away from home.

I point into the forest that stretches from my backyard to my childhood home next door. "Shall we unwind for a few minutes under the stars while I catch you all up on what I found out?"

"Sounds lovely." Sloan places a warm hand on my hip and leads me into the shadows of the trees.

Calum and Dillan are right behind us, and I know they're eager to learn what happened inside the tree.

Discord follows, looking bored. Maybe he already knows what I found out. I don't care. He's the one who wanted to tag along and observe our lives. "There's a lot of nature energy in here." He swishes his fluffy tail like a hand riding on the breeze.

It's true. Dart's and Saxa's energy lingers like the charge of lightning after a storm. The residual magic from our flight through the dragon rings has left a tangible scent and crackle.

"Have you ridden on dragons before?" I hope if we connect

with him, maybe he won't be so quick to screw us over for a laugh.

"No. That was new. It was fun, too."

Excellent. "Our friends are often invited to have fun with us and the dragons. I'm glad you enjoyed it."

Are ye invitin' the demon to be yer friend, Red? Bruin asks me.

Better our friend than our enemy. Don't you think?

I'll wait to answer that until after I see how he betrays ye next.

My bear is a cynic and skeptical.

Settling into my rattan hanging chair, I sit back and wait while everyone grabs a spot. Sloan offers Discord his seat, and he, Calum, and Dillan stand around us in a small circle.

Their anticipation is as palpable as the dragon energy slowly dissipating in the air.

Sloan's gaze meets mine, his worry from earlier replaced with a steely steadfastness that steadies me. He's my rock, my anchor in the swirling sea of magic and chaos that is our life.

"All right. So much to tell you."

I start by recounting the cool, glowing interior of the tree and the conversation we shared. Her warning was dire, but we all understand the critical importance of restoring the veil.

Then I tell them to take out their phones to record the incantation. It's long and involved, but I recite it and am amazed that I remember every word.

Yay me! My English teachers would be so proud. I finally memorized a speech.

"Last, I asked the tree to help us figure out who is doing this so we can counter them."

"What did you find out?" Dillan asks.

"She showed me an array of the faces of our foes."

"And?" Calum asks.

I roll my eyes. "It's a highlight reel of troublemakers. Discord, Loki, Hecate, Eros, a couple of men who looked like Unseelie princes or dark fae leaders, and a few others I didn't recognize."

A heavy silence follows my big reveal. No one speaks. No one moves. We all sit there, each lost in our thoughts.

Finally, Sloan breaks the silence. "Knowing who we're up against is a good thing, no matter who it is. Once Dionysus gets back, we can use his connections to counter some players and possibly unravel the fabric of this insidious cabal."

I nod. "I know Eros is a self-serving dickwad, but I don't think he'd go along with Hecate taking things out on Nikon."

"Agreed. That will be the first thread we pull."

Dillan sighs. "I doubt it'll be that easy. This is an all-star team of dickdom conspiring against us."

"But now we know who, and soon we'll know why."

Dillan snorts. "Then we'll show them the error of their ways, they'll let us reinstate the balance between realms, and we'll all live happily ever after. Easy-peasy."

Calum shrugs. "We've faced worse."

He's right. We have. We've battled creatures of the night, faced down gods and demons, and navigated the treacherous politics of the Fae Court. This is another challenge to overcome, another step on our quest.

"Just another Thursday." I quote Ryan Gosling in *The Gray Man*.

Calum laughs. He and Kevin watched the movie with us the other night, so he gets what I'm saying. "Yep. Just another Thursday."

I yawn and check my Fitbit for the time. "Yikes. We need to get to bed, people. We've still got a long way to go and busy days ahead."

"So, we're calling it for tonight?" Calum asks.

Dillan tilts his head toward the back of the house. "We're good to head home, right?"

I know why he's asking, and yeah, I think it'll be fine for them to portal home. "Yeah, go ahead. I'll text you in the morning and tell you about our next steps. Go kiss your babies and give them a snuggle from Auntie Fi."

Calum's glance shifts from Discord to me. "Are you sure you don't want us to stick around?"

"No. We're good. I need to message Dionysus, and hopefully he'll get back with some news about Nikon. Other than a rescue run, we're in for the night. You two go home."

Dillan scowls. "Let us know if you hear anything about Nikon. If there's a rescue run, we'll be back and ready to battle in ten minutes."

"Understood. I'll keep you posted." I hold my knuckles up for a bump as the two pass.

When they're gone, I pull out my phone and call up Dionysus' contact info. I'm desperate to hear about Nikon, and at the same time, calling will give my brothers time to get through the portal in the pantry and not tip off Discord to our magical gateway to Isilon.

After I leave my fourth message for him today, I tell him where we are, what we found out, and about Eros being involved. Then I sigh and tuck my phone into my pocket. "The end. I'm done and calling it a day. Who's ready for bed?"

"I am." Sloan gets up and offers me a hand to help me. "Are ye comin' inside or sleepin' out here, Discord?"

The fox hops into the swinging basket and curls up on the padded cushion. "I'm fine here. The magic of the dragons feels good."

I'm not sure I like the sound of that, but I figure Dart and Saxa are formidable and can let us know if he tries anything on them. "All right. We'll see you in the morning. I'm sure there will be plenty of chaos for you to enjoy tomorrow."

CHAPTER NINE

I wake to Sloan peeking inside the heavy drapes of King Henry and the soft snoring of a man at my back. From the amusement in my husband's expression, it can only be one of half a dozen men—one of my five brothers, Nikon, or Dionysus.

I glance down at the hand flung over my ribs and the signet ring on his finger. Dionysus it is.

"He got here a couple of hours ago, and ye were still out," Sloan whispers, his voice deep and low. "He looked knackered, so I told him to settle in to get some rest until ye woke. I've got breakfast in the oven when the two of ye are ready."

I gather Dionysus' hand and hug it. "Thanks, hotness. We'll be down in a few, I'm sure."

Sloan nods and ducks back out of the curtains of our massive antique bed. I close my eyes and let the weight of what's ahead of us sink in.

This quest. The veil.

Preserving the balance between realms.

Most important—to me anyway—is bringing Nikon home. *Wherever you are, Greek. Know that we love you and are trying to find you.*

If it weren't Hecate who took him, I'd be all over razing the world to find him. With that bitch in the mix, he could be not only anywhere in the world but held within any *time*.

We ended up in ancient Rhodes the last time she took her frustrations out on him.

"We'll get him back, Jane," Dionysus murmurs behind me. He lifts onto his elbow and reaches over my shoulder to kiss my cheek. "Don't cry. We'll bring him home."

I blink against my tears and turn to meet his gaze. "We have to, Tarzan. He deserves so much more than the life he's led so far. He wants to find love and have a family. He's always wanted kids, and he's been ruined with the guilt of his wife's death.…"

The dam bursts, and I end up dampening Dionysus' shirt with my tears. When I've let out my frustration, he eases back and brushes a chaotic mess of russet waves out of my eyes. "Do you trust me, Jane?"

"With everything I am, yes."

"Then let's get up and get to it. I promise we'll bring Nikky home today or cut a swath through my pantheon like not even the Titans could."

I draw an unsteady breath into my lungs and soak in his confidence. "Thanks, Tarzan. I needed to hear that."

"Anytime. Now, go get dressed and take care of your lady business, and we'll make our plan."

I laugh, swing my feet through the slit in King Henry's drapery, and drop to the floor. Grabbing a clean outfit from my dresser, I hustle into the bathroom to get dressed and take care of my lady business.

"Did you get my message about Eros?" I call as I wet my toothpaste. Then I start brushing.

"Yes. I paid him a visit before coming here. He wasn't in any of his usual hangouts, so I left him messages all over the place. He'll get them, and I know he'll be here shortly."

Good. That will be a step in the right direction.

I spit, rinse, and wipe my face. There's no helping my curls, so I grab a clip and pull my hair back. Once I'm dressed and finished in the washroom, I head back to my bedroom.

Dionysus is lounging diagonally across the huge mattress, looking stressed.

"What's wrong?" I squeeze his foot. "Is there something you haven't told me?"

He shrugs. "Considering the fact that I haven't told you anything yet, yes. But I'm fine. It takes a lot out of me to deal with my family."

"I'm sorry, sweetie. If I could wish you everything you need and deserve, you know I would."

He sits up and shuffles off the bed to stand next to me. "Being an honorary Cumhaill gives me everything I need and more than I've ever had."

Shaking my head, I squeeze his hand. "You are long past being an *honorary* Cumhaill. You're the real deal, Tarzan. We are Borg. You are one of the collective."

His smile is adorable. "Perfect."

The two of us flash downstairs, and I remember too late that I forgot to warn him about Discord. Our unwanted guest is sitting on the kitchen island watching Sloan drink his coffee and scroll through his iPad.

When Dionysus stiffens beside me, I hold up a hand. "It's fine. We have things to tell you about yesterday, too. Have you eaten?"

Dionysus' gaze narrows. "A bit, but I'm always game if Irish is cooking."

Sloan sets his iPad down and slides off his stool. "Shall I make ye both a plate, then? Or would ye like to pick and choose?"

I wave his offer away. "I'll have a plate of whatever you made and will be grateful every moment that you take such good care of us."

Dionysus smiles. "Me too. Thanks."

"Coffee or tea?"

"Maybe one of those fancy cinnamon vanilla teas we got from Myra?" I ask. "Do you want to try it, Tarzan?"

"Sounds perfect."

We take our plates to the table, avoiding fox fur in our breakfast. I set my plate down and double back to the fridge to get… "We've got apple or pineapple tangerine juice."

Dionysus sits straighter. "Door number two, please."

I fill us each a large glass of juice while Sloan steeps our tea. "Since we're waiting for Eros to join us about Nikon, tell us about your last couple of days."

As the two of us eat our breakfast, Dionysus fills us in on how dealing with the gods of the Greek pantheon is like banging his head against a stone wall.

"Hermes told me he's more apt to shove his staff up my ass than to let us use it for an Ostara ritual."

I swallow. "What did you say to that?"

He chuckles. "I told him not to talk dirty. We might only be half brothers, but some lines were never meant to be crossed."

I grin and scoop up another forkful. "Yeah, you did."

"Yeah, I did."

"What about Selene?"

He sighs. "I don't know where she frequents, but I let people know we need to speak to her."

"And Hecate?"

"The Fates say she's been off the grid a lot lately. I'm sure Lachesis probably knows where she is and what she's up to, but she's not saying." He rolls his eyes. "She talks like she's a priest bound by the sanctity of the confessional. I tried to remind her that their dominion is over human lives and they don't have any binding tenets with other gods."

"That didn't help?"

"Not even a little. Pointing out that they have less power than they like to believe pissed them off."

I take a couple of swigs of juice. "What about their mother? Themis made it very clear to Hecate that she wasn't to mess with Nikon anymore."

Dionysus raises his hands to accept the cup of tea Sloan offers him. "Thank you."

"Of course, sham." Sloan joins us.

Dionysus sips his tea and continues. "Themis isn't willing to get involved. She said there is no evidence to prove Hecate did anything to or against Nikky, and she won't be drawn into personal vendettas. She is the goddess of justice."

Now it's my turn to roll my eyes. "It's not us with the vendetta. It's Hecate!"

"I know. Deities are frustrating. I'm sorry."

"Totally not your fault." I finish the last of my breakfast. "The most important thing is that we get Nikon back by whatever means necessary. If Themis can't help us, we'll go after Eros."

"What about him?" Dionysus points his fork at Discord sitting on my counter, watching us. "If he's part of the problem, maybe he can be part of the solution."

I hadn't thought about that. "I figured Hecate took him somewhere back in time and we'd need a god or goddess of your pantheon to find him."

"Probably. Still, there's a chance she's slotted him away behind a magical field somewhere. Hell, if they've got such a hard-on for blending the realms, maybe she's hiding in the fae realm somewhere."

"She's not." Discord hops off the counter and lands silently on the floor with a graceful *swoosh* of red fur. "She finds the fae repulsive and beneath her."

"Of course she does," I remark.

The air around us charges, and a burst of golden mist brings

Eros into my kitchen. The Greek god of Carnal Love stands tall before us, his magical bow and arrow hanging in its pendant form against the bare skin of his chest. "What do you want, *adelphos*? I don't appreciate being summoned like a common servant."

Sloan spins and drops into a defensive position.

Discord vanishes and is gone.

I drop my fork.

Dionysus pushes to his feet and rounds the table. "I want you to explain why in the fires of Hades you're involved with Loki, Hecate, and the rest of them taking down the veil? People are getting hurt. I know you don't care about humanity, but I thought you at least held loyalty toward Nikon."

Eros frowns and takes a step back. "What I do and why I do it is none of your business."

"But it's wrong."

He laughs. "Since you started associating with humans, you've become such an emotional bore."

Dionysus scoffs. "I'm evolving. Do you know what I've learned? Being a god doesn't give us carte blanche to do what we want, regardless of the consequences. The people affected matter."

"Like Nikon," I interject.

Eros scowls at me. "What does screwing with the veil have to do with Nikon? Last I heard, he got a major power boost from it and finally had powers beyond immortality and portaling."

"He's gone missing, and since the Carians attacked us at the bookshop where I work, we're pretty sure Hecate took him."

He holds up his palms. "I had nothing to do with that. Nikon is a friend. He's deserved better than having that crazy bitch stalk him through centuries."

"So where is she? Where did she take him?" I wait, staring him down, willing him to answer me.

"I honestly don't know."

"Do you have a place where you meet with the people involved to plot your efforts?"

Eros breaks into a smile. "Like an evil lair? No. I'm not even sure who all is involved."

Sloan folds his arms across his chest. "Maybe ye could tell us how this alliance came about, and we could get a better idea of what we're up against."

Eros laughs. "Do you think I'm a snitch?"

I roll my eyes. "No, we think you're a selfish dick who screwed over humanity for a laugh and refuses to help us find a friend. If you were half the man Dionysus and Nikon think you are, you'd stop posturing, help us find him, and get him away from Hecate."

He laughs, and I hate that the sound is so deep and sexy. "Does insulting people usually work to convince them to help you?"

"We shouldn't *have to* convince you! This is Nikon we're talking about. You should *want* to help us!"

"There's no I in team, Red."

"But there is in dickwad."

Eros exhales a long breath. "Look. Despite what you obviously think of me, I want to help you—of course, I do—I just don't know if she has him or where."

My phone vibrates in my pocket, and I pull it out to see what's going wrong now.

Except for once, something's going right.

"We're not getting anywhere. Leave, Eros. If you're not with us, you're against us." I pick up my and Dionysus's dishes and take them to the sink. "Since you're on Team Chaos, you're definitely not with us."

Eros looks like he's at a loss, but I don't care.

I finish rinsing the plates and slot them in the dishwasher. "I mean it, Cupid. Go spread some love. Maybe a little caring will rub off on you."

His gaze narrows as his hands ball into tight fists. "Or maybe being sentenced to spread love for eternity makes it a little tough to choke down. Maybe, after millennia of giving everyone else happy endings, I'm done with it."

"Then talk to Zeus and get a transfer, take a vacation, or get some therapy. But you're no use to us broken and bitter."

Eros frowns and looks at Dionysus. "Are you going to let her talk to me like this?"

"Are you going to help us rescue Nikky, stop Loki, and restore peace to the two realms?" Dionysus replies.

The curl of his upper lip says it all.

"Then yes. I stand with Fiona on this. We need to find Nikon. We need to restore the veil. And when the Fates find out you are part of this mess, you better believe they'll come after you."

Eros' expression darkens as his frame grows rigid. "Who's going to tell them—you? We're friends. Family. What's gotten into you?"

Dionysus holds up his hands and gestures at Sloan, me, and our surroundings. "I learned the true meaning of family, *adelphos*. Family is nurturing and kind. It fills my soul. It's about building people up to be their best, not tearing them down for your gain. Nikon is family. Fiona and Sloan are family. I'd love to include you, but for right now, with what you're doing…I can't."

Hurt flashes in Eros' eyes but is gone almost instantly. It's the first time I've ever seen any genuine emotion from him, and honestly, it's reassuring that he is still capable of feeling one.

Dionysus slides his hands into his pockets and meets his gaze. "Fi's right. You should go. We're on opposite sides of this, and it doesn't help either of us to fight about things that neither of us is willing to change."

Eros lowers his chin. "You're drawing a line in the sand here. You realize that, don't you?"

Dionysus nods. "And I have no regrets. I hope, for your sake, you can say the same."

When Eros flashes out, I stride over to Dionysus and wrap him in a tight hug. "I'm sorry, Tarzan. I know coming up against your friends and family cuts you deeply."

He returns my hug and rests his cheek on top of my head. "Not your fault, Jane. When it comes down to it, people must stand for something, and there are consequences for that. I have no regrets. I chose love, and I will continue to choose it for as long as I'm able."

I squeeze him tighter. "Me too."

Sloan surprises me by getting in on the action. He wraps his arms around both of us and kisses Dionysus' cheek. "Ye chose well, Greek. Yer a good man and ye care about the people around ye. Don't ever let others tear ye down fer takin' a different path."

Dionysus draws a deep breath. "Thanks, Irish. I knew this would be a tough one, but yeah, I needed this."

Sloan pats him on the back of his shoulder and eases back. "What did the text say, *a ghra*? The moment ye got it, ye told Eros to take a hike. I assume that was because ye didn't want him to hear what it was about."

I snap out of our love-in and pull out my phone. "Oh, yeah. We've got a lead on Nikon. His cousin Alec needs us to come to the Tsambikos vineyard in Rhodes. He and Papu have pinpointed when and where Nikon is."

Dionysus straightens and holds out his hand to me. "Then let's go meet them."

I nod. "I want to take the dragons home first. I didn't like the attention Discord was giving them, and if he comes back while we're gone, I don't want him messing with them."

Dionysus looks around. "Where did the weasel go?"

"He's a fox, and he left the moment Eros arrived. Likely afraid to have it become common knowledge that he's left his post and is helping us."

"If ye can call it help," Sloan counters.

I shrug. "I think we can."

Sloan is buzzing around in the kitchen, cleaning up the last of our breakfast dishes. "Go get them ready, luv. We'll take them home and tell Calum and Dillan we're on the move."

I grin. "Then we'll find Nikon and bring him home."

CHAPTER TEN

The Tsambikos family villa sprawls across the grassy crest of sheer rock cliffs on the southern tip of the Isle of Rhodes. With the land dropping away at the cliffs and three seas mixing and mingling around the island's point below, the sound of waves breaking is as dramatic as the mist in the air is welcoming.

White marble terraces, tiered and supported by a span of symmetrically spaced columns and archways, run the length of the façade. They give Nikon's family a scenic view of the acres of grapes growing down the southeast slope.

It's spectacular at night, the rising moon casting a silver band across the terracotta rooftops exactly as it did the first time I came here over a thousand years ago.

Time travel is trippy.

The grounds stretch endlessly into the darkness, the boundary lined by a high iron fence holding lit torches at measured intervals. The regularity of the golden flames serves to reinforce the awe.

I admire the surroundings. "It never gets old, does it?"

"Not yet," Papu agrees, greeting us under the covered porch.

"Thank you for coming. Please, join us. I have a carafe of my finest wine breathing. Shall I pour?"

"We would be honored." Dionysus hugs Papu and moves to shake Alec's hand. "Tell us the good news. Tell us we can get Nikon back."

Alec and Nikon don't look a lot alike. They both have the warm, Mediterranean skin of the Tsambikos family, but where Nikon is blond, tall, and rather Adonis beautiful, Alec has dark curls, is slight in stature, and has the long nose and pointed chin you'd see carved in the marble busts of the time.

"Alec, it's wonderful to see you again." I hug him. "Thank you for messaging me."

He steps back and shakes hands with Sloan, Calum, and Dillan. "It's my pleasure. Papu, Thios, and I are so grateful you've come and will help bring Nikon home."

I turn and meet the gaze of the stern-looking man sitting at the table. He nods politely and raises his glass but doesn't rise to greet us.

From what Nikon has said about his father, the two have never been close. Nikon paints him as a narcissistic womanizer, which, being immortal and preserved in the body of a thirty-year-old for a thousand years, could go very well for him.

I return my attention to Alec. "Nikon is our priority. We've been worried sick about him and searching for the when and the where to bring him home."

Alec hands me a glass of wine. "Well, I think I've found that for you. The last time Hecate kidnapped all of you, we put a tracking chip in Nikon's family ring."

"You gave me the idea." Papu grins. "That's how Sloan tracked you to me, but he didn't have a time component. It took me over a year to find a witch strong enough to spell for time and location, but after what happened the last time, I thought it was important."

"Excellent. You know where he is?" I ask.

Alec nods and takes a sip of his wine. "If whoever has him isn't actively throwing us off-course, then yes. He's in 386 B.C.E."

"Excellent. Then we start there."

Nikon's father sighs. "You're putting your lives at risk for his mistakes. You understand that, yes?"

I stop with my glass perched at my lips. "We've all made mistakes, Mr. Tsambikos. Nikon has suffered long enough for falling in love with a goddess. It's not his fault she can't take no for an answer."

Dionysus finishes his glass and chuckles. "Hecate has always been on the psychotic side of spoiled."

"It's time she learns you can't always get what you want." I half expect my brothers to break into a Rolling Stones serenade but the fact that they don't prove how serious we all are about getting Nikon home. "Laying our lives on the line for the people we love is what we do. It's a non-issue."

"A no-brainer," Dillan adds.

"It's what Nikon has done for us countless times," Calum points out.

"He deserves nothing less," Dionysus adds.

Papu and Alec seem pleased with that answer. Nikon's father seems confused.

Whatevs. If he doesn't understand what an incredible son he has, that's his loss.

I hand my half-finished glass of wine to Dionysus and let him finish it. No sense chugging alcohol before we march into battle, after all. "If you're ready to roll, Alec, we are too."

Alec stands, and I give him credit. He's not a fighter, but he doesn't hesitate. "First, we'll have to change. We can't very well show up wearing jeans and T-shirts. Not only will you anger the Fates for influencing history, but we'll also be found out much sooner."

"Good thinking. I guess we are all a little gung-ho to get Nikon home," I admit.

Papu grins and sweeps a hand toward the sliding door into the house. "Fi, I set out some clothes for you in your old room. Go change while we get everyone—"

"No need to waste time changing." Dionysus flicks his hand toward us. "Voilà, we're ready to go find Nikky."

I've seen Calum and Dionysus in formal chitons before, but seeing Sloan and Dillan too is too much. "Just one picture." I reach for my pocket...and realize I don't have any pockets because I'm dressed as an ancient Greek lady.

No, no. This won't do. "Tarzan, I'll need my warrior leathers at least."

"I'll take care of it when it's time, Jane. For right now, you'll draw less attention as a lady."

I adjust the headscarf to cover my red hair. "In that case, I'll try my best to be one."

They all laugh at that.

"Greek, I need my cloak," Dillan advises. "It can pass as old-fashioned, can't it?"

Dionysus nods, and with a flick of his fingers, Dillan is gifted his Cloak of Knowledge.

When that's taken care of, Alec gestures for us to join him on the back lawn and the five of us follow. "Going back this far will give me a brutal migraine. About ten minutes after arriving, I'll be puking and won't be much use to you. Either we get in and out that quickly, or we'll be stuck there until my head clears."

I meet the gazes of my family and friends as I put my hand into the center of the circle. "As much as I want to make this quick, everything in me knows it won't be that easy. Dionysus, when we arrive, take Alec somewhere safe away from the battle."

Dionysus nods. "I'll take him into the private sanctum of my temple. Only I have access to it."

"Good. Alec can vomit in peace and rest, and we'll do our thing and meet him there once we have Nikon and are ready to come home."

Alec seems relieved. "I would stay to help...I just think I'd be a liability."

I wave away his concern. "Our father always says, 'Everyone has a part to play, and every part matters.' You take care of you, or we don't get home. That's help enough."

Alec stretches his hands out in front of him when we've all grabbed hold to complete the circuit. His eyes glow neon blue. The air around us shimmers and shifts, forming a swirling vortex that beckons us into the unknown. I swallow against the discomfort of his power.

Having done this once before with him, I understand that it'll get worse before it gets better.

I clamp my jaw as the nerve endings in my arms ping and crawl with the feel of ugly orange centipedes scurrying over my skin. I'm not sure why they're orange. That's how I picture them.

I swallow against the disgust and fight the urge to let go. All I want is to shake out my arms and legs.

That would be disastrous.

Letting go of the person portaling you is a life-threatening no-no. Doing that with a person portaling you through time is even worse.

Who knows where or when I'd end up or in what condition.

When the world comes into focus again, Alec has brought Dionysus, Sloan, Calum, Dillan, and me back into ancient Greece, to the north end of the island and the walled city of Rhodes.

We're perched at the top of a hill, the landscape below a stunning mix of rugged mountains, lush forests, and pristine beaches. All around us stands the architectural and artistic tributes to the Greek pantheon.

The prayer temples of the gods.

"This is where we first met." I grin at Dionysus.

"The first day of the rest of my life," he agrees, emotion

dancing in his gaze. "Nikky and I waited a long time to meet you again, Jane."

I squeeze his hand. "I hope it was worth the wait."

He winks. "Meh, you turned out okay, I guess."

The two of us laugh. Alec presses a hand against his stomach, reminding me of our plan. "Right. Tarzan, get Alec tucked away safe, somewhere he can recover from the transport. We'll wait for you here."

Dionysus and Alec are gone in a flash.

Calum steps in beside me and lays a heavy arm across my shoulders. "I never thought we'd be back here."

"Me either." I turn to Dillan and gesture across the raised gathering of temples and statues. "Hecate's temple was built among twelve other columned structures littered around the crest of this hill."

"They're kinda ugly," Dillan remarks. "They need to hire a new temple painter."

"Says the man who lives in a cotton candy pink house." Calum laughs.

Dillan's not wrong.

The brightly colored temples and fully painted statues are pigmented from the top of their leafy laurels to the sole of their sandals.

Vibrant orange, gold, green, blue, black, and red.

They are gaudy and over the top. The ancient Greeks had a different sense of color than we do in modern times.

"Is it a holiday or something?" Dillan scans the sea of visitors. "It reminds me of a summer concert at Ontario Place."

I take in the crowds and shake my head. "No, it was this busy the last time, too."

Dionysus is back and casts a wistful gaze over his people. "This is a time when the gods and goddesses of my pantheon are worshipped and often feared. Little did we know it would all end and people would become so ambivalent."

I side-hug Dionysus and lay my head against his bare arm. "You don't need hundreds of strangers to lay gifts at your temple steps to be loved. You have us now."

"Aye, she's right, Greek," Sloan adds.

"Damn skippy." Dillan holds up his knuckles for a bump.

"Anytime you need a drunken cuddle puddle to prove you've still got it, Kev and I are game."

I don't want to think too much about that, but yeah, he's loved. "Let's go get Nikon and bring him home."

When I scan the group, I see the same determination reflected. "Don't underestimate Hecate. She's a formidable goddess and a spiteful bitch. The area around her temple is bound to be protected by powerful wards and traps."

"Let her come. We've got this," Dillan says.

Calum nods. "Yeah, we've faced her before and come out on top."

"Indeed," Dionysus adds with a mischievous glint in his eyes. "Nothing will give me more pleasure than to take her down again."

Yeah, me too.

You ready to do this, Bear?

I was born ready, Red. What do ye need? Am I ghosting to find Nikon?

No, Dionysus will do that so he can portal him somewhere safe. You're on recon and battle.

Oh, ye say the sweetest things. My favorite.

I chuckle. *Yeah, I thought you might like that. Good luck, buddy. I love you. Be safe.*

Right back atcha, Red.

There's a flutter in my chest as Bruin shuffles to readiness, and when the building pressure releases, a gentle gust of a breeze encircles me before my battle bear ventures off.

"Bruin's gone to check things out. Tarzan, any chance you get to find Nikon and get him to safety, take it. We'll take care of whatever else she throws at us."

Dionysus nods. "Don't get dead, guys. Any of you."

We all nod our agreement to that.

"Cool. Now, let's do this."

The five of us waste no time merging with the masses. We keep our pace steady but try not to stand out as we make our way toward Hecate's temple. More than a hundred chiton-, stola-, and toga-clad locals have come to pay their respects, carrying boughs of evergreen, food, and small coin purses.

They kneel at the altars of the Greek god or goddess they hope will look upon them with good fortune.

At the temple of Hephaestus, a man—likely a maker of armor and shields—worships the god of fire.

The thinking is, as a prodigious and revered craftsman, Hephaestus might bless his armor in an upcoming battle or perhaps help him craft fine armor if he's a craftsman.

At the temple of Hermes, women pray together. As the herald of the gods, Hermes is the messenger. Perhaps they're awaiting word of a loved one who hasn't returned from the wars, or they have family traveling and are worried about their journey.

It hurts my heart that Nikon taught me all this and he's here somewhere hurting. At least I hope he's here…but *not* hurting.

"Who's this handsome fella?" Dillan chuckles as we pass a nakey statue of Dionysus. "Dude, they don't flatter your manhood, do they?"

Dionysus rolls his eyes. "It's not anatomically correct. Sculptors of the day believed men driven by mighty endowments were foolish and short-sighted. It was better to be depicted with a modest male package and be known for intelligence."

"Or add a fig leaf and be done with it," Sloan adds.

We leave it at that and pass the temples for Persephone and her mother Demeter, for Heracles, and Poseidon.

"Wow, he's popular." Dillan points at the crowd gathered in front of the temple with Poseidon standing at the peak. With his trident raised, he's an amazing and imposing sight.

"This is a Greek island of fishermen," Dionysus points out. "Poseidon is incredibly important in the lives of these people to grant them good catches, calm the seas and return their husbands, and watch over them on long journeys."

As we skirt the crowd, I point at the temple straight ahead. "There. The one next to Apollo."

Sloan and my brothers follow my indication and nod.

Hecate's temple faces a different direction, so we can't get a good look at it yet, but it's similar to the others. It's a tall marble building with measured columns along the front and sides, an ornately carved frieze over the entrance, and a sculpture of the goddess being honored perched on the roof's peak.

As we approach, my shield wakes, and the tattoo on my back heats. "Heads up, boys, my shield is weighing in. Something wicked this way comes."

Or maybe not.

I hold my hand up and clench my fist. The guys stop immediately and take stock of our surroundings. "Look at the people coming to honor Hecate. What's different here than at the other temples?"

Sloan frowns. "None of them are climbing the stairs to go inside to the altar. They're all laying their tributes on the steps."

"Why is that?"

Bruin returns to our group. *Because a barrier surrounds the entire temple.*

I gather my hair as it kicks up in the breeze and meet my team's knowing gazes. "Bruin says there's a ward up around the entire temple."

"To keep us out or to keep Nikon in?" Calum asks.

"Maybe both."

Dionysus steps forward and raises his hands to test the wall of the barrier. The bubble around the temple shimmers with iridescent swirls when he touches it. "I can weaken it, but I'll need time."

Dillan's eyeing the crowd gathered at the temple's front steps. "Did nobody notice the appearance of the barrier when Dionysus touched it?"

Dionysus shakes his head. "Our magic in this time is masked, so only the empowered can see it. These people have no idea they're being spelled not to climb the steps and go to Hecate's altar."

"Well, it's not going to work on us. The moment you break through her warding spell, we're walking through this barrier and finding Nikon."

There's a round of male grunts of agreement.

"Dillan, hood up," I instruct. "While Tarzan does his thing, why don't you check the perimeter and see if you find any hidden access points or discoveries?"

Dillan pulls up the hood of his green cloak and grins. "Happy to. Don't start the fun without me."

I watch Dillan move off and disappear around the corner of the temple. Sloan squeezes my shoulders from behind. "Keep the faith, *a ghra*. He's going to be fine. Alec tracked him here—"

"Or at least his ring." I voice my fears.

Sloan steps closer, pressing his chest against my back as he whispers in my ear. "No, luv. Nikon's here and we'll find him and bring him home."

"If Hecate gets her ass kicked, all the better."

He chuckles. "All the better. That's the spirit."

"If the Fates are with us, maybe they'll see Nikon being held prisoner and tell their mother. Themis promised to act against Hecate if she targeted Nikon ever again."

"From your lips to the goddess' ears," Dionysus interjects

while working on the ward. "The world would be a better place with that bitch's powers bound."

"They took *your* powers. Surely, they'll do the same to her once we prove what she's done." I hear the words coming out of my mouth, but even I'm skeptical we'll ever get justice. I'm about to say something about that when the ground beneath us rumbles.

"Does Rhodes have earthquakes?" Calum asks.

Dionysus straightens and calls a sword to his hand. "No, but it's about to have one helluva battle. Look!"

I follow his gaze up the temple's stairs to where a seven-headed hydra emerges from the shadows, snarling and snapping at us.

"Looks like Hecate's welcoming committee." I spin Birga before me. "It would be rude not to introduce ourselves."

CHAPTER ELEVEN

The moment the hydra is visible on the front steps of Hecate's temple, I call my armor forward and swing Birga to stretch before the fight. Pressure builds in my ears and there's an audible *crack*, followed by magic snapping in the air.

"The barrier is down." Dionysus grins. "I burst her bubble."

I laugh and race up the steps. "Yeah, you did. Give me my battle leathers and go find Nikon."

Dionysus snaps out as the gladiator leathers Nikon had crafted for me appear on my body. I stretch a little, pleased at my increased movement. "Thanks, Tarzan."

He's long gone, but I know he heard me.

Bruin materializes beside us, and the sudden appearance of a massive Kodiak bear goes unnoticed. With the spell of gentle diversion broken, the people of Rhodes are now fully aware of the reality around them—and are already in full freak out.

Not that I blame them.

A seven-headed mythical monster screeching and hissing is alarming. Cue mass hysteria and the rapid slap of sandals racing in every direction.

"Hey, I said not to start without me." Dillan rounds the temple at a run and joins us on the fly.

The five of us spread out, taking the beastly obstacle from all sides. "You're here now, and you didn't miss anything."

"No thanks to you guys."

Sloan and I head straight at the thing. Dillan calls his dual daggers and is on my right, Bruin is on our left, and Calum has climbed onto a marble pedestal. He's firing arrows while sitting on a globe perched on the shoulders of a hunched-over Atlas.

Bruin calls forward his battle armor and lets out a ground-trembling roar.

The hydra doesn't seem intimidated by our show of strength. If anything, it seems more determined. The heads are rolling and swinging like the out-of-control air dancers you see outside the carwash. You'd think that would imply a scattered focus.

It doesn't.

This thing is fast and relentless.

The three front heads thrust forward, jaws snapping. I swing Birga and bat away the snout of one and fight to hold my ground against the others.

Sloan has unsheathed the sword at his hip and is swinging in long, smooth arcs to force distance between us. "Remember. Don't cut off the heads or more will grow back."

Dammit. Right. I totally forgot that, and by the wild growl rumbling from my bear, Bruin did, too.

"Just hack the hell out of them, Bear." I adjust my attack. "You love to shred your opponents."

Aye, that's true. I do.

Over the next few minutes, we continue to battle, not engaging wholly on the offensive but gleaning the strengths and weaknesses of our opponent.

The hydra is physically strong, has tremendous reach, and a daunting field of vision. It doesn't have amazing pivot and spin abilities—especially because its attention seems fragmented by the conflicting wills of the heads being attacked on several fronts at once.

When another head bears down on me, my shield burns hot, and I dodge to the side. Hot breath washes over my face, and I groan. "Dude. I think you've got the leg of a centaur caught in your teeth. Have you ever heard of mouthwash?"

"I don't think it's been invented yet, Fi." Dillan laughs and slices at the head attacking him. "Maybe mint."

"Yeah, that might work. Or Greek yogurt. Is that a thing now?"

"You'd think so, wouldn't you? It's in the name."

Calum snorts. "Yeah. I think that's here now."

I meet its next charge head-on, thrusting my spear toward its chest with all my strength. Birga's jagged spear tip digs into the beast's tough hide, and I feel her glee as she drinks its blood.

Having an enchanted necromancer weapon takes some getting used to, but Birga rocks, and hey, everyone has their thing, right?

As Birga sings, the hydra howls.

Two other heads come at me, and I spin. Launching to the side, I avoid the angry one I stabbed, but there's no way I can outmaneuver two more.

This is going to hurt.

I'm about to cast an Impenetrable Sphere when Sloan swings his sword, slicing off one of the hydra's heads. The creature shrieks as the toothy noggin *thuds* on the ground, and oogy mauve blood washes me.

I blink at the dead head and frown. "You broke your rule."

The hydra thrashes and screams as two more heads grow in the place of the first, and it charges again.

"Ye didn't have yer defenses up, and the thing was about to make a meal of ye. Thank me later."

I chuckle, vault into a front somersault, and duck as a volley of arrows screams toward me. "Incoming!"

Calum's barrage of arrows hits several eye sockets, and the hydra wails again.

At some point, Dillan mounted the neck of one hydra and is now being swung and flung all over the place.

"Added points for difficulty if you can nail the landing," I shout.

Dillan laughs. "Did the eight-second buzzer go off?"

"Yep. You win the title."

With that, Dillan releases during a particularly wild head fling and soars through the air with a whoop. He almost lands it—and I'm sure if he were wearing his tactical boots, he would have—but the sandals and the fact that we're fighting on marble steps throw him off.

He topples off-balance, and one head gets a chomp on his chiton. The hydra pulls him into the air and swings its head like a dog whipping the stuffing out of its favorite toy.

My heart thumps at the base of my throat, blocking my gasp. Instead of snapping him in two, the fabric gives way, and he flies backward.

I avert my gaze, but being stripped doesn't bother Dillan. He jumps back into the fray unabashed.

If only I had my phone to capture this moment. He'd never live this down. "Penalty for nakey battling!"

"Cover that shit up, brother," Calum calls.

Dillan grunts. "Do you think I want my junk flinging around in the breeze when talons and teeth are slicing the air? That would be a *no*."

Then something occurs to me. "We don't have to fight or beat this thing. Dionysus has been gone long enough. Either he can't get to Nikon, or he's facing his own troubles. Sloan, we need to portal inside the temple to help him."

The moment I make the demand, he *poof*s to me and *poof*s me inside the temple. He disappears and is back with Calum a moment later. Then Dillan.

Thankfully, my hubby is a quick thinker in battle. He grabbed the swatch of torn fabric from the steps and tosses it to Dillan. "See what ye can do with this."

While Dillan wraps his hips and fashions himself an impromptu cotton kilt, I assess our surroundings.

Instead of stark and white like it is in our time, the temple's interior is opulent and gold. Richly colored tapestries hang along the roofline, depicting Hecate throughout history.

I follow the chronology of the images woven into the fabric, and my gaze winds around the space. In none of these do I see a reflection of the woman I know.

The spiteful stalker.

The petulant goddess.

The bitch who can't get it through her head that she's not all that and none of us care.

The *clash* and *clang* of swords have us racing toward the inner sanctum. Dionysus has a sword in each hand and is fighting in the round, defending against five angry women in scarlet and gold gowns.

Carians.

Because Dionysus is goofy and chill with my family and me, I sometimes forget he's also an incredible, seasoned warrior and immortal god—until moments like this.

Seeing him like this never fails to suck the oxygen from my lungs.

He's fierce.

He's focused.

He's a fighter on fire.

Upon noticing our arrival, a senior woman warrior wearing all gold swings her hand through the air and shouts something in Greek. Another wave of Carian warriors floods in from all sides.

Shitshitshit…they heavily outnumber us.

Bruin. You're the best at finding hidden rooms. Alec says Nikon's here somewhere.

Or was, Bruin replies. *The witch might have already taken him and gone.*

I know he's right, but the thought makes me ill. *Just try, buddy. We need to rescue him.*

Bruin ghosts out, and I windmill Birga in front of me as Hecate's warriors approach. "They're warriors *and* witches," I remind my brothers and Sloan. "Be ready for anything."

The second wave of this battle begins, and the four of us join Dionysus. I weave through the chaos, using my staff to deflect blows and magical assaults as I force my way toward him.

A roar brings the hydra crashing through the opening into the inner sanctum, and the gang's all here. Several of the Carian warriors screech and shuffle quickly to reestablish their position so they don't have their backs to the mythical beast.

If luck is with us, the hydra isn't loyal to them.

That would even out the battle nicely.

It lunges at us with a roar, and one of the eight heads snatches up one of Hecate's warriors. The woman twists, trying to fend off the beast with a flurry of spells and magical bursts of energy.

Excellent. Now all we have to do is avoid the hydra, battle the psychotic warrior women, find Nikon, avoid the wrath of Hecate, and get out of here and back to our own time.

Easy-peasy.

Dionysus laughs in my mind. *I love how your mind works, Jane. It never fails to crack me up.*

Glad to offer you comic relief, Tarzan, but really, we can do this.

Yeah, we can.

We push back against the creature and the warrior witches, the five of us settling into our groove. There's something to be said for fighting with people you love, trust, and thoroughly understand.

In the biggest of big battles, I have the battle crown Fionn gifted me. It allows me to follow my team's thoughts, emotions, and health on the field. I can do that instinctively when it's only the five of us.

I know how each of them thinks, fights, and feels.

I know their strengths and weaknesses.

And I know their tells.

Even if these warrior chicks fight together and consider themselves a unit, they aren't a family. That makes us better.

Not that I'm biased or anything.

The battle rages on, a whirlwind of magic, steel, and beastly roars. We're outnumbered but not outmatched.

I duck as one of the hydra heads lunges for me and opens its toothy maw. At that exact moment, Dillan lifts his leg and kicks one of the witches he's facing toward me. The Carian fighter stumbles sideways, her arms coming up as she flails to catch her balance, and the hydra snatches her up.

"Substitution," Dillan shouts as if he's a referee at a sporting event.

I giggle and get back to fighting.

A moment later, Bruin returns. He materializes and speaks so my brothers and Dionysus can hear him as well. "She's got him rigged to a bladed noose and set to fall the moment someone enters. I can't tell if it's meant to strangle or decapitate him. They warded the entire room up the wazoo. I can't find a way through her spell or to get ye in there without him dyin' and losin' his head in the process."

My heart kicks up in my chest, and my mind stumbles over that image. "But he's immortal. Would he really die, or would he regenerate?"

"I don't know."

"Is she there to watch?" Dionysus releases the sword in his right hand so the blade drops, and he can use the hilt to club one of his attackers in the head.

"Aye, the bitch is stretched out on a chaise, drinking wine, and smiling like a Cheshire cat."

Dionysus frowns. "Then I'd say there's a good chance he'll really die. If she's enjoying herself and wants a front-row seat, she's planning on making people suffer."

I want to disagree.

I want to believe a woman who loved Nikon couldn't plot to watch his death simply because their love didn't survive the test of time.

I want to…but I can't.

"We can't risk it. We have to think of something else." I raise Birga with both hands and brace her over my head to stop a downward strike. "What about you portaling in and not entering via the door?"

Dionysus spins, swinging his sword at shoulder height, and lops off the head of one of Hecate's warriors. "She'll be expecting that. We need something she won't expect or that will negate her threat."

"Like what?" I swing my gaze to check on my brothers. The hydra is advancing on Dillan and Calum, but Sloan dashes forward, slashing at the creature's chest before *poofing* out and reappearing at a safe distance.

"I'll think of something."

While he thinks, I rush toward my brothers with my spear raised above my head. Together, we drive the hydra back toward Hecate's warriors.

The golden warrior—who undoubtedly is the woman in charge—looks frustrated and worried.

Yeah, we have that effect on people.

Sorry, not sorry.

The beast screams, and I turn in time to see Sloan and Bruin ghost out as the heads of the hydra try to defend against their attackers' sudden appearance and disappearance.

The creature stumbles back with a serious gash across its chest. It staggers sideways and slumps to the floor as its feet fail. Sloan and Bruin take another run at it, Sloan's sword and

Bruin's claws working in unison as they hack away at its scaly hide.

"I've got an idea," Dionysus announces and disappears.

In the vacuum left by his abrupt exit, the two women he was battling leap over their fallen sisters and come at me.

Lucky me.

From my position in the chaos, I see how their sudden run catches the attention of two of the heads. I might warn them if I was in a better mood and they weren't holding one of my closest friends prisoner and threatening his death.

Too bad, so sad. You reap what you sow.

My incoming attack gets eliminated with two quick *snaps*, the spine-shivering *crunch* of bones, and a muffled gurgling that triggers my gag reflex.

The golden matron warrior shouts something in Greek and the two remaining Carian fighters disengage and retreat. We let them go without issue.

We're not here for them.

That leaves us, a dozen dead females, and a badly injured hydra. With the pressure of the battle over, I signal for Calum and Dillan to end their attack. "He's had enough. Look at him. He's barely able to move. Sloan, can you move some of these bodies close enough that he can lie here and munch?"

"Ye want me to serve the hydra that's tryin' to kill us an all-it-can-eat buffet?"

I nod. "He's not trying to kill us now."

"Because we've bested it," he points out, his breath still ragged and fast.

"Please, hotness. I really think he's had enough. It would be cruel to kill him now. We've proven we have the upper hand."

Dillan snorts. "Leave it to you to think that a murderous, mythical beast is a wounded stray that needs your attention. You're not bringing that thing home."

"I hadn't even thought about it until you said that."

Calum laughs and shakes his head. "No, Fi. We've got kids there, and even if it's docile now, it's because it's near death. It's not a bucket of eels you can put in the bathtub. You're not bringing it home."

Sloan makes a face at me. "Ye put a bucket of eels in yer bathtub?"

I nod. "Emmet and I caught them at the creek. We took turns flicking them out of the water with sticks and putting them in a pail. We lugged that pail all the way home and got them settled in the tub. Then Aiden came home from high school and lost his shit."

Sloan arches a brow. "I'm with yer brothers on this one, luv. The hydra is not a pet. It doesn't have a place in Isilon."

I sigh. "Fine. Will you at least heal that big gash in its chest?"

"Ye mean the gash I almost died makin'?"

"Yeah, that one."

"Yer serious?"

I'm about to argue mercy for a fellow warrior when Dionysus snaps back—and he's not alone.

Themis, the goddess of justice, is an elegant and poised woman with smooth features and long, dark hair she keeps swept up the back of her neck and pinned atop her head. Only the most perfectly coiled tendrils fall loose against her bare shoulders.

Her daughters, the Moirae, the goddesses of fate, look like her. Because goddesses don't age, the four look more like sisters than a mother and her three daughters.

These women weave the fate of humanity and gods alike with no one powerful enough to influence their judgments.

Clotho is the origin of life, and her thread is spun upon the birth of all.

Lachesis is the second sister and allocates the fate of lives in progress.

Atropos is the cutter of thread. With her shears, she determines how and when a life will end.

"Bruin, show us where Hecate is holding Nikon," Dionysus requests.

"Is that safe?" I ask.

"Perfectly." Themis offers me a reassuring smile. "I told you at the end of your trials that Nikon would live free from a life of Hecate's torment. I do not give my word lightly. If Hecate is truly doing what Dionysus claims, we will end it. Show us where, Bear."

Bruin ghosts out, but before I can wonder how we'll follow them, we've all been transported into the room in the temple where Nikon is bound at the top of a precarious perch.

In the flash of a moment, the magic around us snaps, and the narrow pedestal Nikon is balanced on disappears. Lachesis raises her hands, and a blast of magical energy radiates from her palms, encircling Nikon.

A moment later, he's free of his bindings and kneeling on the marble floor. I rush to him, wanting to comfort and hug him, but welts and sores cover him. "Shit, sweetie. What did she do to you?"

Nikon looks at me, and his gaze is much too glassy for my liking. "Later, Fi. I want to go home."

I kiss the top of his head and straighten. "Sloan? Can you help him?"

Sloan frowns when he sees the damage up close. "I'm not sure I can, *a ghra*. I'll try, of course."

"How dare you invade my private space!" Hecate launches to her feet, her green eyes flaring. "Get out! You have no authority here! You are trespassing!"

"No, Heckie, this is us rescuing, not trespassing," Dionysus replies, speaking slowly as if she won't understand.

Her glare is terrifying. "You meddlesome half-breed. What have you done?"

"Nothing but inform Themis and the Fates that you're up to your tricks again and you've ignored Themis' decree."

"You *idiot!* You ruin everything."

Dionysus claps. "Excellent. Ruining everything you do is a favorite pastime of mine." He turns his attention toward Themis. "As you can see, the Heckster is tormenting Nikon. She took him from his life in the twenty-first century, transported him back here against his will, and is inflicting her cruelty on him yet again."

Hecate's gaze narrows on us as she balls her fists and magical energy crackles in the air. "This is my last warning. Get out. All of you!"

Themis raises her hand, and golden shackles bind Hecate's hands. "I warned you at the end of the trials that you were to leave this man to his life. It seems you didn't take my warning to heart."

"I did nothing wrong. I didn't bring Nikon here because he's mine. I brought him here because he's a direct threat to a project I'm working on in his time."

Themis frowns. "What are you up to?"

"She's allied with half a dozen gods from different pantheons to cause chaos," I answer. "They brought the veil between worlds down and are actively working against us to keep us from repairing it."

Hecate's eyes widen, and her mouth falls open. "Lies. You know nothing, human."

I laugh. "Actually, we know everything. We know about Loki, Discord, Eros, and the others. Your cabal has unraveled, and we're about to undo the damage you've done. Kidnapping Nikon won't stop it and you saying he's a threat to your plan because of his powers with spatial magic is lame. You're a bitch who can't admit he's not into you."

Hecate lunges forward and throws her hands up, but she's all bluster with her wrists shackled together.

Themis shakes her head. "Apologies, Fiona. It seems, once

again, our pantheon has disrupted your lives in progress. Be assured it won't happen again."

Dionysus meets my gaze and tips his head in a subtle nod. I take the hint and accept her apology. "Thank you, ladies. It's always a pleasure to see you, but I would prefer it if it weren't during a moment when someone I love is being tortured and threatened with death."

Atropos graces me with a wry smile. "Wouldn't that be nice for you?"

It would.

Dionysus nods. "Thanks, ladies. If you've got everything in hand, we'll take our leave."

With that, he portals us back to his temple.

CHAPTER TWELVE

"How is he?" I rush to stand in front of Sloan and wait with my fists clenched. "Why did he pass out? Did she do something to him? We should have found him sooner. We should have thought of something, some way to find him and not just wait."

Sloan pulls me into his embrace before I have a total fall apart. "Breathe, *a ghra*. We did what we could, as soon as we could, and now Nikon's safe."

"But is he all right?" I plead for him to tell me and put me out of my misery.

"In time, he will be."

"What does that mean?" The words clog my throat. "What did she do to him?"

Sloan grimaces. "That's his story to tell, I'm afraid. The fact remains that he'll need time to recover from the emotional impact, if not the physical."

"Can I see him?"

He kisses my forehead and releases me. "Aye, he asked me to send ye in before yer head explodes. He knew ye'd be concerned."

Concerned?

I'm more than concerned—I'm devastated.

I meet Sloan's warm, mint green eyes and rein in my emotional cyclone. "Do you mind if I spend some alone time with him? If he needs to talk, it might help him if it's only me."

"Of course, luv. Be with him and comfort him. Take as much time as ye need."

I pull him in for another long hug. "I'm so thankful you were here. You're my rock. You know that, right?"

Sloan winks. "No need to thank me. Nikon is family."

He is. I turn to go in, and Sloan catches my arm.

"Try to get him to drink. He's had a shock to his system and his fluids are down. If we were in our time, I'd have him on an IV."

"Will do." I squeeze his hand and hurry into Dionysus' private quarters at his temple.

The door pushes open with a whisper and I tip-toe inside. It's exactly as I imagined.

Nakey statues, lush grapevines magically growing along lattice screens, a wine station with an amphora of wine on the floor, and crystal carafes on a marble table. Beautifully woven tapestries hang over marble walls and between glossy columns.

Then I round the screening.

Nikon lies on his back with deep burgundy satin sheets draped over his hips. His eyes are closed, and I'm glad because I wasn't prepared for the damage done to him and he didn't see my reaction.

It's the first time I've been in Dionysus' sexy domain in his old hangout, and it's Nikon lying in the sheets. The funny thing is, he's got the same ageless, timeless Greek beauty thing going on as Dionysus.

He looks as at home here as he does in his mansion in Toronto.

I ease into the room and look him over, trying to figure out if he's asleep or awake.

Sloan only left the room a few minutes ago and said Nikon asked to see me. Maybe he is that exhausted that he couldn't stay awake one more minute.

Maybe Hecate hasn't let him sleep.

Maybe—

"Come over here and lie down before you have a complete meltdown, Red."

I meet Nikon's gaze and exhale. "I didn't want to wake you. But yeah, I won't say no to a chance to make sure you're really here, and you're all right."

I rush over and climb onto the bed, and he makes room for me to settle in against his side.

"You *are* all right, aren't you?"

"I won't be battling in the next few days, but I'll survive. I always do."

I hear the aching sadness in his tone, and my heart breaks a little more for him. "Well, I'm all yours for as long as you can stand me. We'll lie here, drink honeyed water and wine, and convalesce."

I settle beside him and hesitate, unsure where to put my arms or if I should touch him. The lesions on his skin are raw and angry. "Do you hurt, sweetie?"

"Nah. Dionysus made sure I was good before he left. He shared a bit of ambrosia with me, which I gotta say is good shit. It's like being drunk and high and basking in the afterglow of great sex, all at once."

"Yay, Tarzan." The first of my tears break free as I get a close look at the damage he sustained. "I'm so sorry this happened to you. We would've come sooner, but we couldn't find you."

Nikon slides his arm under me, pulling me against his side so we're lying together. "Red, if there's one thing I know as a constant in this world, it's that if someone in your life is in trouble, you and our family and friends are razing the Earth to find them and bring them home. It's what kept me going. I wasn't timing you. I was holding out until you came because I *knew* you'd come."

The dam of my emotions breaks, and all my anger, fear, helplessness, and frustration pour out.

Nikon gathers my head on his shoulder, and I wrap my arm around his chest. I need to hold him and know he's okay. He didn't escape unscathed. His usually perfect, smooth, tanned skin is raw, and had Bruin not assessed his situation before our infiltration, he might be dead now.

Really dead.

Like…*dead* dead.

Even thinking about that is unbearable.

"I love you, Nikon Tsambikos. I love you, and I need you in my life. You're not allowed to have some crazy ex-lover witch-bitch take you away from me."

His amusement jiggles both of us. "I'll remember that, and yeah, I love you too. You already know that."

I do. But while we're discussing Nikon's emotions… "Why didn't you mention that you and Sarah aren't dating anymore?"

He rolls back and looks up, studying the ceiling. After a long silence, he exhales. "I guess I didn't want you to worry. You and Sloan are happy, and I know you want me to be happy too."

"I do, but I also want you to tell me what's going on in your life. You don't need to filter. Despite what it looks like, my circle of close friends is very small. I cherish the people on that list."

His head lolls to the side, his long, flaxen hair back to how it was when I first met him, and Hecate wouldn't allow him to cut it. "I appreciate that, but it's not your job to make sure I'm happy."

"Maybe not, but it is my job to make sure you're not unhappy. That's what loving someone is all about." I shuffle closer and lay my head close to his. "You're mine, Nikon. Not romantically, but in all other forms of the word. It's not only me who loves you. Calum and Kevin, Sloan, and Gran, and so many of us love you."

"And me," Dionysus adds, stepping in from the door. "Don't forget me."

"I could never forget you, Tarzan."

"Of course you can't. I'm unforgettable."

I chuckle and point at the empty glasses on the drinking station. "Bring over a glass of honeyed water, would you? Sloan wants Nikon taking in fluids."

Dionysus course-corrects and pours a glass before bringing it to the bed.

The bed in Dionysus' love den is three times the size of a king, so even with another body, there is room to spare.

Dionysus climbs in behind me and reaches over me to hand Nikon the glass of sweet water. "I'm sorry it took us so long, *adelphos*. We figured out the who off the block, but the *when* and *where* were tougher."

Nikon accepts the glass and sits up enough to sip. "I take it Alec helped with that?"

I grin. "Yeah, he said they chipped you after our last kidnapping adventure with Hecate."

"They did."

"We're thankful they did," Dionysus adds and grins. "He's in my guest room, by the way. He has a massive migraine, and I soundproofed the room so he can rest undisturbed. He said he'll stop puking after a few hours, but he won't be upright until tomorrow or the day after."

Nikon finishes his glass and hands it back to Dionysus, who magically projects it to the marble table. "Yeah, coming this far back does a number on him. I'll owe him big for centuries to come."

"We all will," I correct.

The door opens again, and Calum, Dillan, and Sloan come inside. "Looks like Fi's loosening up on the Greek orgy idea." Calum smacks Dillan's arm. "She's already in a Greek sandwich."

I laugh, too comfy to move and too tired to care. "I said toga party, not Greek orgy."

"What's this now?" Dionysus props up on his elbow behind me. "Did I miss party planning?"

Calum and Dillan split apart and climb onto the bed too. "Fi said for her birthday in May, she's thinking of having a toga party. Dillan and I might have morphed her plan a little for the afterparty theme."

Dionysus snuggles in tighter to give Dillan room and kisses my cheek. "Leave all the planning to me. Greek orgies are my specialty."

I'd protest more, but Nikon is laughing and looking genuinely happy, so I let them get away with it. "That's the afterparty plan. My actual birthday will be a lovely Greek toga party with family and friends."

Nikon nods. "Understood. I'll plan the birthday part, and Dionysus can focus on the afterparty."

Dionysus reaches across me and high-fives Nikon and Calum. "Deal. Get ready for the best party evah!"

Sloan laughs and stretches out at the end of the bed. "Everyone, get some rest. It was a long battle, and we need to be ready for retaliation if it comes."

"Always the voice of reason." My voice sounds distant and tinny. "Good night, Mackenzie."

"Good night, *a ghra*."

"Good night, Elizabeth," Dillan says.

"Good night, John-boy." I giggle.

"Good night, Jim-Bob," Calum adds.

Dionysus flicks his hand, and we're all covered by a comfy blanket. "I don't know what that was about, but you guys crack me up."

The next morning, I wake in a messy mashup of hands and feet and squirm to get free. Sloan notices my struggle and stands from the bench against the wall to help with the exfil. He reaches over, chuckling as I clasp his wrist, and portals us across the room.

Dionysus flops forward without my back to support him and inches closer to snuggle with Nikon.

Who looks much better.

"Thanks for the save, hotness."

He chuckles. "Ye didn't look like ye suffered too terribly much."

I shrug. "What can I say? I'm a snuggler."

"I'm surprised ye didn't suffocate."

I giggle and finger-comb my hair in the high-gloss shine of a marble column. "Believe it or not, I've been there before."

Sloan's eyebrow arches. "Do tell."

I finish with my hair and sidle over to pick a low-hanging bunch of grapes. With my bounty in hand, I tilt my head to the outer room, and we leave the sleeping heap of men to their snoring.

In the next room of the temple, I sit at the top of three steps and pluck a grape from my bunch. "When I was like…eighteen, I think…the boys had an end-of-summer party when Da and Aiden were on nights. We got waaaay too drunk and were playing Shot Twister."

Sloan scoffs. "Because the people in yer family would think that's a perfectly sane idea."

"It was awesome."

"Of course, it was."

I pop another grape in my mouth and let the burst of fruity juiciness wake me up a little more. "I have no recollection of how the evening ended, but we must've collapsed during the game. I woke up with my head resting on Marcus Breen's abs, Tommy

Barren's hand on my boob, and Emmet snoring in my ear…*loudly*."

Sloan shakes his head. "Yer brothers should've been more protective of ye in situations like that. Lettin' ye get banjaxed with men there and none of ye in possession of yer faculties…I hate to imagine what could've happened."

I chuckle. "If your crotch remembers, I have always been able to take care of myself. I believe I did a fair job teaching you that lesson the first time we met. Besides, they were there, and no matter how drunk anyone got, I was the chimp with the white tuft on its butt."

He blinks and snags a couple of grapes for himself. "Am I supposed to know what the hell that means?"

I chuckle. "Hasn't that one come up yet?"

"Not that I recall, no."

I finish chewing and swallow. "When chimpanzees are young, they are revered and adored. They are also mischievous and annoying as hell to the older chimps."

"And this is how ye see yerself?"

I laugh at his expression but continue. "Chimpanzees are born with a white tuft on their butts that signal to the older chimps that they're off-limits. They're just learning and therefore are untouchable."

"A primate 'get out of jail free' card?"

"Yeah. So, with five brothers and Da being who he was, the guys in our neighborhood knew better than to try anything unwelcome. Hell, they were leery of trying anything even when it would've been *very* welcome."

Sloan grins. "I like this story."

I laugh. "Of course you do. It was probably about the same time you were at university busily sexing up your succubus."

"She was never *my* succubus, luv. Besides, if ye believe our paths were walked to bring us together—which I know ye do—we can't regret the choices made or the people who came into each other's lives because they all led to this." He taps the platinum Claddagh band on my ring finger and flashes me a smug smile.

"Fine. I won't gripe about your time with the succubus." I pop another grape in my mouth and bite down, the little globe exploding in a wash of flavor. "Besides, I'm sure she taught you a thing or two that I now benefit from."

He chokes on a grape and casts me a sidelong glance.

"Don't reply to that, Irish." Dionysus sweeps in behind us. "There's no winning a conversation like that. Trust me. It's lose-lose."

I laugh. "No reply necessary."

Dionysus grins and waves, signaling for us to get up and follow. "Come on. Everyone is up. We're going to have breakfast and check on Alec. Maybe we can get home today."

"Are you tired of hosting us in your godly temple, Tarzan?" I rise.

"Never, but like Dorothy says, 'There's no place like home.'"

Alec joins us for breakfast, and it's heartening to see he's moved past the tinge of green phase through the ashen gray phase. Now he only has purple bags under his bright eyes and looks a little hungover.

"Feeling better, it seems." Calum echoes my thoughts as he shifts his chair over at the table and gives Nikon's cousin more room to sit.

Alec accepts a plate from Dionysus and sits, eyeing the selection. "Much. Good to see you, cousin."

"It's good to be seen. Thank you for the rescue."

Alec replies in Greek, and the two have a quick conversation in their native tongue before returning their attention to the gathered group. "Tell me about the rescue. What did I miss?"

Dillan takes the lead on recounting the highlights of our battle with Hecate, the hydra, and the Carian warrior women.

When he's finished, Alec looks a little green again. "I can't say I'm sorry I missed that. You'd think after living as long as I have, I would've found my inner warrior…but no, I'm glad I had a sick note."

I wave away his self-recrimination. "It takes an army, and everyone has their talents. There's nothing wrong with preferring to be a non-combatant."

Dillan grins. "That leaves more for us. Right, Bear?"

Bruin lifts his snout from his trough of wine and his platters of quail and raw fish. "Damn straight. Those little women were plucky, but the hydra was the beast of the hour. A worthy foe, indeed."

"Now that you're well again, we can get home," Dillan remarks. "I've got a baby boy who will be missing his da and a wife who's likely getting worried."

Sloan sets his cup down and holds up his finger. "I've been thinking about that."

Dillan rolls his eyes. "Why do I feel like I won't be snuggling with my angels anytime soon?"

Sloan shrugs. "This is a democracy, of course, so yer welcome to reject my idea."

"Which is what?" Dillan asks.

"I was thinkin' that maybe we make a pit stop between here and home."

I pop the last bit of goat cheese into my mouth and chase it with some grainy bread. "A pit stop when, hotness?"

He swings his gaze to Dionysus. "Could ye find out the exact date and location of the moon demon's attack on Selene?"

I grin. "So, we can claim the moonstones before she destroys them. Noice, Mackenzie. Point to you."

"Aye, if it's possible to intervene, we could take them home with us and Selene wouldn't have to worry that anyone will even attempt to use them against her again until at least the twenty-first century."

I focus my attention on Alec. "Is it possible?"

He shrugs. "I time portal, but if Dionysus or Nikon can get us to the right place, it should be doable."

Sloan nods. "Excellent. Then all we need is for Dionysus to pinpoint the when and where, and we're in business for the moon ritual."

"Maybe making a pitstop will prevent you from getting so sick," Calum suggests. "Like scuba divers needing to stage their ascent back to the surface."

I chuckle. "Yeah, to keep you from getting the time-traveling bends."

"Exactly," Dillan agrees. "Win-win."

"Assuming Dionysus can nail things down fer us," Sloan says.

Dionysus flicks his fingers at Sloan. "Pfft, nailing things is my superpower. Consider it done."

CHAPTER THIRTEEN

Coincidently, Selene was born on the Isle of Rhodes, so the "where" of our interception is easy enough. It's the "when" that remains a bit foggy. As confident as Dionysus was that he could nail down the time and date of the hell demon's attack on Selene, when it comes down to it, history and the documenting of events back then wasn't an exact science.

"What would make anyone think usurping the tidal powers of the moon and going up against Selene was a good idea?" Dillan asks. "Pantheon gods and goddesses are powerful enough, but she's a Titan goddess. Sounds like a recipe for suicide to me."

Dionysus grins. "She's tough, but demons can be tough too."

"How close was the battle?" I ask, wondering what we might be up against.

Dionysus shrugs. "There are gaps in my knowledge of Greek history. Some because I was drowning my sorrows, some because the human historians got it all wrong, and some because I just don't care."

I chuckle. "Fair enough. But obviously, Selene wins."

"She does." The gentle smile dancing in his eyes isn't something I often see when discussing Greek deities.

"You like her."

He grins. "I do. She is fair, and she never lauds herself over others."

"Good. It's nice to know not everyone was horrible to you, Tarzan." I raise my hand to keep from bumping into the back of Calum. We've reached the crest of the raised plateau where the prayer temples of the gods sit high above Rhodes and are looking down at the walled city below.

Calum points at a massive bronze statue to the east. "Wow. That's new since the last time we were here."

"Colossus of Rhodes," Dionysus says. "A seventy-cubit tribute to Selene's brother Helios, god of the sun."

"That's one big nakey man." I tilt my head to get a better view. "At least they gave him a cape."

"And a laurel of sun rays," Calum adds.

"How tall is seventy cubits?" Dillan asks.

"Just under a hundred and ten feet," Sloan answers, awe twinkling in his eyes. "It's one of the seven wonders of the ancient world. I'd like to take a closer look. Anyone want to join me?"

It's unanimous, so Dionysus snaps us down to the harbor as a group. When we materialize, no one seems to notice, which is a joy of Dionysus. He can be as subtle or flamboyant as his mood suits and is usually very deliberate about it.

The sound of crashing waves greets us on the docks of ancient Rhodes, the late morning sun bathing the area as if the massive statue of Helios is watching over us.

The harbor is bustling. Fishermen tend to their nets and unload their wares. The voices of merchants hawking their goods carry from the distance, and so do the heavy footfalls of the sailors marching toward the taxi boats taking them to the massive ship waiting inside the breaker wall.

I step back from marveling to watch Sloan. As a druid historian, he apprenticed with Granda for years. When I first met him, I thought maybe he did that because my grandparents were the only ones to nurture him, and he wanted to share Granda's interest.

In truth, Sloan is awestruck by history. Events, artifacts, personalities of the past…it doesn't matter.

He loves it all.

He's seen images of the statue before, but to behold the Colossus in person is entirely different.

I take a moment to be mesmerized by the sights and sounds around us—the vibrant colors, the bustling activity, and the harbor's salty air. "Sorry, Nikon. Is it wrong that I don't totally hate that we ended up back here again?"

Calum smiles like he's thinking the same thing. "Sorry, Greek. It's amazing to experience moments like these."

"Right?"

Nikon shrugs with a doting smile for us. "It's nice that you love our history. Honestly, it would be amazing if we could spend moments like this without suffering the torture that accompanies it."

Alec offers his cousin a sad smile. "I can make that happen for you. All you have to do is ask."

Nikon waves that away. "I said without the torture that accompanies it. I know what you go through to come this far back. I would never ask you to do that on a whim."

Alec nods. "I appreciate that, but I'm here if you need me. Besides, once the torture passes, I enjoy being back here again."

We take in a few more precious moments in the harbor before getting back to our task of the day.

"Where was the battle between Selene and the moon demon?" I ask.

Dionysus checks that everyone is ready to leave, and we portal as a group to a rocky area on a remote part of the island. "If I'm right, it'll be here."

"You think it'll be tonight?"

Dionysus shrugs. "Give or take a day or two. It was said to be during the full moon. Scientifically, the moment the moon is full lasts only an instant, but to the naked eye and to a scribe in 226 B.C.E. that could have been up to three days."

I release Bruin, and he materializes at my side. "We think this is where the battle between Selene and the demon will be, buddy. Can you give the area a once-over and tell us what we're dealing with?"

"Happy to, Red."

"And maybe an opinion on why this is the location," Sloan adds. "I understand the raised vista and the open space, but I have a feelin' there's more to this bein' the place than privacy."

"I can help you there." Dionysus squints at the sunny sky overhead and moves to a spot about thirty feet to our right. "When the moon is full tonight, this will be where the most direct concentration of its radiance will fall."

"And you know this how?" Dillan asks.

Dionysus shrugs. "It's a god thing, I guess. Sun, moon, stars, magnetic north, Earth's axis, planetary alignment, it's just…accessible."

"Just when I don't think you can get any cooler." I grin at him.

"So, what is our plan, exactly?" Nikon looks from me to Sloan. "Are we attempting to stop the altercation altogether? Are we mugging the demon for the stones? Are we stealing the stones before Selene can destroy them? What's the plan?"

"We haven't really worked out the minutia," I admit, looking at Sloan and Dionysus. "Should we tell Selene and give her a heads-up? Would that tamper with the timeline?"

Dionysus shakes his head. "Not really. In deity circles, the timeline thing doesn't really apply. Since most of Zeus' offspring and the Titans can move through time, we can pop back and leave a note for ourselves. It's not advisable—because it's a bit of a ripple in the pond scenario—but there are no rules against it."

I consider that and meet Sloan's gaze. "In that case, maybe we tell Selene and lobby for the moonstones beforehand. Then she can claim them after our ritual back in our time."

Sloan considers that for a moment and nods. "Agreed. I think that makes the most sense. If no one sees a better course, we'll go that route."

When no one offers a different plan, Dionysus nods. "All right. I'll visit Selene and see if she'll receive me. If I can, I'll work it out."

The night is draped in the rich velvet of a deep indigo sky, spangled with a million winking stars. As Dionysus foretold, the centerpiece is the moon, gloriously radiant and full, filling the heavens with her silvery light—and the goddess commanding her power.

Selene is at her most potent on a night like this, but by looking at her, all I can see is her radiance. She doesn't seem deadly and powerful. She seems elegant and graceful.

"Where does a moon demon come from?" Dillan whispers, scanning the surrounding darkness.

I grip Birga a little tighter. "Hell?"

He rolls his eyes at me. "I meant how will he emerge to this realm? Dumbass."

I chuckle and stretch my neck from side to side, listening to the soft *pops* of my vertebrae as they release. "Sorry. I can't help you."

We settle back into silence, and I envision how things will play out.

We're spread out across the grassy ridge, hidden by shadows and ready for the confrontation that's about to take place. My pulse throbs in my ears, matching the rhythm of the moonlight that shimmers through the air.

A quiet *crackle* of energy hangs around us, as palpable as the imminent threat we're here to intercept.

I watch as Selene, a luminescent figure, prepares her altar in the open space below. She's ethereal, bathed in the celestial glow of her moon. Her robes billow around her, moved by the ever-present sea breeze.

"Are ye ready, luv?" Sloan murmurs, his hand resting lightly on the hilt of his sword.

"As ready as I'll ever be." The hard edge of resolve steels my voice. "I'm not a fan of demons. Give me an angry sasquatch or an evil warlock any day of the week over a demon."

"I don't think yer meant to like them, luv. It's kind of in their job description that they'll be unpleasant."

Yeah, I suppose that's true.

Before I respond, the ground rumbles beneath us, and a sense of pure malice crawls up my spine like an icy serpent.

With my fae vision engaged, I watch the black depths of the night change as the moon demon emerges. He's a creature of shadows and a stark contrast against the purity of Selene and the brilliance of her moon.

The demon roars, a sound that shakes the earth beneath our feet. Selene doesn't flinch. She raises her hands, her very presence defiance against the encroaching darkness.

The battle is imminent, the air electric with the tension. "Get ready to rumble, folks. The moment he makes his move, we're in this hard and fast."

I'm not sure if Selene would look so confident if we weren't here, and she was taken by surprise. I'm sure, like all deities, she'd never admit to wanting or needing the help of a mere mortal, but after Dionysus filled her in, she has to be glad we're here, doesn't she?

Doesn't matter.

If it gets us the magical moonstones, she can front all she wants.

Her altar glows with the moon's power at its peak, and she holds out her arms. The demon roars again, and Selene turns from where she's begun her ode to the full moon. "Ah, Muzak, I've been expecting you."

The spawn of the hell realm grins and raises his clawed fist. Something within his tight grasp casts orange sparks from the sides of his hands.

I'm willing to bet it's the stones.

"I'd hate to be predictable," he gloats.

The hair on the back of my neck stands on end as the ass crack of hell opens, and a horde of three-foot-tall creatures with long ears and beak noses scrabble through the opening to join the fight.

"What the hell is this?" I glance at Dionysus. "This was *not* in the sitrep."

Dionysus shrugs. "I told you history is faulty."

"Looks like we're rewriting history," Dillan observes.

I scowl at the horde of Harry Potter house elves, scanning the gnarled, grotesque features with my fae vision. Their energy is olive green and chaotic but not nearly as powerful and vile as other raiders we've dealt with.

"The demon is a big deal, but his gremlin fan club isn't. We've got this."

"Yeah, we do," Calum agrees.

"Dayam, those things are fugly." Dillan flashes me a wry grin and twirls his twin daggers.

"Right and tight, everyone," I shout, catching their attention. "Sloan, Calum, and Dillan—you guys handle Gremlin Central. I'll keep the demon busy with Bruin and Nikon. Dionysus, you're with Selene."

A chorus of affirmatives echoes around me, punctuated by the sharp *twang* of Calum's bow releasing an arrow. He nails a gremlin in the chest. Dillan grins like a madman, and Sloan's face hardens into that focused look I love.

"Bear, cut us a path."

Bruin's roar vibrates through the night air, a promise of force and fury. He charges ahead, plows into the gremlin horde, and tosses them aside like rag dolls.

I steel myself as we break through the last of them and are within striking distance of the moon demon. He's a towering monstrosity of darkness and anger, his eyes burning with malice.

His gaze meets mine, and his lips curl into a vicious smile. "Oh, look, a tasty little morsel of meat. I love it when my food delivers itself."

"Yeah no, I don't think so," I mutter and surge forward.

The demon roars, launching at me, and I brace for impact. The world narrows to the rush of wind, the gleaming arc of my spear, and the impending clash with the demon.

We need this win because I need those stones. Whether we confiscate them, steal them, or pry them from his curved dead claws, I don't care.

Bruin roars beside me, and we go at the demon hard. "Did I hear Selene right? Your name is Muzak? As in the boring music played in elevators to lock you in tedium?"

His look of confusion doesn't stop his next attack. He squeezes sparks out of those stones for the second time and I'd swear the moon gets bigger. It's like he's drawing it toward Earth until it's a gigantic globe about to collide with the planet.

That has to be an optical illusion, right?

Wind howls past me, a primal scream in the night as I run full tilt toward the demon. Bruin thunders beside me, a roiling mass of muscle and fur. His growls echo across the moonlit battlefield.

Over in the mosh pit of gremlins and chaos, Calum aims his bow, arrows nocked and gleaming under the moonlight. Dillan spins with his daggers glinting wickedly. Sloan, my sexy hubster, is a blur of motion as he portals himself in short bursts from one side of an opponent to another to attack fast and furious.

The demon in front of me roars as Bruin lands a well-placed

swipe of his claws. The two grapple and roll and I'm thankful my bear has his armor on.

A Celtic god gifted him that armor.

Surely that will keep him safe from a demon, right?

While the two of them roll and fight, Selene looks on from her altar. She's still running through the motions of her full-moon ritual, and I'm a little taken aback.

We're here to help her, but she doesn't feel the need to pitch in? Dionysus is keeping all hellspawn away from her, and by the look on her face and the way she's lazily sweeping her hands through the air over her altar, you'd think she was waving to butterflies in her herb garden.

Hello? We're battling here.

In a display of raw power, the moon demon throws out his clenched fist and sends a wave of darkness crashing toward us. It hits like a physical blow, sending us sprawling on the grass.

I grit my teeth, ignoring the pain that flares through my body. Pushing up on my hands, I glance toward Selene. The goddess stands tall, her face a mask of calm as she works her magic.

Seriously? Still nothing?

Dionysus either hears my inner voice or reads my expression because he shrugs one shoulder.

Yeah, I know. Deities do what deities feel like. The rest of the world be damned.

You need to get those stones away from him, Dionysus says into my mind. *We don't need to win this fight—Selene can do that. We just need those stones.*

Good point. Okay, I change gears on my battle plan and rethink. When he threw out that wave of darkness, Muzak punched forward, extending his arm far enough from his body that I might've been able to do something. Maybe we can get him to do that again.

Tarzan, I need you to come at Muzak and make him use those stones. I have a plan.

Dionysus grunts. *And it starts with me being the target of his magical assault? Thanks a lot, Jane.*

I chuckle, but there's no humor in it. *With Nikon sitting this one out, you're the most durable of us. Sorry, sweetie.*

I get it. One magical assault coming up.

Bruin, I'm borrowing Dionysus for a moment. You've got Selene.

Aye, Red. I'll do what I can. Watch yerself.

Yep. I intend to.

When Dionysus turns to rush Muzak, the moon demon spins and thrusts out his glowing fist. A beam of magical energy streams from his hand, and the bolt of raw power catches Dionysus square in the chest.

I hear the impact and the rush of breath that escapes Dionysus' lungs. That packed a powerful punch. I push the worry of that down for now and focus on my plan.

Brandishing my spear, I charge, swinging Birga with all my might. She whistles in the night air as I arc her in a downward stroke, aiming for the demon's wrist.

I don't know much about demon physiology, but Birga has never let me down. She loves to bite into flesh, and she's enchanted with powers of her own.

The next moment is when everything stops, and at the same time, everything happens all at once.

Muzak blinks as his clenched fist falls to the ground, either in shock or disbelief.

I release Birga and race forward, grab the severed hand, and roll away from its demon owner.

As I spring to my feet, a bison barrels into the demon, his claws digging deep into its shadowy form.

Dionysus crumples to the ground, and his face contorts in a horrifying mask of pain.

Then all the gremlin minion creatures turn, see me with the hand, and launch after me.

My instincts kick in hard and tell me only one thing…

Run!

CHAPTER FOURTEEN

With the demon's severed hand still clutching the moonstones, I break into a run and beeline for the cover of the few trees lining the hilltop. It won't offer much of a barrier between me and those gremlins, but it's better than standing in the open and getting clawed to shreds.

Behind me, the enraged chittering of the gremlin minions grows louder. I don't dare glance back. They're hot on my heels. Adrenaline pumps through my veins, propelling me faster as my mind scrambles for my next steps.

As I duck under the branches of a lemon tree, I cast a spell I hope will put some distance between me and them. *"Tree Travel."*

The power surge that bursts from me is more than my druid magic—much more. Somehow, clutching the moonstones has amped me up.

I race into the trunk of the nearest tree and come out of another twenty feet in front of me and to the right. I keep running, calling on the same spell three more times so I've got a decent lead.

At the hillside's crest, I scramble in a rapid sidestep, dropping down the slope toward the streets of ancient Rhodes.

The city is a maze of narrow, winding streets flanked by towering stone buildings adorned with ornate statues of the gods. I tuck myself in a fertility altar for Venus and try to pry the demon's fingers open so I can carry the stones and not his ichor-dripping hand.

"Why won't you let go?" I hiss, pulling with all my might but getting nowhere.

Whatever the reason, there's no loosening the grip.

Focused as I am, I lose track of how much time has passed and nearly get my throat ripped out as a hellspawn launches at me.

My first instinct is to call Birga, but this alcove is too small. The grunt and growling of incoming minions mean I'm about to be swarmed.

With a sharp kick, I knock the little bastard back into the open street. *"Wall of Stone."*

The ground rumbles, and the alcove's walls close me in. I've got a moment's reprieve from the gremlin attack, but I've sealed myself into a stone cylinder. They'll likely stack up to create a gremlin ladder and invade me from above in a few seconds.

I frown at the wall's upper edge. It'll take effort to scale that. What do I do with the demon fist?

I need these bloody stones.

An idea strikes, and before I can think better of it, I drop to all fours and call for my transformative form. I don't often access my sabertooth cat, but she never fails to heed my call.

My body tingles with magical energy, and my racing heart continues to pump hard. The sensation is odd but not as frightening as I found it the first time.

The tingles morph into a burn, which erupts into an explosion of my cells. I watch my fingers curling against the packed earth change to massive paws with russet red fur and claws.

The last thing in this world I want to do is take the demon's hand into my mouth, but there's no help for it. I take one for the team and snatch it up with my extended fangs. *Gawh...it's nasty.*

Fighting back my gag reflex, I sit back on my haunches and launch up, reaching for the top of the alcove wall. My cat's strength and grace make the leap easy.

I soar up, grip the wall's lip with my paws, bring my back feet up to gain purchase, and launch again.

I'm out of the alcove and running along the second-story rooftops of the city homes.

My cranium floods with animal impulses I don't fully recognize. Random scents and instincts flash through my brain like some kind of baffling evolutionary remix. Without slowing down, I scrabble over the roof I'm on and leap down to the next street.

Bruin? Dionysus? A little help would be nice.

I'm comin', Red, Bruin says across our bond. *Can ye give me a landmark to go by? All these feckin' streets look the same.*

I'm racing on all fours, trying to stay in the shadows and out of sight. One of the gremlins lunges at me, claws flashing in the moonlight. I drop and roll, bringing my back feet up to rabbit-kick the fucker and send it flying.

Its scream rings in my ears as I roll back to all fours and keep running. Bruin's right. Everything looks the same. I need something unique.

The Colossus. I'm almost at the harbor. I'll meet you at the Helios statue.

Perfect. On my way.

My heart pounds in my chest as I zigzag through the city, praying to any god listening that I won't hit a dead end. My footsteps are silent as the pads of my paws absorb the weight transfer with each lunge.

The snarls and hisses of the gremlins close on my tail punctuate my predatory silence.

I vault over a pile of crates stacked in an alleyway and nearly lose the fist from my mouth. When I land, there's an awkward moment as it rolls in the alley's dirt before I clamp my mouth around it again.

Gross, gross, gross. Oh, my gods...

I try not to think about the grit and ichor coating my tongue and focus on closing the distance to the massive statue at the harbor.

The market square is in front of me, filled with stalls overflowing with fruits, vegetables, and all sorts of goods. I weave to evade, but two demon minions drop onto me from nowhere, and we tumble through one of the stalls.

Lemons, artichokes, pears, and olives fly everywhere.

I growl deep in my throat and swipe my paws, dicing one gremlin across the belly and ripping a hole in the throat of another.

I roll back to all fours when they're down and keep running.

Sorry! I apologize over my shoulder, knowing the store owner will be pissed in the morning.

I round an ornate fountain decorated with mosaics of Poseidon and glance up to get my bearings.

Almost there.

I race through narrow streets lined with homes and shops, and down a long set of stone stairs. Eventually, I reach the city's harbor, where the cobbled roads give way to sandy beaches and wooden piers.

Panting heavily, I skid to a stop at the mighty statue's base. Bruin materializes in front of me, and I drop the fist and haul oxygen into my lungs. *Thanks for dropping by, buddy.*

Ye know, it would be a damn sight easier keepin' ye safe if ye weren't always runnin' off and gettin' yerself into trouble.

True story.

I consider changing back to my human self, but after watching Dillan fight naked in battle, I'm going to avoid a repeat performance. *Any chance someone can grab my battle leathers on their way down to the harbor?*

The ground beneath my paws rumbles before my thought is even out of my head. The thunderous *crack* and *pop* of the earth heaving precedes a massive fissure opening and another legion of gremlins climbing out of Hell's crack.

Oh, crap.

To the harbor, everyone—all-call to Colossus.

The moment the air snaps with Dionysus' signature power, I release my cat and resume my form. "I need clothes, Tarzan!"

Dionysus blinks at me, but a momentary distraction is all it is. The next moment, I'm back in my battle gear and spreading my stance, ready to rumble.

"Rude!" Dillan snaps, forming a wall with Sloan and Calum to keep the incoming force at bay. "You never covered *my* nakey bits when I lost my clothes in battle."

Dionysus shrugs. "You never asked."

Nikon snaps in a moment later, scanning our surroundings. "Where do you need me?"

"You're supposed to be resting."

"You shouted a telepathic all-call. I'm not about to ignore that."

I wipe my tongue with my forearm, but it does nothing to reduce the foul taste of dirt and death in my mouth. "We've got what we came for. Let's get Alec and get the hell gone."

"We need to close this fissure before these assholes sink the island," Sloan instructs. "Fi, Dillan, and Calum, yer with me. Nikon, Bruin, and Dionysus, keep them off us."

Beside me, Sloan drops to his knees and presses both hands to the ground. I do the same, pressing my left palm to the ground and my right over the clenched fist of the moon demon to activate the stones.

If it works the same as when I was casting earlier, I should get a boost from the stones and maybe make this a little quicker and easier on us.

Dillan and Calum are beside me in a heartbeat.

Dillan has blood dripping down the left side of his face and pooling in his eye. Calum looks clammy and pale. Neither of those things makes me a happy camper.

"*Wall of water,*" Dillan calls, pulling up a solid screen of water from the harbor.

The gremlins shriek, and I grin. "I don't think the hell creatures like water."

Calum regains a little color. "Isn't that sad? Maybe they need a swimming lesson."

"Yeah, I think that's a great idea."

From the corner of my eye, I see Muzak climb out of the crack in the earth, and my heart sinks. He's whole again, his right hand in place as if I never chopped it off.

Glancing down at the severed appendage in my grip, I wonder how he did that. Is it like a gecko getting a new tail or a starfish growing back a leg?

Cool, but unfortunate. It would've been better for us if he remained on the injured list for a little longer.

"Give me back my stones, witch." He throws out his hand from thirty feet away, and I curse and grab the clenched fist with both hands, crushing it to my chest as if it was the football in the Super Bowl playoffs.

"Guys, we need to go…like now." I fight to hold on as the power of his magical call drags me forward even with my heels dug in and fighting him all the way.

Sloan abandons his efforts to close the fissure and grabs me around the waist. I wait for him to *poof* us out of the demon's tractor beam, but he doesn't.

"Get us out of here, hotness!"

"Oh, that I could, luv," he grits out and switches his hold on me to grapple both me and the severed fist. "Greek, get us out of here."

I'm unsure which Greek he's referring to since both have

more portal power than him, but I suppose it doesn't matter. Either of them would work.

Muzak is growing more and more furious, and the rumbling of the ground is growing into an all-out quake. I glance at the Colossus of Rhodes, the giant statue standing tall against the night sky, an eternal symbol of human resilience and ingenuity.

It's swaying, and the stone base is cracking under the extreme tremors, rattling us to the marrow of our bones.

"What do historians say took down the statue?"

Sloan frowns and follows my train of thought. "A feckin' earthquake."

"You mean like the one Muzak is causing?"

He grunts. "Aye, luv. Like that."

"Well, if it's going down, we might as well use it to our advantage."

"Feckin' hell, Fi. It's one of the seven wonders of the ancient world."

"And we're trying to save two realms. That's more important than a bronze god smiling at the boats."

A rush of air gusts past us and Bruin materializes in a grappling tackle, his mighty claws wrapped around Muzak in a violent bear hug.

The tractor beam stops, and we collapse to the hard ground before recovering enough to get to our feet and gain some distance.

I scramble back to the statue and place my hands on the crumbling surface of its stone base. Calling on the deep, earthy power of my druidic magic, I use the moonstones still trapped in the severed fist to give an extra push to my power.

The ground rumbles violently and the statue sways. "Brace yourselves, boys!"

A terrible screech fills the air, and I wince. It's the moon demon. He's furious about his stones and cluing in to my audacious plan. I grit my teeth and send another massive magical pulse.

A groan echoes through the darkness of the night and the Colossus begins to topple.

The ground beneath me cracks and shifts, lurching violently. Sloan and I get thrown off our feet, but it doesn't matter. The Colossus is toppling into the water.

"Impenetrable Sphere." I flop onto my back, clutching the moon demon's fist and the moonstones locked in its grip.

The thunderous *crack* of the hundred-foot bronze statue crashing into the water sends a tidal wave rippling over the harbor wall, swallowing the shore and the remaining gremlins.

Our sphere gets thrown around like a bubble on rough seas, and I enjoy the moment of bobbing around. Yes, it's a little nauseating, but no one is actively trying to kill us, so that's a step up.

"Do you see anyone?" I search the streets rushing with water.

"No. Perhaps they portaled back to Dionysus' temple to rendezvous."

I search the wreckage of the damage we caused, and the only good thing is that the fissure has sealed, and the hell beasts are no more. "Yeah, let's try the temple. I'm sure that's where everyone is."

Sloan *poofs* us back to the private quarters of Dionysus' temple, and I exhale a ragged breath. I toss the severed hand to my hubby as I run and hug my brothers, Nikon, and Dionysus.

"Is everyone okay?"

"Okay enough to get the hell home," Dillan replies.

Calum looks peaked, and my gaze falls to his bloody fingers clamped over his side. "I wouldn't mind a trip to Wallace's clinic if Alec can get us home."

I want to peel his hand back and look at the damage but think better of it.

Home is a better idea. Let Wallace sort it out.

When I scan the room, only one member of our party is missing. I close my eyes and reach out over my bond. *Bruin? Where are you, buddy?*

"Right behind ye, Red."

I rush over and wrap my arms around his neck. Pressing my face into the lengths of his fur, I take a moment to be thankful that we're all here. "Glad you made it back, buddy."

"Och, it was a near thing. That demon bastard pulled me into his fissure, and I almost got sealed up with them in hell."

The thought of it being that close makes me ill.

Bruin nuzzles my cheek. "Don't panic, Red. We've gotten through worse scrapes and come back ready to rumble."

"Yeah, we have." I pat my chest. "Now, if there are no objections, I need to get home and spend half an hour with my electric toothbrush and a bottle of mouthwash. I have demon breath, and it's disgusting."

CHAPTER FIFTEEN

The playful roar of dragons in the distance wakes me, and it takes a moment for my mental hamster to get in its wheel and catch me up. Right. We're back in our own time, safely home in Isilon.

Sitting up, I smile at Sloan's side of King Henry. It's empty, of course. His sheets and duvet are straightened and left as tidy as possible with me still sleeping on my side of the bed.

I stretch and roll to the end of the bed to curl around Manx lounging by the footboard. "Hey, Manxy. How are things on the home front?"

He blinks and twitches the black tuft of one ear at me. As a lynx, he's got a stunning, thick coat, but the black tufts of his ears are dramatically beautiful, not to mention silky soft.

Him flicking them generally means he's annoyed.

It doesn't take much to figure out why. Manx is Sloan's animal companion, and he doesn't enjoy being left behind when there are adventures to be had.

He expressed his discontent when we left, but it hasn't dissipated since we've been gone.

"Manxy, come on. You know why you couldn't come on this one. We were time-traveling. The people of ancient Greece wouldn't have known what you were. You're too exotic. You would've drawn too much attention to us. We were going for stealth."

He wriggles his nose, and his whiskers tickle my cheek. "Ye think I'm exotic, do ye?"

I chuckle and stroke a gentle hand over his head and into the deep fur around his neck. "How could I not? You're lithe and majestic and too beautiful *not* to draw attention. Greeks and Romans were known as collectors of rare and exotic creatures. We couldn't risk you being sought after."

He uncurls his body a little and lifts his head to look at me. Hurt and frustration swirl in his golden eyes. "I hate being left behind."

I press a kiss onto his velvety nose. "I know you do, puss. I promise it had nothing to do with anything other than needing to avoid notice while we found and rescued Nikon. He was the focus."

He considers that for a moment before he sighs. "Sloan said ye got him back with little fuss."

I hear the hope in his voice and swallow. Sloan's a better liar than I am about these things. I'm sure he said something very comforting so Manx didn't feel like he missed out on a grand adventure.

"Once we got into Hecate's sanctum, Themis and the Fates took care of her, and we took Nikon back to Dionysus' temple to rest until we could travel."

I intentionally leave out the battle with the hydra and the Carian warriors to make it sound less exciting.

"Bruin mentioned ye made an unplanned pit stop on the way home. Ye got the stones?"

"We did."

"He said that got dicey."

"A little, but we got the job done and are here now. Is that where Sloan is? Is he working on the stones?"

"Aye, he called Merlin at the crack, and they've had their heads down ever since."

Ah, thus the curled-up companion pouting at the end of the bed. "Well, give me five to freshen up, and we'll go find them and see what they've figured out. Then maybe the three of us can train for a bit. We've got some big battles coming up. I don't want you going soft on us. We'll need you for the big finish."

His eyes glitter in the morning light. "Ye mean that?"

I scrub the underside of his chin, causing him to close his eyes and stretch out his neck for more. "Of course, I mean it. You're an integral part of this team, Manxy. I know you get sad when you have to stay behind, but it makes Sloan and I feel so much better to know you're here watching over the family."

"It does?"

I smile and let him see the truth in my words. "It absolutely does. Knowing you are here is one of the main reasons we feel safe to go off and do what needs to be done. You're our rock, Manx. Our secret weapon."

It's true. He might not have the strength or killer instinct Bruin has or the ability to fly and breathe fire like Dart and Saxa, but he's no less of a warrior. Manx is noble, brave, and loyal, and won't ever quit fighting for the ones he loves.

Just like his bonded companion.

Thinking about Sloan makes me smile, and I scoot to the opening between the heavy drapes of our bed and drop to the floor. The hardwood floors are warm from the sunlight coming through the window, and I pad over to my dresser to grab clean clothes.

"Give me a few, puss, and we'll see what Sloan and Merlin have figured out."

Neither Sloan nor Merlin is downstairs when Manx and I go looking, but a note on the fridge door says to meet them at the Light Weavers' temple when I'm up and about. I pop down two pieces of cinnamon raisin toast and grab the open fruit punch juice box Ireland left in the fridge a couple of days ago.

Whatevs. It wouldn't be the first time I got toddler cooties from one of the monkeys.

"Heading down to the Light Weavers' temple," I call to Bruin, who's basking in the sun.

He's snoring soundly, so I don't bother waking him. If he wakes up worried, he'll reach out and find me.

Manx and I head down our cute little cul-de-sac, and I chuckle as I always do at seeing Dillan puttering around tending to his pink house.

Today he's using his druid powers to work on his garden, and I gotta say, even Gran would be proud. Beside him sits the Pack-n-Play with a sunshade over the top and a sweet baby boy angel cooing and kicking his feet.

I'll never get enough of that baby.

He is cuteness overload.

I wave as we head down the cobbled street, but Dillan's too focused on his gardening and his boy to notice. That's fine. I love that he's absorbed in his life.

Bizzy and Meg are playing with the twins in the side yard of Aiden's big blue house, and I'm happy to see that Haniel's fairy godmother, Micky, is watching over them.

The woman is an angel. Literally.

She loves the kids and takes such good care of them that Kinu, Eva, and the others can relax and take a few moments to care for themselves.

It's a win-win all around.

"Do you think maybe we'll have kids soon?" Manx asks, noticing me notice the monkeys.

I meet his gaze and shrug. "I don't know. Maybe once the

world is back on its feet again. Why? Is that something you're looking forward to or worried about?"

We turn the corner at the end of the street and continue toward the main city center. Isilon is a big place, but the main corridor runs straight down from the palace, past our neighborhood, and into the city square.

"Looking forward to. I think it's nice that Daisy gets to snuggle with Bizzy. I'd like to do that too."

I reach down and stroke the top of his head. "You're a great snuggler. No matter when they come, our babies will be lucky to have you love them."

Manx grins at me. "I hope it's soon."

I chuckle and pat his shoulder as we walk. "I'll keep that in mind."

The two of us continue toward the city square, waving a friendly hello to the odd person we see. The city has slowly been coming back to awareness after over a thousand years of being dormant, so we have yet to explore huge sections.

Bit by bit, beings from other realms who need a haven have found us and are building new lives here.

It's good. People need to know that if the worlds turn on them, there's a safe place they can go.

Isilon is that for dozens of people and one day that will be hundreds…maybe even thousands.

My brothers stand at the helm of it all.

The Hidden City is lucky to have them because Emmet and Brendan are the best of the best. They'll ensure that whatever went down the last time, with the Dark Weavers killing and destroying the city's inhabitants, never happens again.

We arrive at the Light Weavers' temple, and I yank the handle of the huge, twenty-foot door and open the way inside. By the sound of male voices echoing off the hard, polished surfaces of the outer area, we're not the first to arrive.

"Good morning, all," I call as we enter the room.

I glance around and realize I've never been in here before. It seems like a magical workroom. There are shelves of jarred ingredients, dried herbs, leather-bound books, and candles of every color and size.

A four-foot round table occupies the room's center, and the moon demon's severed hand sits in the center of it.

Merlin, Sloan, Da, and Granda are all gathered around the table, staring at the grotesque appendage, its fingers still clasped tight with the moonstones locked away.

Da straightens and opens his arms to welcome me, but the air is thick with tension.

"I take it things aren't going well." I kiss Da on the cheek and move to Granda.

"We're still in a stage of observation," Granda replies. "We didn't want to start in on the stones and cause a reaction we didn't expect."

That makes sense.

I slide in between Granda and Sloan. "What have we heard about Calum?"

Sloan meets my gaze, and the tension knotted in the pit of my belly eases a little. "I spoke to Da this morning. Calum suffered several deep punctures from the claws of those hell beasts, and there was some poison involved as well. He's all fixed up now and should be home fer dinner if Da continues to be satisfied with his recovery."

"I hope you thanked him and told him how much we love and appreciate him."

Sloan nods. "Aye, I did. I also promised we'd come to stay next weekend once all this Ostara ritual business is over."

"Oh, yeah. I'd like that."

With that settled, I return my attention to the clenched fist on the polished oak table. "Do you think it's possible for the moon demon to track these stones? Might we end up with him here on our doorstep?"

Merlin waves me off, his gaze still focused on the hand. "I thought of that. I cast a concealment spell on the stones as soon as Sloan handed them over. The demon will find nothing."

I draw a deep breath, relieved. If Merlin is confident we're safe from the moon demon, I'm happy with that. "Are demons capable of time travel?"

He lifts one shoulder. "I'm not sure how time works in hell. Either way, between the magical cloaking of this island and the concealment spell and the time change from the point when you took possession of the stones, I'd say there's no chance that demon is finding us or trying to reclaim these stones."

"Speaking of reclaiming the stones," Dionysus interjects, appearing at the table with us. "I've got good news and bad news. Which do you want first?"

I groan and drop my head back. "Give us the good news first, Tarzan. What's happened now?"

"Selene claims ownership of the moonstones and says we interfered in her life course. She's demanding them back so she can destroy them, as she would have had we not altered history."

I blink at him. "That's the good news?"

He tilts his head from side to side. "The good news is that I convinced her to let us keep them until after the full moon ritual when we try to reinstate the veil."

"No. Until we *reinstate* the veil. There is no try."

Da chuckles. "Is that wisdom from Yoda?"

"Maybe."

Dionysus rolls his eyes. "Anyway, I told Selene I would surrender the stones to her once it's done and we stabilize the realms. She's not pleased, but I think she'll give us our chance."

"I suppose that is good news." Granda scratches his nape. "So, what's the bad news, then?"

Dionysus turns to Sloan and me and gives us double thumb guns. "Helios is majorly pissed about you two taking down his statue and he *is* coming after you."

Sloan lets out a throaty groan and drops his head. "Och, if there were any way to go back and not take down the Colossus, I would. Honestly, I can't believe Fiona and I are the reason that statue fell."

I shrug. "Hey, we didn't alter history on that one. It was the right timeframe and the right way to bring it down. Who's to say we weren't always the reason and history played out as it was meant to?"

Sloan rolls his eyes, looking ill.

"I'm not sure what that part of the story is about, but is there any chance we can circle back to it later?" Merlin asks. "We're trying to unlock some majorly powerful magical objects here."

I straighten and get with the program. "Right. Sorry. Okay, so where are we on this?"

"We were about to cut away the hand," Da answers.

I make a face. "Ew. Seriously?"

Sloan shrugs. "We don't want any magic to affect the stones or cause a chain reaction. Cutting away the fingers seemed the easiest way to free the stones."

"Still, that's gross."

Merlin chuckles and holds up a wickedly sharp tool that looks like a Dremel with an extreme attachment. "If you're squeamish, avert your eyes, girlfriend."

While I don't have to look, the high-pitched drilling whine and grinding of bone still paints a vivid picture in my mind's eye.

It gives me the heebs, and I shake my shoulders and step away for a bit. Dionysus chuckles and places a pair of noise-canceling headphones over my ears.

The world around me goes silent.

It's shocking, really. I'm not sure when I last spent time within a cone of silence, but yeah, this is nice.

Wow. Thanks, Tarzan. These are amazing. Do you mind if I hang onto them for a bit?

He grins. *They're yours. Enjoy.*

Thanks. I love them.

The two of us hang out in the public worshipper's area of the temple until Dionysus nods at something behind me and swirls his finger in the air to gesture for us to turn and go. *They're ready for us now.*

Cool. Let's do this. Reluctantly, I remove the headphones and hand them back to Dionysus. "Will you put them on my nightstand so I don't lose track of them?"

"Of course." The next moment, they're gone.

When we return to the workroom, Merlin has his hands up and his focus locked. He's murmuring a series of incantations while his hands weave intricate patterns above the fingerless palm of the severed hand.

I didn't think it could get grosser, but yep—it did.

There are four stones embedded into the flesh of the demon's palm. They're all the same shape and size but different colors—blue, green, amber, and silver.

"Did they burn into his flesh?" I ask.

Sloan bobs his head. "Aye, it looks that way, but I don't think it was recent. My guess is the demon has used those stones so often and so long that they've become part of his hand."

"I suppose that's handy to avoid misplacing them."

Da nods. "Aye. And likely the reason his fingers remained clenched long after ye severed the hand."

I don't want to think about what happened after the severing part. Like clutching the thing to my chest with it oozing black ichor or worse, carrying it in my mouth...

I gag and lurch forward as my stomach heaves.

Dionysus is ready, though. He pushes his favorite barf bin under my chin and holds it against my chest. "Do you need Captain Jack?"

I hug his *Pirates of the Caribbean* garbage can against my chest and close my eyes. "I think I'm okay. Just a visceral flashback of that thing in my mouth."

Sloan flashes me a pitying look. "Yer all right, *a ghra*. Ye took care of that last night with the two tubes of toothpaste and the bottle of mouthwash."

I nod. "You'd think I took care of it, but when I see grossness like that, I can still taste it."

Dionysus holds up a selection of lollipops, and I grab the red one, unwrap it, and shove it in my mouth. He takes purple and does the same.

"Better. Thanks, Tarzan."

With that settled, we return our attention to Merlin's progress. Light is shimmering around Merlin's hands, radiating a soft, warm glow that illuminates the fronts of the men standing around the table.

For a moment, I'm pretty sure nothing is happening. Then, like ice slowly melting over time, I see more of the stones around the edges.

Bit by bit, the stones are released from the demon's fibrous flesh.

"Now that they're gaining their freedom, can we pry them loose or cut them out?" I ask.

Granda frowns. "We tried that when Merlin first cut away the fingers. The stones didn't appreciate bein' dislodged so abruptly. They gave Merlin a bit of kickback."

Sloan nods. "We opted for a bit more subtlety for the dislodging the second time around."

Good call. "Do you think they are bonded to the demon or simply don't like to be jostled?"

Granda shakes his head. "I don't know. It's all a bit odd. I've never known demons to use magical stones."

"That's because they don't," Patty snaps, marching in to join us with a scowl. "Those are fae elemental stones, likely stolen when an elf or one of my kind was tricked or killed to take them."

When Patty joins us in the room, the stones burst into brightness as if being lit from the inside.

The room falls silent, and we all freeze. Merlin stops chanting and takes a step back. We all wait for something to happen—all of us except Patty.

Patty grabs a stool from against the wall and drops it beside me at the table. When he climbs it and reaches across the table, the gemstones pop free of the demon's flesh and roll toward him.

"Aye, I've got ye now ye poor wee ones."

They roll into his meaty palm and settle as if they are sentient and have sought out an old friend. I scan the faces of the others.

Am I the only one who's not following?

Nope. The same blank look of surprise and confusion is mirrored around the table.

"How'd ye do that, sham?" Sloan asks.

Patty is still shaking his head, but I don't think his annoyance is aimed at us. At least, I hope it isn't. "How'd I do what? Know to come? Know what they are? Get them to trust me?"

"Yes." I nod. "All of those."

He lays his arm on the table and opens his palm. "I knew to come because I came to feed the kids and heard them cryin' fer help. I know what they are because I was raised in the fae realm and I'm not an eejit. They trust me because they sense I'll not let ye keep torturin' them like ye were doin'."

The group falls still.

"Torturin' them?" Granda looks distraught. "We thought we were freein' them."

Patty frowns. "Aye, well, that might be so, but ye were doin' a piss-poor job of gettin' it done."

CHAPTER SIXTEEN

Angry Patty is wildly passionate, but he settles down once we explain the entire story and how the elemental stones were embedded within the demon's hand. "Merlin wasn't trying to harm the stones," I repeat. "He was trying to free them."

"Aye, I understand. It was just a lot to hear them cryin' out like they were."

Elemental stones must communicate on an inaudible frequency like a dog whistle because Patty heard them when none of us did.

Then again, strictly speaking, none of us are from a fae race. Druids are guardians to the fae, but we are still human.

"I wonder how many others within the city heard them call?" Granda muses.

"Should we be concerned?" I ask.

Patty shrugs. "I can't answer ye that, but I can tell ye they were wailin' with a great deal of power."

I don't know everyone who has been accepted into the Hidden City, but I hope we can trust them not to overstep in this matter. "Maybe it's best if you keep the stones with you and take them back to the dragons' lair when you go."

Sloan meets Granda's gaze and Merlin's, and they all agree. "Aye, perhaps that's best, but guard them with all ye got. They are part of our plan to get the veil back into place."

"Och, ye can count on it, lad. They'll be as safe as safe can be."

Good. I lean forward on my elbows and inspect the pretty stones. "Now explain to us what elemental stones are and how they work."

Patty grabs the corner of a black altar cloth and tugs it across the table to smooth it out in front of himself. Then he sets out the four stones and lines them up in a tidy row.

The stones are beautiful, each one shimmering with an inner light that reflects its element.

"Ye can probably guess by their colors which stone is which without me sayin'. We've got earth, air, fire, and water."

I study the stones as he points them out one by one.

The earth stone is a deep, rich green and looks like the essence of a forest compressed into a tiny space.

The air stone is a clear sparkling silver. It almost looks like a prism, shifting colors subtly, as if capturing the dance of a cloudless sky.

The fire stone is a deep red but pulses with a warm glow, like the heart of a flame.

The water stone is a pure crystal blue with tiny swirls that flow like a river.

"I assume four is a complete set," Merlin remarks.

Patty nods. "Aye, but a complete set is incredibly rare. I haven't heard of anyone possessin' a set of four fer a thousand years or more at least."

Sloan grunts. "We stole them from a demon back in ancient Greece. He didn't seem too pleased about losing them, either."

Patty chuckles. "I imagine not."

He strokes his stubby fingers over the four of them, and they each glow brighter under his touch. "They're content now. No harm done." He nods and smiles at Merlin.

That's a relief. I'd hate for the magical stones to think we were trying to hurt or force them into servitude of any kind. We're the good guys.

"Ye mentioned that yer people and the elves might use stones like this, but what of elemental fae themselves?" Da asks.

Patty meets his gaze. "Elemental fae and these stones contain the same source of magical energy. That's like askin' if a puddle would use a glass of water to make somethin' wet. The answer is no. There's no need. They have the elemental power within them."

"So other nature-based races used them," I say.

Patty nods. "Aye, elves use stones to augment their power in jewelry or the hilts of their weapons. My people are much more like the druids. We'd never smash these up to set in a pendant. We'd carry them in a pocket or a gem pouch."

"And each stone harnesses the power of its element," Granda says.

"Aye, individually, they are powerful. Combined, their potential is extraordinary."

"Yeah, no kidding," I interject. "The demon using them had his fist clenched and raised toward the night sky. I'd swear he was drawing the full moon closer to the earth with their power."

Da and Granda both blink at me, eyes wide.

Merlin frowns. "They carry *that* much power?"

Patty nods. "Aye, with stones this size, in a full set, and likely amplified by the demon's natural abilities."

"Can you use them?" I ask. "For the ritual, I mean. If a member of the fae carries and uses them, will it help strengthen our ritual if you wield them instead of one of us?"

Patty strokes his chin and draws his fingers down his long, white beard. "Let me think on that, lass. These stones are beyond anything I've handled before."

"But they seem to like you."

"Aye, but I'm neither the demon who's been abusin' them nor

the man who—no offense, Merlin—was torturin' them. Maybe it's not so much that they want to be with me, but about who they *don't* want to be with."

I feel bad for Merlin.

He wasn't doing anything any of the rest of us wouldn't have done if we thought we could. We didn't realize the stones were suffering.

I didn't know stones *could* suffer.

But here we are.

"Maybe you can bond with them over the next day or so and work with them," I suggest. "We still have a few components to finish gathering before we can perform the ritual. Maybe you'll have a better idea once you spend time with them."

Patty nods. "Aye, I can work on it."

"Grand," Granda says. "So, we have the stones, the incantation, and some of the herbs sorted out. Lara is working on the rarest ingredients fer the incense and is hopeful we'll be ready in time."

"That leaves the celestial map and Hermes' staff," Da adds.

A heavy sigh brings our attention to where Dionysus is rolling his eyes. "I tried negotiating with Hermes while I was at Olympus. He's not interested in getting involved, and he's not one for sharing."

"Not even fer a good cause?" Granda asks.

Dionysus shrugs. "He doesn't consider the balance of humanity a cause that affects him, I'm afraid."

Merlin scratches the dark scruff on his jaw thoughtfully. "Perhaps we need to try a different approach. Pantheon gods are often more susceptible to, well, let's call it friendly persuasion."

Sloan snorts and leans forward with his arms crossed. "Ye mean bribery."

Merlin shrugs. A small smirk tugs at the corners of his mouth. "One man's bribe is another man's opportunity."

Silence hangs in the air for a moment before I break it. "What could we offer him that he'd want enough to make a trade?"

The room falls silent again, all of us lost in thought. This is the problem with dealing with gods. They have very particular tastes.

Patty pipes up. "As for the celestial map, I've got a mate who might help us get a line on it. An ancient artifact collector who owes me a favor."

Noice. "Excellent, because we've exhausted the research route and haven't had much luck. Yeah, let's visit your friend. Thanks, Patty."

The chime above the door emits a strangled wail as we enter, and I'm not sure what kind of welcome that's intended to be. It sounds like a Canada goose got its long neck caught in the door, and I turn back to make sure it didn't. With nothing there, I assume the sound was intentional, or at the very least, not unusual.

Sloan, Patty, Dionysus, and I step into the artifact shop and look around.

Unlike Myra's Mystical Emporium, where everything is orderly and sorted in well-thought-out sections, this shop is like stepping into a hodgepodge of history, magic, and mystery.

Shelves cluttered with objects of indeterminable age and origin stretch from floor to ceiling, laden with curious objects and glowing gems that pulse with ancient energy.

The air is thick with the scent of old parchment, cotton candy, and a hint of something metallic. I draw a deep breath. It has that peculiar mix of iron and silver that only magical artifacts seem to possess.

Everything is softly lit by the warm glow of globes filled with fireflies. They hover mid-air, casting dancing shadows on the aged wood and stone.

A human-sized bird cage occupies the corner opposite the door, its bars crafted from the bones of an unknown creature and currently housing a disgruntled-looking pixie with neon green wings.

Glass cases along the long wall display strange relics—a dragon's tooth, a mermaid's comb, a bottled storm, and countless other items that defy explanation.

In the far corner, a huge grandfather clock chimes, not the hour, but what sounds like a melody from another world. Its pendulum swings irregularly as though keeping time for a realm that does not obey our laws of physics.

Our footsteps softly shuffle over the stone floor as we venture farther inside. Sloan's eyes are wide as his historian's passion inventories his surroundings.

His excitement for all things aged never gets old.

I look around and can't help but feel the creeping tug of trepidation. A sphinx's riddle box here, a gorgon's looking glass there. It's a mix of wonder and possibly danger intertwined.

"Buy or browse?" croaks a voice from the back room.

I'm not sure how to answer that. Neither? Is this guy like one of Brenny's or Da's confidential informants? Should we offer to pay for intel?

"Just a visit from an old friend," Patty calls. "That is, if a gruff old arse like yerself has any friends."

There's a bit of shuffling behind a black curtain and a gnome with features as craggy and worn as a mountainside comes through.

He has the same fluffy white hair as Patty, but where our friend's is full and long like a dandelion gone to seed, this man's sprouts in tufts from his ears and chin. His rheumy eyes hold a glint of shrewd intelligence.

He searches our faces, and the dawning clarity hits as he recognizes Patty. "Well, well, well. It's been too long, Red."

"Long enough that no one calls me Red anymore." The two

embrace and Patty slaps the man's back, sending a cloud of dust wafting up. When they step apart, Patty gestures at his friend. "Bilbus, these are my dear friends Fiona, her husband Sloan, and the Greek."

It strikes me as strange that he introduces Dionysus as "the Greek" instead of giving his name, but hey, this is his show. He can play it however he wants.

Bilbus peers at us from beneath his bushy brows. A hint of a smile tugs on his lips. He claps his small, wrinkled hands, sending another puff of dust into the air.

"To what do I owe this unusual pleasure?" His eyes twinkle under the pulsating firefly light.

Patty is the one to field that, and he jumps right in. "Weel, we're on a bit of a quest, ye see, and I thought ye might be the man to help us out."

Bilbus strokes his sparse beard and hobbles around his shop while Patty explains. "Ah, I see." His eyes brighten when Patty gets to the part about the map. "I've heard tales of the map, though I've never had the pleasure of beholding it myself."

"Do ye know where we can find it?" Patty asks.

"Stories say 'twas housed in the Great Library of the Norsemen."

"The Norsemen?" I repeat. "Like the Vikings?"

A thoughtful hum reverberates from deep within him as he strokes his beard. "Exactly like that. The Vikings charted the seas and stars with equal fervor, mapping realms both known and unknown."

Patty raises a brow at that. "But the Great Library of the Norsemen is said to be in Valhalla."

Bilbus shrugs. "I can only tell you what I hear."

I sigh. "Well, we can't just march into the afterlife of the Vikings. Do you think Hel will help us? Are you two in a better place these days?"

Dionysus nods. "Yeah, Jonah and I sent her a cask of mead for

Yule, and she sent us a lovely set of aurochs drinking horns with an invitation to join her sometime."

"You aren't taking Jonah to Helheim, are you?"

He chuckles. "Of course not, Jane. I have more sense than that. Vikings would take one look at my cowboy and eat him up. No, I just meant things are good."

I pat my racing heart. "Excellent. And if her father is up to no good again, I'm sure she'll want to know."

Dionysus chuckles. "She gets so frustrated with him."

Sloan frowns, his green eyes piercing as he glances at Dionysus. "Hel might be the only one who can get Loki back on side. He doesn't seem to obey the wishes of his pantheon, but he loves his daughter."

I agree. "She's always been reasonable, even helpful at times. If she has access to the map, I'm sure she'll tell us, but I have a sneaking suspicion Loki probably snatched it and either stashed or destroyed it already."

Sloan sighs. "Aye, if he's aware of its significance to reinstating the veil, he's likely taken it off the board of play. Still, it would be irresponsible not to find out."

I read the text that buzzed in on my phone. "Agreed. So, if it's cool, Tarzan will handle the visit with Hel, and we'll update Garnet and Merlin. As well, Andromeda needs me to check in with Nikon."

"That works," Dionysus agrees. "It's likely easier for me to handle the Helheim issue and visit the realm of the Viking afterlife without two living mortals, anyway."

With that, we thank Bilbus and take our leave.

When Sloan and I step out of the portal into the kitchen, I feel a familiar foxy presence. I glance at the reading chair by the front window, and there he is. Discord is in his fox form, curled up like he owns the place.

"Well, look who showed up while we were away," I drawl, crossing my arms.

Discord's golden eyes blink open, and a teasing grin curls up on his fox snout. "Miss me?"

I can't help but roll my eyes. "You could say that. We could have used your help with Hecate."

The fox's ears flatten at the mention of the goddess. "Oh, Red, I love a good brawl as much as the next trickster, but when gods get involved? No, thank you. That's a one-way ticket to a world of hurt."

"You're afraid of Hecate?" I tease, feigning surprise. "I thought you were a badass in your own right?"

"Not afraid, but also not stupid. Hecate is a mean bitch with a long memory."

True story. "We know that better than most."

"Because of your immortal friend."

My gaze narrows on the wily being. "What do you know about Nikon and his situation?"

The fox's mouth falls open in a laugh. "I know Hecate has been biding her time, waiting for an opportunity to get back at him for rejecting her."

"Yeah, that much is obvious."

Sloan shuffles around in the kitchen, unloading the dishwasher and setting out a frying pan, a whisk, and a bowl. "It's a moot point fer now, anyway. Hecate violated the terms of an agreement with Themis and is in custody with her powers bound."

"For how long?" Discord asks.

"Long enough for us to reinstate the veil." I hope that's accurate. "After that, well, we'll see."

Discord whistles and jumps up on one of the breakfast bar stools to watch Sloan crack a couple of eggs and pour milk into the mix. "Taking Hecate off the board is a good move. Well played, Red. Who's next on the list?"

I slide behind Sloan to pull out the bread he'll need to make French toast. Then I bring down the cinnamon sugar, butter, and syrup.

I'm still gauging how much I should share with him when I turn back. "Are you going to screw me over the first chance you get?"

His gaze softens as he stares toward the wall as if considering it. "I don't think so."

I think I have a way of reasoning with him. "Let me put it this way. If you screw us over, the veil will stay down, and you won't have accomplished any new chaos. It'll be the same social unrest and awakenings that have been occurring for the past fourteen months."

Sloan gives me a weird look, but I ignore it. Strange as it is, I understand how Discord's mind works. He's not evil. He's like a spoiled, bored toddler that wants to cause the maximum amount of drama.

I continue. "However, if you don't screw us over and we outplay beings like Hecate, Loki, Eros, and whoever else is behind this, they will be so raving mad I'm sure there will be all kinds of hostile fallout."

His golden gaze narrows on me. "I do like the sound of that."

I thought as much. "You see… Switching sides is the right move for you. It'll be more fun."

Sloan slides the first three slices of French toast onto two plates, and I dress mine up with butter and syrup. "We've already taken out Hecate and have our sights on Eros and Loki. By the time we finish, we will overthrow this entire coup."

"When the veil goes back up, there will be another period of chaos," Sloan adds, seeing where I'm going and playing along. "Not only will those behind it be furious and out fer blood, but the fae communities will also be cut off from the easy access to prana. And the human communities will have to readjust to their world changing again."

Discord's eyes widen. "Wouldn't it be fun if we seal a bunch of human communities on the other side and trap them in the fae realm?"

My mouth hangs open mid-bite, and I catch myself before I dash his hopes. He won't be on my side if he realizes I won't let him have any fun. "Maybe. Or maybe we'll think of something even more disruptive. I'll put my thinking cap on and see what I can come up with."

Discord grins and lowers his snout to his plate, licks his breakfast, then picks it up with his teeth and inhales it in a few quick chomps. "What's our plan?"

"We need Hermes' staff and the celestial map," I answer. "We figure Loki's already taken the map, so we need to figure out where he'd stash it and how to get it back."

"Ah, Loki," Discord murmurs, his tone somewhere between respectful and wary. "Now things are getting interesting. He's not going to be as easy to beat as Hecate. He's a trickster, like me, and we're a different breed altogether."

Ain't that the truth?

"Then we're fortunate yer willin' to teach us the ways of the wily mind," Sloan interjects. "Especially if we're to outsmart him and restore the veil."

Discord swishes his fluffy tail and sits taller on his stool. "Yes, you are."

We don't need Discord's help as much as his participation in not getting in our way, but he doesn't need to know that.

Yeah, maybe he'll share some of what he knows if we can convince him it'll stir up trouble.

Can we trust him? I'm not sure. Right now, it's a "keep your enemies closer" kind of moment.

"Let's assume we can't convince Hermes to lend us his staff, and Loki destroyed the map. What then?" I ask.

Sloan frowns. "I suppose that leaves us with one of three options. One, seek other magical objects that might offer a similar level of power and purpose to use as replacements. Two, try to track them down despite the overwhelming odds. And three, to find another ritual or solution to reinstate the veil."

I groan. "And start all over again?"

"It's not ideal, luv, I know. We might not have any other choice. While you check on Nikon, I'll go to the shrine and do some research. Maybe I can find other artifacts or enchanted objects that might equate to the staff and the map."

I brush my fingers over the silver crescent moon hanging against my sternum. "I don't think the amulet would've come to me if this wasn't our path."

"We won't give up, *a ghra*, but it would be irresponsible not to consider all options."

"All righty, then. Go team."

CHAPTER SEVENTEEN

Walking through the front door of Nikon's mansion is like walking into a storm cloud. The air crackles with pent-up frustration, and Andromeda lifts a shoulder, her long, flaxen blonde hair loosely falling as she shrugs. "It's a spatial energy thing, I think. He's in his room. I made a tray for you to take up. Try to get him to eat something. I'm heading downtown for court."

I see the tray she's talking about on the table at the bottom of the stairs. "Not a problem. Is Politimi home?"

Andy chuckles. "You battle monsters and irate gods but are afraid to be left alone with our little sister?"

"Um…maybe."

Andromeda laughs and grabs her leather folio case and keys. "Well, fear not. You are safe. Timi's spending a few weeks in the Alps at the yeti compound."

"Oh yeah? How are things going there?"

"From what she's said, good. Kimne is leading the group while the young queen grows to maturity, and Timi says raising her and protecting her has brought the community together even closer than before."

"Outstanding. I'm relieved to hear that." After Mingin and Melanippe killed the yeti queen in a twisted charade devised to have me kill innocents, their community was left reeling. I'm glad things are working out.

Andromeda wraps her scarf around her neck and pulls up her elegant cashmere coat's collar to protect against the February bite. "Don't let his attitude get to you. He regrets ever getting involved with that woman and hates himself for everything she's done."

"Thanks for the warning."

She sends me a sad smile. "He'll listen to you, Fi. Reach through his anger and convince him he's not the problem."

"I will."

When the door *clicks* shut, I unzip my coat and take off my boots. After dropping my purse and keys on the bench at the grand entrance, I grab the handles of the serving tray and head upstairs.

I hate that Nikon is suffering at the hands of Hecate again as he did for over a thousand years. And as he did when she killed his wife and unborn child.

Hecate seems to think that kidnapping and torturing him is how to ensure he never forgets her.

What she's too fucking selfish to understand is after everyone she's hurt in the pursuit of reclaiming their love, he never *could* forget.

My socks make no sound on the plush ivory carpet of the second floor. It's a comforting, squishy sensation, and I gather my thoughts as I walk. I saw the physical damage of what Hecate did to him, but I have no idea what emotional wounds she's lashed open again.

When I get to the door to his room, I slide the weight of the tray to the palm of my hand and knock with the other. "Hey, Greek? Mind if I come in?"

There's a muffled curse in the distance. "Fi, I'm in a shit mood and will be shit company. Can I catch up with you later?"

"If you truly want me to leave, I will, but I'd like to come in and spend some time with you." I wait a few beats and listen at the door. There's been no sound of movement, but who are we kidding—he can teleport. If he snapped out of here, I never would've heard him go.

"I'm taking the lack of answer as an invitation." He doesn't object to the warning, so I take the liberty to open the door and let myself inside.

I find him hunched over on the couch with his elbows on his knees and gripping an open bottle of Scotch. "That bad, is it?"

He sighs and runs his fingers through his tousled bed head. "I tried to warn you."

I set the tray on the glass and marble coffee table and climb onto the couch facing him. Settling in, I cross my legs and lean forward to reach for the bottle. "Are you sharing?"

He chuckles and hands me the bottle. I tilt it in the dim light that wormed in from the sides of the blinds. It's three-quarters empty, but no other bottles are lying around, so it's not as bad as it could be.

"Do you remember the first time you brought me to your home? We shared a bottle of booze then, too."

He meets my gaze, and yeah, he's wrecked, but he's also angry and frustrated. Good. It would've scared me even more if he was defeated.

Angry I can work with.

"Discord had killed a cop and blamed it on me. The entire station house was beating on the door, and I didn't know how I would get out of there."

He meets my gaze and sighs. "I remember."

I take a long swig from the bottle and let the burn of the amber gold warm my belly. "Brendan was dead. My father and my brothers were being investigated because of me. It seemed like my decisions were endangering everyone I loved."

He holds out his hand, and I hand him the bottle. "You landed on your feet."

"Damn right. Because you snapped in, brought me here, and fended off the world while I fell apart. Then, when I found my footing, you dusted me off, and we tackled what needed to be done."

He grunts. "You didn't need much dusting. You only needed a moment to pull the pieces back together."

"Right. And I trusted you enough when I was hurting to keep me safe while I sorted through it all. I didn't only land on my feet because of my endless awesomeness. I landed on my feet because you caught me and held me steady until I was solid again."

He's trying to keep it tight but can't hide the raw edge of his feelings. "I hate her, Fi. I hate her so much I feel like she's poisoning me."

I unfold my legs and shift along the seat to get closer. Giving his chest a gentle shove, I push him back toward the couch's padded arm. He doesn't object.

He also doesn't object when I crawl up the inside of the couch and lay alongside him. I rest my cheek on his soft cotton T-shirt and lie there, listening to his heartbeat. "One time in the tenth grade, I got suspended for fighting. Have I ever told you that?"

He sighs. "No. I don't think so."

I pat the flat plane of his stomach. "Bear with me. It'll make sense in the end, I promise." When he doesn't object, I continue. "So, you know how I'm not great with other girls?"

Okay, so that at least makes him chuckle. "Yes. I might have noticed that a time or two."

"Right, so in elementary school, I had a best friend. Her name was Carrie. She and I did everything together and were besties. Then, when we went to high school, she discovered boys, and everything changed."

Nikon examines the bottle of Scotch. "Am I drunk or is this story setting me up for an after-school special?"

"Carrie thought boys were these magnificent beings of strength and attraction, and I didn't see it. I had five brothers and Liam at home, and they had their friends. Boys were just, well...boys."

"I take it this was before the discovery of sex."

I chuckle. "Even then. In grade nine, it was obvious we were traveling in different circles. By grade ten, she was a different person. All she cared about was drooling over guys on the football or soccer teams and hanging out with bubble-headed Barbies."

"What were you doing?"

"By that time, Aiden, Brendan, and Calum were all on the force, and Dillan was about to join the academy. Emmet and I were working at Shenanigans and trying to keep the household running smoothly."

"No time for drooling over the soccer team?"

I laugh. "I didn't need to. My brothers were all captains of the soccer team, and between them and their weekend parties, those guys practically lived at our house. They were my friends."

"So, Carrie was jealous you had the inside track?"

"Yeah." I point at the tea tray still sitting unappreciated on the coffee table, and Nikon hands me one of the ginger cookies. "I knew we weren't close, but I thought we were still friends. Turns out, Carrie was a vindictive shrew."

"Okay, I take it we're getting to the suspension?"

"Yep. So, if she'd come after me, that would've been bad enough, but she went after two guys she knew I spent time with. She figured the three of us were fooling around, but we weren't. They were only friends, and we enjoyed hanging out."

Even remembering it makes me furious. "Evan was arrogant, but he was one hell of a fullback, and Antony was one of Emmet's close friends. Carrie started this smear campaign, spouting off stuff about them being drunk at a party and getting handsy with her, even when she told them to back off."

"Shit. That's messed up."

"Yeah, and when several bubbleheads backed her up, it spread throughout the school. Both of them got hauled into the office and kicked off the team."

"And they hadn't done anything?"

I shake my head. "Nope. Just the innocent targets of a vicious bitch. Even the implication of sexual impropriety was enough for them to be dropped."

"So, you beat the stuffing out of her, I take it."

"Yep. I caught up with her after school the day the guys got kicked off the team and asked her what happened. I knew she was lying the minute she opened her mouth. When I called her on it, she just laughed."

"She didn't even bother to deny it?"

"Hells no, she was gloating. She asked me how I felt knowing my boyfriends were now nobodies because of me. She said if they'd made better decisions, they would've given her a chance and they'd still be on top."

"Cue the fiery Irish redhead."

I grin. "I punched her in the nose, and Jackson Pollocked her pink midriff shirt like a fucking artist. Then I grabbed her ponytail and took her to the ground, pressing her face to the lawn saying, 'If you want to talk dirt about people, then dirt is what you get.'"

Nikon's arm tightens around me. "How long was your suspension?"

"A week."

"Well, I'm glad you hit her."

I brush the cookie crumbs off his shirt. "I haven't told you the worst part."

"Oh?"

I take a moment and draw a deep breath. "So, after the fight, I told the coach and the principal why I hit her and explained that she lied. It didn't matter. It was my word against her and her friends. They said they would look into it further and for me to keep my head down and stay out of it. So, I went home and left it to them to handle."

Nikon is running his fingers absently down my arm and stops when I stall out. "What happened, Fi?"

I wriggle and lift onto my elbow to look at him. "Emmet said the bullying in the halls and the comments that week were brutal. Evan had been in line for a soccer scholarship to a great university, but the two schools fighting over him dropped him like a hot rock. His dad lost his mind. His mom found him in his room. He hung himself."

Nikon's image wavers behind a wall of tears. He brushes his thumb over my cheek. "Aw, Fi, I'm sorry."

Yeah, me too. I swipe the tears running hot on my cheeks. "For a long time, I hated her. I wanted to strangle her every time I saw her in the halls. I couldn't believe someone I cared about could be so heartless. How could she know the devastation she caused and not care? How could she see Evan's younger brother at his locker and not tell the truth?"

"She never made things right?"

"No...and for months it festered inside me. Then one day, Da cleared out the house, stretched out on my bed, and patted his chest. Together, we laid there, just like this."

I press my hand to Nikon's chest and meet the pain in his eyes. "Da said, 'There are people in this world that deserve to be in yer head and yer heart, and there are others that don't. Don't ever let someone undeserving take root because soon enough, they'll take over.'"

With that said, I lay back down, and we stay quiet with our memories and the pain they cause.

After a long while, Nikon hugs me to his chest and kisses the top of my head. "You know, you could start a YouTube channel called 'Da said' and make the world a better place."

I chuckle. "Yeah, we lucked out with him."

We lay together for another few minutes before I try again. "There's no way I can know what she's put you through or the depth of your pain and anger after what you've lost—but I do know the love of family and friends can heal all wounds.

"Hecate is a bitch. She hurt you over and over, but you have us now, and we will stand by you and heal you over and over. She'll never have that. If she comes at you, we'll take her down. We'll make sure Hecate regrets ever crossing paths with us."

It's more than a promise—it's my vow.

Nikon might be immortal, but I have dragon longevity and will be at his side for centuries and possibly millennia. I'll never give up on him, and I'll never let Hecate take him down.

An hour later, Nikon is showered, fed, and ready to fight back. Since I drove my SUV to his place, we drive it home and he portals us to the Batcave. When we get there, I use my security pendant to get inside and meet the frustrated gazes of Merlin, Sloan, and Garnet.

"First off, where is Discord?"

Sloan hikes his thumb toward the blustering snow outside. "He got bored upstairs and said he was going to have some fun."

"What does that even mean?"

Sloan shrugs. "Black ice? Pushing old ladies down in the snow? I don't know, luv, but I don't have the powers to stop him, so there was little I could do."

"No. Of course. Totally not your fault. So, back to the long faces when I got here. Do I even want to hear what those are about?"

Sloan straightens and greets us with a kiss for me and a

squeeze of Nikon's upper arm. "I don't suppose so, no. Still, it won't change a thing, so ye might as well be informed."

"Fine. Let's hear it."

"Well, I combed through my database, the one fer the Order, and talked to Myra as well. As far as I can tell, there are no enchanted objects we can swap out fer Hermes' staff and no other rituals to reinstate the veil."

"Awesome."

The elevator opens in the outer part of the entrance, and Andromeda comes in, brushing snow off her hair with her leather gloves. Nikon strides over to let her in and the relief on her face when she sees him gives me the warm fuzzies.

"I take it he needed a friend?" Sloan whispers, brushing my wrist with a gentle finger.

"Yeah. And I needed to be there for him. I've spent so much time focused on getting back to myself since being cursed and missing months of my life that I dropped the ball on my friendships."

"Och, I think yer likely bein' too hard on yerself, but if it helps, I'm glad yer both feelin' better about things."

Andromeda and Nikon share a couple of whispered words near the door. Then she heads to her office. With Nikon following her, she presses her fist over her heart when she looks at me.

I give her a subtle wink, pleased he's feeling better.

The air snaps with a spray of golden mist, and Dionysus returns with a grave expression. "I've got bad news and worse news. Which do you want first?"

"Seriously, dude. You've got to work on your delivery. Would it kill you to materialize in a room, throw up your hands, and say, 'Great news, everyone?'"

Dionysus doesn't pretend to feel bad. "The celestial map is gone, and Loki is a dick."

"Tell us how you really feel, Tarzan. So, is that the bad news or the worse news?"

"Oh, that was the bad news."

Amazeballs. "Okay, give it to us. What's the worse news?"

He draws a deep breath as panic swirls in his gaze. "I've been summoned on high, and Daddy Dearest has told me to bring you, Sloan, and Nikky."

My mouth falls open. "What's that now?"

Sloan's hand tightens on my wrist. "Why would Zeus want to see us?"

He shakes his head, looking blank. "No idea, but there's no way it's good. I'm to take you all to Mount Olympus right now."

CHAPTER EIGHTEEN

With no time to prepare for our trip to Mount Olympus, we arrive with a mind full of questions and our hearts pounding with panic. Summoned to appear before Zeus. Dionysus is right. This can't be good.

When we arrive, I press my hand to my stomach and try to breathe. If Zeus ends us…

"I didn't have time to say goodbye to my family." Blinking past the sting of tears fighting to surface, I take Sloan's hand. "Did I do this?"

Sloan looks almost as alarmed as I feel but cups my jaw in his palms. "Whatever the reason…whatever happens…we stand together as one."

"As one," I repeat, lifting my chin.

I draw a deep breath and study our surroundings. We're standing on the balcony of a silver and blue spire rising from a palace below. The air is cool yet somehow imbued with a warmth that's inviting and comforting.

It does nothing to ease the icy chill tingling down my spine. Before us, spread like a canvas of divine beauty, are the pantheon lands of Mount Olympus.

This is the heart of ancient Greek mythology, the home of the Olympians, a place of power and immortality. White marble structures, intricate and grand, stretch as far as the eye can see, gleaming under the sun.

The entire landscape is bathed in an ethereal glow, lending a divine aura to everything in sight. The ground below us is a vibrant, lush green carpeted with wildflowers in a riot of colors. The sky is a stunning canvas of pink and gold.

"It's incredible." My voice is barely a whisper.

"It might look that way." Dionysus sounds unconvinced. "I apologize now for whatever happens. I wouldn't have brought you if I had the choice, but ignoring the summons would do nothing but make him angry."

Facing Dionysus, I squeeze his hands. "Not your fault, sweetie. Like Sloan said, we stand as one. No matter what happens, we're here together."

After another moment and a shared smile of encouragement, I gesture at the open archway leading into the spire of the palace. "After you." He's the Greek god here, after all. It seems only right that he gets this party started.

The four of us climb a vast staircase carved from sparkling white marble. As we ascend, we pass a few divine locals—nymphs flitting about with playful laughter, muses strumming lyres, and gods walking around with an air of effortless grace.

We emerge onto an open courtyard with wide, polished columns reaching skyward, holding up a round, domed structure covered in stained glass arches.

Intricate carvings depicting epic tales of heroism, of gods and goddesses, monsters, and men adorn the walls. An aura of timelessness imbues everything, a testament to the eternal power of the Olympians.

"This is the celestial amphitheater." Dionysus indicates the round structure. "Zeus holds his meetings here so there is an audience. I don't know what he has planned, but I'll try my best to diffuse it."

"Maybe it's nothing." I hope to soothe Dionysus a little. My words sound empty even to my ears. "Okay, so maybe it's not horrible."

Nikon snorts. "You're really selling it, Fi."

Yeah, well, I'm trying.

We cross the courtyard's polished floor. The soft murmur of a nearby waterfall joins the trilling of birds and the rustle of the laurel trees, creating a symphony of peaceful sound.

Sweet and intoxicating scents fill the air, blending with the fresh fragrance of citrus trees.

My hand instinctively finds Sloan's, our fingers lacing together. We exchange a glance, a shared moment of awe and apprehension.

We are in Olympus, a place of myth and legend.

I'm not half the history nerd Sloan is, and it's almost too much for me to take in.

He must be losing his freaking mind.

"Should we change or something?" I check with the guys. "I know guys don't always worry about what they're wearing, and honestly, I don't always either, but with the amount of porcelain skin and flowing skirts passing us, I think we're not putting our best foot forward."

Dionysus waves and a shimmer of magic sweeps over me. In an instant, my stretch pants and knit sweater transform into a flowing emerald gown.

The fabric clings and drapes in all the right places, and the neckline's cut shows off the swells of my boobs. "Well, maybe distraction is the way to go." I chuckle.

Dionysus waves my comment away. "You look stunning, Jane. Never hide beauty behind modesty."

"He's right." Sloan slides my hair behind my shoulder. "The

color makes the red of your hair even more vibrant. It's a dress fit for a goddess."

I check in with Nikon, and he winks. "If you've got it, flaunt it."

"All righty, then. Go big or go home." I stand taller, pull my shoulders back, and lift my chin high.

Sloan stands beside me, equally transformed. He's in a chiton of deep indigo, a shade that complements his warm, mocha brown skin and pale eyes. The fabric gathered over one shoulder accentuates his muscular form perfectly.

He looks every inch the ancient scholar.

Nikon is wearing a rich burgundy chiton that sets off his golden hair and tanned skin. He looks impressive, his brooding demeanor of this morning replaced by a look of stern resolve.

Dionysus passes his hand down his body and is wearing what I can only guess is the royal version of the same garment. Although, he doesn't look happy to be in it. "We're in the lion's den. Who knows, maybe playing nice will help."

I hope so.

Together, we step inside the celestial amphitheater, ready to meet the king of the gods.

We stand at the center of the vast, domed space and I'm glad it's empty for the moment. I'm trying not to look like a tourist. Trying…and failing miserably. Head thrown back, eyes wide, I take it all in. The celestial amphitheater is a grand rotunda with arched doorways arrayed in a circle around us, with each doorway opening to a private seating area with a low front rail facing the arena.

They're like the private boxes at a hockey game, or in this case, maybe more like the opera.

Frescoes depicting scenes from the lives of the gods, their

exploits and victories, and their loves and rivalries adorn the rotunda's walls.

Some images subtly move as if they are living scenes rather than paintings. I study Zeus hurling a thunderbolt, Hera sitting on a throne surrounded by peacocks, and Dionysus with a retinue of maenads and satyrs.

"Look at that. You're famous," I whisper, tilting my head toward the piece featuring him.

The sadness in his eyes sobers me. He's not enjoying anything about this. Where Nikon was always proud and excited to share his place of origin with me, Dionysus would rather be anywhere but here.

The golden glow becomes brighter, almost blinding, as the gods enter one by one. My heart hammers as I look up and watch Themis stride forward with Hecate in tow.

I stiffen at the sight of the witch. She meets my scowl with hers, her dark eyes gleaming with an unspoken promise of vengeance and suffering.

In the box next to Themis, the three Fates emerge. They stand tall and elegant, Clotho, Lachesis, and Atropos. As the keepers of lives, do they know what's about to happen? Is Atropos here to cut the threads of our lives short? Would she do it?

If Zeus ordered it, I'm sure she would.

The mere sight of them sends a chill down my spine. Their presence is a grim reminder of how helpless we are to stop whatever Zeus has planned.

A soft light blooms and Eros strides forward farther down on the right. The god of love has his golden bow slung over his shoulder and refuses to look our way.

Selene appears next. She materializes in a cascade of silver light, her luminescent eyes sweeping over us with a look of haughty disdain.

Next to her stands a man I've never met, although his likeness to the bronze statue in Rhodes tells me who he is at a glance.

Helios, the sun god, radiates a heat that reaches us on the arena's floor. He sears us with a gaze as fiery as the sun chariot he rides.

Hermes materializes last. His winged sandals twinkle, and he clutches his staff. The messenger of the gods scrutinizes me.

The realization hits me like a punch to the gut. We've been meddling in the affairs of the gods. Interfering, intervening, and as I consider our interactions, offending.

Looking at them now, gathered here in their divine glory, I can't help but wonder…have we gone too far?

Zeus is the last to arrive, appearing with a burst of golden mist, but a hundred times more dramatic than Dionysus. His gaze narrows as he stares us down. He is every bit the king of the gods, intimidating and majestic.

I swallow hard, the question heavy in the air around us. Whatever this is about, there's no escape. We're here and have no option but to see it through.

"Dionysus." Zeus' voice rings out, echoing off the golden walls. He fixes his gaze on us, his stormy expression heavy with an ancient authority. "Introduce your pets."

Dionysus tightens his hand around mine, his face pale and lined with worry. He loves us more than he'd ever admit to his family. If he did, they would use us as leverage against him or to hurt him.

They think they are his family, but they're wrong.

We are. We have given him a home and filled him with love and acceptance in a way the gods on Olympus never have. While he likely doesn't fear his father outright, I can see in his eyes that he's terrified Zeus, in all his divine might, will harm us.

Dionysus steps forward with a reassuring squeeze from me, placing himself between Zeus and us.

He gestures at Sloan first. "This is Sloan Mackenzie. He's a…" Dionysus hesitates, and I see him struggle for a moment. Likely, not because he's unsure of what to say, but because he's worried about saying too much, revealing too much.

"He is a druid, a scholar, and a warrior. He fights as a guardian of the fae and a keeper of humanity."

Dionysus moves to Nikon next. "This is Nikon Tsambikos of Rhodes. He is an immortal born in the time of the Macedonian Wars. He is empowered with the blessings of the Earth Mother, a friend, and a brother-in-arms."

Nikon's eyes are hard as flint, and his jaw is clenched tight. He stands tall, his warrior pride shining through. I feel a rush of gratitude for him. If there's anyone I'd want at my side in a standoff with gods, it's Nikon.

Dionysus' voice softens as he turns to me. "This is Fiona Cumhaill Mackenzie." He takes a moment, his gaze warm. I know that he's torn between protecting me and allowing me to stand my ground. "Chosen successor of Fionn mac Cumhaill, leader of the Fianna druids, mother of dragons, and a champion for the innocent and the oppressed."

He returns his gaze to meet his father's. "These are my friends, not my pets. They are honorable and brave, and I am proud to stand by them."

With introductions done, Dionysus steps back to my side, and a heavy silence falls over the rotunda.

Zeus casts an unreadable gaze over us and locks on me for a long moment. The sound of my racing heart pounds in my ears, but I lock my knees to keep from shrinking under the scrutiny.

After a long moment, he gestures at Themis.

The goddess of justice turns to us with a neutral smile. "We meet again, young warriors. Zeus has summoned you here today because several members of this pantheon claim you have wronged them in one grievous form or another."

She pauses, and I let the weight of that sink in.

We've wronged *them*? Seriously?

"This is ridiculous," Dionysus snaps. "You are gods. To imply that three humans upset you so profoundly that you need to have them summoned is beneath you."

Themis inclines her head. "Perhaps if the slights were isolated instances, but mounted together, we found there to be enough evidence to warrant a hearing."

"Is that what this is, then?" he asks. "Is this a celestial hearing? What are the charges? What punishments are being called for? Who is to stand as their champion?"

Themis raises an elegant hand to stave off his questions. "I assumed you would stand as their advocate."

"You assume correctly." Dionysus straightens, all business and looking murderous. "Let's get this over with. Who is claiming what?"

Themis raises a roll of parchment and pulls it open. "The charges against your friends read thusly.

"Hecate: interference in godly affairs causing irreparable loss.

"Selene: theft of that which was to be hers, causing loss of power.

"Helios: the wilful destruction of a symbol of his grandeur causing loss of face.

"Eros: character assassination and causing loss of long-term friendships.

"Hermes: making false spoken statements damaging to his reputation.

"Zeus: usurping the familial bond of his blooded heir."

When Themis finishes reading the list of grievances, the goddess of law and justice gazes upon us with her stern, clear eyes. I see no malice in them, no joy or sadness. Only the unwavering commitment to fairness and balance. "How do you plead?"

Well, shit.

I study the faces of the plaintiffs and consider what Themis said. Then I meet the gazes of Sloan, Nikon, and Dionysus.

You're totally being set up, Dionysus says.

Yeah, and everyone here knows it, I respond. *Not getting your way isn't a criminal offense. How can they even claim it is?*

They're gods. Everything is about getting their way.

"How do you plead?" Themis repeats.

I draw a deep breath and relax my pose. "We are honored to witness the grandeur and the glory of Olympus and to be given the chance to speak to the claims waged against us. We will not deny the actions that lead to the slights you speak of, but we unequivocally deny them as actionable grievances to be held against us."

Themis doesn't blink, doesn't even move. Only her lips purse slightly at my words. "How can you accept the charges yet dispute the grievance?"

"Because each case is subjective when seen through the lens of a god or goddess versus the lens of a human. If you speak to the morality of what happened, you'll see that our actions are always based on an individual's rights, justice, or survival."

Themis doesn't respond, and I get the sense that she's giving me the opportunity to plead my case. "I never go into a situation wondering how we can alienate or offend people. It's the opposite. My team and I are working to reinstate the veil between realms."

Helios grunts. "What do we care about mortal realm issues? Fae, human, vampire, werewolf...they are of no concern to us."

"But obviously they are," I argue. "Otherwise, why would Hecate, Eros, Loki, Discord, and a bunch of other gods and empowered folks pull the veil down and fight us tooth and nail to keep it down?"

Zeus looks confused. "What does this have to do with the grievances against them?"

"I think she's trying to make her point, sire," Themis interjects. "She's saying she trespassed against us in the pursuit of a higher purpose."

Exactly. Thank the gods someone can follow the bouncing ball.

"Fourteen months ago, a group of empowered elites rocked the balance between realms. During the Winter Solstice, during the Time of the Colliding Realms, they removed the division between humans and magic."

Zeus frowns. "To what end?"

I shrug. "To expose magic to the mundane? To cause maximum chaos? To screw with the little people and laugh while dormant genes are triggered and powers awaken? I can't speak to their motives, but I can tell you the world is in trouble if we don't restore the balance."

"Again," Helios huffs. "Why do we care?"

"Because people are being targeted and killed," I reply, exasperated. "Magical awakenings are causing divisions in communities and families are being destroyed. If half of the world becomes enhanced, what will they do with those powers?"

"You're saying that the magic of the fae has become common knowledge?" Zeus says.

"Yes."

"What about gods? Do they understand we are more powerful than fae magic?"

I fight not to roll my eyes. "I'm not sure the comparison of who's more powerful has come up. Still, with the world erupting in empowered people, a great many now believe themselves to be gods in one form or another."

"Blasphemy!" Zeus shouts.

"She's taking this hearing off-course," Hecate snaps, her venom cracking off the walls. "We are gods! They are bugs. We can squash them if we so choose. The point of us being here is to punish them for getting in our way."

"Exactly," Helios shouts.

Themis arches an elegant brow. "No. The point is to hear the grievances and allow Fiona, Nikon, and Sloan the opportunity to explain and defend their actions."

Hecate thrusts her bound wrists into the air between us and scowls. "She has interfered more than once and meddled where she has no business."

Themis nods. "All right. Let us begin with Hecate's argument. Fiona, how do you respond?"

I gesture at Hecate. "Millennia ago, Nikon and Hecate shared a love affair. When it ended, Hecate declared Nikon her possession. She cursed him, stalked him, and centuries later when he dared to love again, she killed his wife and unborn child."

Themis and her daughters know this, so there is no surprise there, but I watch Zeus, Selene, and the others, hoping to see any sign of compassion.

I don't see any.

"Then, a few years ago, Hecate kidnapped us from our time, mistaking me as Nikon's lover. She intended to continue Nikon's suffering by torturing me, except I called for a challenge of trials and won his freedom. Themis oversaw the trials, and the outcome was cast. Hecate was ordered to leave Nikon in peace, allowing him to live his life without her interference."

Zeus' eyebrow arches slightly. "Is this true, Themis?"

"It is. Hecate was warned that to interfere or assault Nikon of Rhodes again would result in me binding her powers and exacting a heavy penalty, ensuring justice."

Zeus looks at Hecate. His face twists as if he's swallowed a mouthful of chunky, sour milk. "You are a goddess. To crawl after a man who is beneath your station and rejects you is shameful. Gods don't seek affection. We are sought! This ends now."

Zeus flicks his hand, and Hecate is gone. I'm not sure where she went, but honestly, I don't care. The important part is that Zeus is annoyed, and it seems he has dismissed her grievance.

Zeus meets Nikon's gaze. "That you reject a female as powerful and gifted as Hecate speaks to your flaws but should not have cost you the lives of your wife and child. I have suffered that pain and wish it upon no man, god or otherwise."

Nikon drops his gaze. "Thank you, sire."

After a moment's pause, Themis gestures at Selene. "Next up: Theft of that which was to be hers, causing loss of power."

CHAPTER NINETEEN

Over the next hour, I stand in the center of the celestial amphitheater with Dionysus, Nikon, and Sloan, explaining the circumstances of each grievance against us. The slights levied against us aren't exactly trumped-up—they are legit—but it feels like schoolyard politics where I'm arguing with entitled children about their hurt feelings.

We didn't steal from Selene. According to history, she took possession of the moonstones and destroyed them after the battle. We retrieved them before she destroyed them to use them to restore the balance of the realms.

We regret the loss of the Colossus. Again, according to history, the statue fell into the harbor during an earthquake in the same year. Using it in battle helped us push back a horde of demons and close a rift to the hell realm.

I slide my gaze to Eros and shake my head. Schoolyard politics at its best. It's the old "You stole my friends" argument. Sorry, that one doesn't fly.

When we get to Hermes, I stall out. "I'm honestly baffled by the grievance you claim against us, Hermes. We've never met. We've never had a conversation. The only time your name has come up in our circles has been the past week while dealing with the reinstatement of the veil between realms."

Themis frowns and looks at Hermes. "Making false spoken statements damaging your reputation," she reads off the parchment. "What is your basis for your grievance?"

Hermes strikes the base of his staff against the stone of the floor. "I'm the messenger of the gods. I know the news. I hear the whispers. You think I'm petty for not letting you take my most prized possession and possibly damaging or destroying it?"

"Petty seems harsh," I respond in my defense. "Do I wish you'd reconsider allowing us to use your staff during the moon ritual? Absolutely. Are we frustrated you won't help reinstate the veil? Definitely. Have we badmouthed you and spread unfavorable tales of cowardice or indifference? No, we have not."

Having spoken my piece, I stand tall, unflinching under their heavy gazes. I know they might not accept our pleas, but we have spoken the truth, and there's a certain power in that.

A power that even gods cannot deny.

As the silence stretches on, I clasp my hands and wait for Themis' judgment. This is her domain, and while I consider us polite acquaintances, I am under no illusions that we are friends.

Still, I believe her to be fair and her judgment sound.

There's a level of comfort in that.

After deliberation, Themis, the goddess of divine law and order, gazes down at us with an impassive expression.

"By the laws of this pantheon, these humans' actions, while inconvenient and at times disrespectful, do not cross the line into the criminal. Annoying the gods, while not recommended, is not an unjust act. This proceeding is thus dismissed."

Her words echo through the grand amphitheater, bouncing off the statues and pillars of the majestic arena. A sigh of relief washes over our group, and tension seeps from my shoulders.

We know better than to celebrate, and Dionysus's look reminds me that a fast exit is best.

I expect us to snap home in the next instant, but that doesn't happen. The growing annoyance clouding Dionysus' expression tells me there's a problem preventing that from happening.

Zeus rises from his throne.

The ethereal light streaming in from the arched windows silhouettes his imposing form. His gaze settles on me, and a dagger of dread slices through the relief.

"Fiona," he announces, his voice filling the vast chamber. "I wish to speak to you."

As Zeus' thunderous voice reverberates throughout the great hall, I swallow against the lump of dread in my throat. His golden eyes, filled with centuries of wisdom and power, bore into mine.

I see Dionysus' features reflected in the square of his jaw and the set of his shoulders. His son has a great deal more softness in his eyes, though…at least usually.

As Zeus approaches, Dionysus goes full momma bear and looks like he might be about to Hulk out.

I press a gentle hand against his arm. "Easy, sweetie. S'all good. If your father wants a word, that's fine."

Sloan doesn't agree.

Nikon either.

Okay, so it's three against one in that opinion.

Zeus stops before our group and dismisses the three of them with a haughty wave.

They glance at me, concern clear in their eyes, but I nod at them to leave. Dionysus lingers, shooting me a worried look. I wink with a reassuring smile. It's enough to convince him to leave, however reluctantly.

The heavy stone doors close behind them with a resounding *boom*, leaving me alone in the celestial amphitheater with Zeus.

An intimidating silence stretches between us. It's not every day you get singled out by the king of the gods. The reality of that sends a shiver down my spine.

"It's good to finally meet you," I remark, pleased my voice is steady. There's no doubt in my mind Zeus would exploit any weakness of fear if he were to spot it.

I'll be damned if I give him that opening.

His eyes flicker with interest, a hint of a smile tugging at the corners of his mouth. Is this the conversation he wanted to have, a silent summing up of the size of our *cojones*? If so, he's in for a surprise.

"I sense Celtic royalty in your bloodline." He eyes me curiously. "You're descended from the Tuatha de Danann."

"Distantly, yes. Boann, the goddess of the river Boyne, mentioned it when we first met."

He watches me for a moment longer. "You're not like most human females, are you?"

"I couldn't say. I expect not."

"You don't fear me, nor are you awed by the pantheon's members."

"No."

"Why?"

His question doesn't sound facetious, so I take the time to consider it and give him a genuine answer. "I've seen humans who shine with greatness and gods who lack the decency of common civility. I've battled alongside demons who fight for justice and witnessed members of the Choir of Angels support evil and death. In my experience, what makes a person awesome and powerful has nothing to do with their station and everything to do with their actions and convictions."

He takes a moment to consider that and offers me his elbow. The gesture seems courtly enough, and my shield isn't weighing in more than a buzz of power, so I accept his offer and we walk.

At a lazy pace, we stroll toward an exit below the platform where Zeus sat during the proceedings. The tall, double doors are elaborately carved and topped with a stained glass transom window depicting Zeus as a heavenly body overseeing a group of cherubs.

"There was one grievance against you which was never addressed, Fiona, and which you have yet to defend yourself against."

The tone of his voice is hard, and I'm not sure I *want* to defend against his grievance. My instincts say he won't be as impartial as Themis.

That won't bode well for me.

We stride across the wide balcony and stop at the railing overlooking the beauty of the Greek lands below.

"I've been watching you, Fiona, and I admit, I've almost removed you from existence more than once for your trespasses against me."

My head turns on a pivot as I peg him with a look. "Excuse me? Trespasses against you? What have I done?"

"Ever since Dionysus met you, he rarely comes home, and when he does, he displays nothing but hostility and disdain for any of us here."

His gaze is intense, almost penetrating, and I meet it squarely. "He has potent feelings about how the pantheon's members treat him. It might not be my place to render an opinion, but I don't think his feelings are unfounded."

"You're right. It is *not* your place. Living among gods and immortals isn't the same as living the blink of history you mortals do. Over time everlasting, there become entanglements and complexities that make relationships more difficult."

I snort. "Please, that's a cop-out. I live with gods and immortals. I live with mortals too. In my family and with my circle of friends, compassion, love, and respect go a long way in ensuring that the entanglements and complexities of relationships don't grow toxic."

Zeus' gaze narrows. "Don't think yourself qualified to form an opinion. That level of arrogance is liable to get you killed."

I shrug. "It's not arrogance to say I know Dionysus' heart and mind better than you. It's a fact. We've spent years together, sharing, laughing, and loving one another. I've heard his confessions. I've witnessed his pain. And he has suffered a *lot* of pain and disappointment."

Zeus doesn't appreciate my observations, but I don't care. "He has also *caused* a lot of pain and disappointment."

"Maybe, but if you whip a dog long enough, it will either curl up and submit or bare its teeth and bite back. Dionysus isn't about to submit. I would think, as his father, you'd be proud about that."

Energy crackles around us as stormy clouds swirl in Zeus' eyes. "Don't pretend to know my feelings about my son, female. No matter how many pajama parties you share, Dionysus is *my* son. *My* family."

"Biologically, yes. But by choice, Dionysus is part of *my* family," I retort, my voice echoing in the vast open space beyond the balcony. Heat rises in my chest, sparking my ire. "In my home, he is cherished, and we appreciate his contributions. Can you say the same about his time here?"

Zeus' eyes widen, and he grimaces as if he'd swallowed something bitter. "He is a god. This is his home. Like it or not, we are his family."

"He didn't choose to be a god," I snap. "And from what I've seen, you haven't made it a home for him. Maybe you need to revisit your definition of family. In my book, it's the people who love you and watch out for you. The people who want the best for you and will go out of their way to protect you and ensure you thrive."

Zeus regards me with an unreadable expression. "He is my son. I won't lose him."

His words hang in the air, and his frustration takes me aback. I expected this to be about his ego or superiority, but despite his stern exterior, Zeus is a father who fears losing his child.

"Dionysus found a family with us," I murmur. "That's not a bad thing. He's a warm and magnanimous man with a joyous side that makes him perfect to be the god of good times. That doesn't mean he can't have a relationship with you or other pantheon members. It just means you must earn it."

He grunts and grips a thunderbolt in the air between us. "I am the king of the gods!"

"That doesn't make you a good *father!*" I shout.

Will Zeus ever understand what family means?

"Is all well?" Themis' voice rings out, clear and confident, slicing through the tension between Zeus and me.

Zeus turns at the sound of her voice and gathers his composure. "Do you need something, Themis?"

She brushes her fingers down the column of her long neck. "I wish to speak to you regarding another matter, but if I can be of aid in this discussion, I am at your disposal, sire."

Her stern gaze falls on Zeus, who meets it with a frown. "Fiona has strong views about Dionysus and the failings in our relationship."

"Fiona has powerful feelings for those she cares about."

"She implied the estrangement between Dionysus and me is *my* doing."

I shrug. "I've only heard his side of things, that's true, but I've witnessed his suffering at the hands of the pantheon. I also watched him almost die, and nothing was done, and no one stepped in to help him. It took my sister-in-law exerting a dangerous amount of her angel power to keep him alive long enough for us to stop the attack on him."

Zeus chuckles. "Dionysus is a demi-god of the Greek pantheon. No matter the suffering you think he has endured, there was no true peril."

I shake my head. "Except that the Fates were punishing him for saving the life of one of us and his powers were bound, and his immortality blocked. I assure you, if we hadn't moved heaven and earth—literally—Dionysus would not be alive for us to argue over."

A crease of tension forms between Zeus' brows and he looks at Themis. "Is this true?"

"It is. The girls failed to recognize the dangers of him living among mortals during his period of punishment. By the time I realized the issue, the guardian angel Fiona mentioned had nearly perished in keeping him alive while Fiona and the others battled the necromancer and destroyed his hold."

Zeus looks genuinely confused. "Yet I heard none of this."

I scoff. "Do you really expect people to report to you when they've almost killed your son? If you had a relationship with him, you might have noticed something was wrong, like we did."

His gaze narrows. "Don't preach, child. There are intricacies in our lives you can't possibly understand. One incident doesn't mean I haven't been paying attention."

"Except it isn't one incident. Dionysus has been targeted more than once, and it's my family and I who have been there for him."

Zeus turns his attention to Themis. "Targeted by whom? When?"

Themis lifts her chin. "Dionysus was tortured and weakened by Loki a few years ago. He was poisoned, captured, and tortured. It was Fiona and her family who came to his aid."

Zeus blinks, clearly taken aback. "You challenged Loki to save my son?"

"Of course we did. Dionysus is a member of our family, and we fight for our own."

There's a long silence as Zeus absorbs this, his face unreadable.

Themis catches a coiled spring of dark hair and flicks it over her bare shoulder. "Dionysus can be difficult, juvenile, emotional, and frustrating—no argument—but I have witnessed how Fiona, her family, and their friends accept him and stand by him."

I exhale the breath trapped in my chest, and the tension in my lungs eases a little.

Themis continues. "You might have taught him a thousand

lessons about being a god of this pantheon, but Fiona taught him lessons too…lessons he never could learn here. Because of his situation growing up, he never learned about compassion, devotion, loyalty, and love. Now he has."

She takes a step back, her eyes never leaving Zeus' face. "Perhaps it's not Dionysus who abandoned his family. Perhaps it's we who failed to show him what it means to be a family."

Her words hang like a beautiful song in the silence, and I can't help but think that she's right. We might not be gods, but when it comes to family, Clan Cumhaill is powerful.

"If you want a relationship with him, coming after me isn't the way to achieve it," I advise. "Treat him with kindness and respect his contributions to a situation, defend him when he's unable to defend himself, and do things for him because it will make him happy."

Zeus' gaze narrows on me. "You are not what I expected, Fiona Cumhaill."

I chuckle. "Yeah, I know. I get that a lot."

CHAPTER TWENTY

The room spins as we're flung from one world to another, the grandeur of Olympus instantly replaced by the comfortable familiarity of our Toronto home. I stumble, the residual power from Zeus' dismissal tugging at me, but Sloan is there with his arm around my waist, grounding me.

He searches my face with his gaze, concern etched in the lines of his brow. "Are you all right, *a ghra?*"

I absorb a bit of his strength and straighten. "Yeah, I'm fine."

Nikon shifts uncomfortably while glancing at Dionysus, who's watching me with a thoughtful expression. "What happened with Zeus?" Nikon asks.

I exhale slowly, shifting over to settle on the couch. "Zeus has taken exception to us considering Dionysus our family. He didn't see the value of our relationship, and I think he intended to scare me off with the threat of suffering his wrath."

Dionysus curses in Greek, and I set my hand on his knee. "I think I worked all that hostility out. By the time we parted, I think he had a much clearer understanding of our relationship and why we love one another."

"We shouldn't have to explain anything to him," Dionysus

retorts. "He had millennia to care about where I was and who I spent my time with. He never gave two shits unless it inconvenienced him."

I hate to see him so twisted up. Not that we're not used to it. He always gets like this when he's forced to spend time with members of his pantheon. "He's also unhappy about you spending so much time away from Olympus."

"Well, tough titties," Dionysus snaps.

"Were ye able to smooth things over?" Sloan asks.

"I don't know about smooth, but I think he genuinely wants to understand Tarzan better."

Dionysus snorts, a bitter edge to the sound. "Zeus? Understanding someone other than himself? Now that'd be a sight."

"Sweetie, I know you've had a rough time with him, and you have every right to wash your hands of the lot of them. Still, he's your father. I think he really wants to be better. He just doesn't know how."

"He could start by not threatening you at a tribunal and calling the three of you my pets."

"I think he got the picture on that. Honestly, by the time Themis and I—"

"Themis was there?" Dionysus asks.

"Not at first, but yeah, she had something to discuss with him and joined us after a bit. She has a way of speaking to him that calms him down."

Dionysus chuckles. "She's wholly impartial and sees things with logic and from every angle. Even if he wants to, he can't argue against her observations. He gave up trying a lifetime ago."

I lean back and sink deeper into the couch. "Then it's likely good that she happened upon us."

Dionysus grins. "Don't for a moment think that was a coincidence. I'd bet my nuts that Lachesis was tracking the conversation and sent her mother to intervene on our behalf."

"You think?"

He nods. "The Fates are still trying to make it up to me. They almost got me killed, and they know I love you. There's no way they'd let Zeus harm you if they could help to stop it."

Good. They need to make up for more than a few things. Letting out a long breath, I realize how much worse things could've ended up if I hadn't been born into my family.

When Mam died, I had Da and five amazing brothers.

When Dionysus' mom died, he had a narcissistic god for a father and a dozen self-entitled half-siblings that wanted daddy's attention for themselves.

"Hey, Tarzan? Maybe don't close the door on him all the way just yet. If what I saw was genuine, maybe a relationship with Zeus isn't totally crazy. He might never be the father you need, but the two of you might salvage something."

Sloan makes a soft noise in the back of his throat. "She's right, Greek. Three years ago, if someone told me I'd love my father and enjoy spending time with him, I would've said they were off their nut. Now my Da and I are thick as thieves. Once he truly understood what I needed and saw the mistakes he'd made, we worked on building a better relationship."

Dionysus is quiet for a long moment, staring at the two of us. I see him wrestling with the idea, his emotions warring across his face.

Finally, he nods. "All right. I'll leave the door open a crack... but only a crack."

"That's fair." I lean to the side to bump his shoulder with mine. "Honestly, it's likely more than he deserves. You're a good man, Tarzan. I hope he realizes what a gem you are and gets his head out of his ass before it's too late."

Maybe Zeus can bridge the gap.

Maybe even gods have room to grow.

Stepping through the double security doors into the Batcave, we're greeted with the sight of Discord lounging on one of the high-backed chairs, swishing his fluffy russet tail. A smirk plays on his lips. "Look what the fox dragged in," he quips, tilting his head in greeting.

"What are you doing here, fox face?" Dionysus asks.

"Fiona and I were having adventures until you took her away and ruined our fun."

I smile at Garnet and Merlin in apology. "It wasn't Dionysus' fault. Zeus summoned us."

"Is everything all right?" Garnet asks.

Merlin's gaze washes over me, and I know he's searching for any sign that the mighty smiter might have smitten me. "S'all good. We came to an understanding. So, where are we on reinstating the veil? Did we learn anything by having the elemental stones?"

"Not much, no," Merlin answers. "Although your father texted me and said Lara has the herbs and dried ingredients we need for smudging and cleansing the ritual area."

"I don't like smudging," Discord interjects. "The scented smoke gets up my nose and makes me sneeze."

I shrug. "Sorry, dude. It's part of the master plan. You'll have to steer clear or suffer the sneezy fate."

"I thought you were supposed to be nice to me. I'm on Team Trouble now. Aren't you supposed to praise in public?"

I blink at him. "You're on Team Trouble?"

He nonchalantly swishes his tail. "If I'm aiding you in the next phase of causing chaos, I'm part of the team. And if I'm part of the team, you can't keep disappearing and leaving me behind."

My cheeks warm at his admonishment. "My bad. You're right. If you're switching sides, you're on Team Trouble now." I sweep an arm toward the conference table. "So, shall we get started?"

Discord's smirk widens at my words, but he doesn't say anything. Instead, he hops off the chair and trots toward the conference table in front of the monitor wall. "Finally, a place at the table."

I exchange glances with the others. Garnet scowls, Merlin and Sloan shrug, Nikon grins, and Dionysus rolls his eyes. Since none of them object, I follow the little fox and sit beside Discord.

"Welcome to the team, Discord." I settle in. "Now let's get to work."

I'm a little worried. With Discord officially in the mix, there's no telling what kind of chaos is in our future.

Then again, it's not like we didn't have chaos before.

When we're all seated, the seven of us sit back and review our situation's status. It doesn't take long because we all know we're stuck.

"I don't suppose we found any other rituals?" I ask.

Merlin shakes his head. "There's nothing. This is our only play."

"What about a staff replacement?" Nikon asks.

"I might have some good news there." Merlin holds up a finger. "A powerful magical conduit might work much the same way as Hermes' staff."

"What kind of conduit?" I ask.

"I found a spell that might give Birga the power boost we need so you can use her in the ritual."

"Really? That's great news. Will it work?"

"There's no way to know for sure until it all plays out, but I'm hopeful."

A hopeful Merlin is good enough for me.

"So, with the pendant, the elemental stones, the staff, and the cleansing herbs, it's only the location we're missin'," Sloan says.

There's no way Loki will be stupid or careless enough for us to get our hands on it.

"You don't think using the power of one of the rings of standing stones or a place of power will be enough?" I ask.

Merlin makes an uncertain face. "It's not ideal and considering we're already substituting with the staff, I'd rather not substitute the location as well."

Agreed.

Sloan nods. "We still have a little time."

A very little time. Between going back to ancient Greece and being summoned to Olympus, the hour is almost upon us.

I sigh. "Okay, let's brainstorm. We need to pinpoint the location to give us the strongest chance of success. No idea is too out of the box. Go."

Discord sits up and taps his little paws on the table. There's a mischievous glint in his eyes. "You want the celestial map, Red?"

"No, we *need* it. Without it, we won't be in the optimal location at the precise time that's best to complete the ritual."

"That's important to you?"

"We can't just wing it when aligning the energies of the full moon," Nikon explains.

Discord's laughter bounces off the walls, a sharp contrast to the somber atmosphere.

"Something funny, fox?" Garnet growls.

His lips turn up in a toothy grin, and his eyes sparkle with mirth. "You're all a bunch of Gloomy Guses. All this fretting about a missing map."

"The map is incredibly important to our ritual. There's a reason we're frustrated."

He puffs up his chest, his fox tail twitching behind him. "You look for a map, drawn and inked, while in my mind, its lines are linked. I might not know where your precious map lies, but I have seen it with these very eyes. Photographic memory, my dears. A nifty trick over the years."

I blink as my mind catches up. "Are you saying you can reproduce the celestial map?"

His grin widens, and he nods, relishing our surprise. "Why, yes, Red, that's exactly what I'm saying. If you need a map, I can draw it for you."

Seriously? Could it be that easy? When has anything been that easy for us? Still, part of me hopes the missing puzzle piece is finally fitting snugly into place.

Not a moment too soon.

"All righty then." I grin at the cheeky chaos god. "Let's get you a drawing pad."

Dionysus' gaze narrows. "How do you expect a fox to hold a pencil?"

I soon find out it's more magic and less cartography. We all huddle around the conference table, eyes wide, as Discord finishes his work. "Ta-da! One celestial map, freshly plucked from the halls of my magnificent mind."

The map sprawls across the table, an intricate weave of lines and symbols I can't comprehend. But it's magnificent and undeniably a work of genius.

I'm in awe. I'm also a little skeptical. "Dionysus, from what you know of constellations and bisecting realms, does it seem accurate?"

He squints at the map, taking in the details. "I hate to say it—because that fox is a dick, and he made you stab Nikon—but it's perfect. We'll be able to get to the right place at the right time and kick the ass of this veil issue."

Amazeballs.

"Love the enthusiasm." I chuckle. "Before we go kick the ass of this veil issue, we owe Discord a moment of gratitude. This is a game-changer. Thank you."

The others can barely muster up a grunt or an acknowledgment of appreciation, but our trickster friend doesn't notice.

He's too busy feigning nonchalance. "Oh, it's nothing, really. I only wish I could see Loki and the others' reactions when they figure out you've got the map. They'll be furious!"

Yeah, I wouldn't mind seeing that either.

A small frown creases Discord's brow. "You don't think they'll know I told you, do you?"

Despite how much Discord loves chaos, he's a coward when it comes to being in the line of fire. Must be all that time being beholden to the greater demons of hell.

"Your secret is safe with us," I assure him. "We're so grateful for the turn of the tables that we'll tell no one it was you. We wouldn't want to disrupt your reward. You deserve to be the man of the hour."

His eyes narrow, but then he chuckles. "I do deserve that, don't I?"

I see the annoyance in the others' gazes, but I ignore it. Hey, we've got a fighting chance now, a real chance of getting this done and restoring the veil.

For the first time in over a year, we're almost at the end of this mess.

"Sloan, Merlin, and Dionysus, figure out the where and when. Once we have that, I want to walk the site and get familiar with it before the full moon tonight."

"Do you think that's necessary?" Discord asks.

I chuckle. "Oh, yeah. Loki and the others won't simply let us perform the ritual in peace. Without a doubt, they'll be gunning for us. They might even be in place already. This is going to come down to who wants it most and how prepared they are to get it."

The sun blazes straight overhead as we stand atop the highest point of the Giza necropolis. At the edges of the Western Desert, west of the Nile River, and southwest of the city center of Cairo, the pyramids at Giza make an impressive ritual site for us to take our stand.

I'm not sure if it's a boost of prana from the intersection of ley lines below or that we're standing on top of the Great Pyramid, but a frisson of excitement runs the length of my spine.

"Shit is getting real," I remark.

Sloan feels it too. I can tell by the way he's taking everything in—with that look he gets when he's geeking out—that he's in historian heaven right now.

"Okay, hotness, tell me all the things. Give me the National Geographic documentary. I'm ready."

He grins, strides over to stand behind me, and points over my shoulder. "From our position, we have a commanding view of the sandy expanse of desert meeting the architectural marvels of Cairo."

I chuckle at the sheer delight in his narration.

"The ancient pyramids, themselves made of sandstone, rise majestically from the sea of golden sand, standing sentinel over the passing millennia."

"Uh-huh, go on. You're killing it, hotness."

"Beyond, the modern city thrives, a glittering oasis of lights and movement against the desert's timeless tranquility. Date palms and the life-giving Nile River carve a ribbon of green through the desert, a testament to the resilience of life in this stark landscape."

I twist and meet his lips over my shoulder. "If you ever get sick of druiding, you've got a real future in tourism, Mackenzie. I felt like I was standing on the top of the pyramid, seeing what you see."

He chuckles. "You are there."

"Oh, yeah. How freaking cool is that?"

This life takes a lot from us, but it gives us a lot, too.

All fooling aside, we've got work to do, so I pull out the celestial map. The lines and symbols dance before my eyes as I try to make sense of them.

To my left, Sloan paces out the altar's location, stepping carefully over the uneven terrain as he charts the ley lines coursing beneath our feet.

"I think here." He points at a spot where the energy feels strong. We all follow him and plant ourselves at various points around the imagined altar.

"Now, we need to think about defense." Nikon rakes his gaze over the stark landscape. His eyes linger on the sand, the river in the distance, and the other pyramids in the surrounding area. "Over there. That's a good spot to watch from."

We spread out and assess the terrain, noting each dip, rise, and potential hiding place. It's a dance of strategy and anticipation, each of us silently preparing for the battle to come. The sun disappears, and the moon emerges, casting a silvery glow over the land. A fitting backdrop for the night's preparations.

It's eerily quiet, the only sound being the occasional rustle of wind or the distant howl of an animal. The silence stretches on, broken only by our quiet exchanges and footsteps.

As we stand under the blanket of stars, the reality of what we're about to do begins to truly sink in. Despite the odds stacked against us, despite the inevitable chaos to come, I feel a surge of hope.

This is it.

We're as ready as we'll ever be.

"All right. Let's get everyone here and get ready to rumble. It's do or die time."

CHAPTER TWENTY-ONE

In the hushed silence of the Egyptian night, our family and friends take our stand, a united front against the malevolent godly forces conspiring against us. High atop the Great Pyramid, the vast expanse of desert spreading out beneath us, there is nothing to do but wait.

I scan the readiness of my team. Patty, his eyes sparkling with fierce determination, stands beside me.

Sloan is beside him, his expression solemn in the moonlight, a quiet intensity simmering in his eyes.

Manx is silent, his gaze fixed on the horizon.

Merlin stands at our prepared altar, exuding an air of calm that soothes my frazzled nerves.

Discord, our wily wildcard, bounces on the pads of his feet. A wicked grin spreads across his face as he surveys our preparations. "This will be fun."

I shake my head at his strange enthusiasm. "This isn't about fun for us. It's about righting a wrong and setting the realms of the world back into balance."

His excitement doesn't diminish. "It will be fun. Trust me. I know things."

"Yeah, I know you do."

Across the way, atop the Pyramid of Menkaure, I check on Dillan, Eva, Da, Nikon, and Garnet. They stand ready, their silhouettes sharp against the backdrop of the starlit sky.

"Safe home, everyone," I whisper into the night.

My gaze shifts to the Pyramid of Khafre next. That's where Xavier, Calum, Diesel, Aiden, Dan the Djinn, and Dionysus have taken their positions.

Bruin is pacing the perimeter of the smaller pyramid, battle armor gleaming in the moonlight.

Take care of them, buddy.

His boxy head turns to meet my gaze across the expanse. *Ye know I will. Take care of yerself and yer group.*

I promise.

Call if ye need me.

Will do.

The moon hangs heavy in the sky, casting long shadows across the sand. It's full tonight, so hopefully, the illumination will keep things well enough lit that things can't gather in the shadows.

A chilly gust sweeps across the pyramids, stirring up the sand and sending it swirling around us. I watch it dance in the moonlight, sparkling like tiny diamonds, before it dissipates into the night.

"It's time, Fi." Merlin holds his hand out for the map, and when I surrender it, he spreads it across the altar table and pins it open. "Everyone ready?"

"Yeah, let's do this." I take one of the many barbecue lighters we brought tonight and join Sloan in cleansing the site.

With careful precision, we light the series of torches arranged around the pyramid's apex. Each torch bursts to life with a warm, welcoming glow, casting dancing shadows across the stone platform.

Infused with a special blend of cleansing herbs, prepared with loving care by Gran, Granda, and Da, it is the first step in the success of our night.

I hadn't heard of several of the ingredients, but the mixture of sage, sweetgrass, cedar, and lavender wafts in the air, the scent intoxicating.

Be with us tonight, Mother Nature. We can use all the help we can get.

After repeating the process one by one, Sloan and I meet at the pyramid's far side. With the torches lit and Merlin performing the smudging spell, we're a go.

"Be careful, luv. Promise me."

I wink at my hubby and blow across the top of my lighter. "I promise. That goes for you two as well."

"Aye, we'll be fine. Won't we, sham?"

Manx calls his battle armor forward and smiles at me. "Aye, we will."

"Ye'll need to bring yer pretty necklace into play, Red," Patty says.

I hand Sloan my lighter and pull the Blind Moon Crescent from under my battle vest. Striding over to where Patty is standing ready, I check in with him.

The elemental stones shimmer with unearthly energy in his hands, and unless I'm totally off-base, I think they're happier to be working for him than they were for the moon demon.

I smile at the kaleidoscope of colors and call Birga into my palm. This is as good as it gets. She's not the staff the ritual called for, but she's amazing, and I'd never underestimate her—especially with Merlin's booster spell at work.

The air around us shifts, growing thick with the electric charge of magic as the herbs purify the ritual site and Patty, Merlin, and I begin the ritual.

We take our positions, forming a triangle around the altar. I stand at the western point, Birga ready and the amulet in hand.

Patty whispers a few comforting words to the elemental

stones. His voice gets lost amid the whispering desert wind. As he speaks, the stones flare brilliantly, their colors intensifying.

Merlin has the ritual and the map laid out before him. "Okay, our shields are as strong as Dionysus and I could make them. Let's do this."

I press Birga's green marble spear tip into a crack in the stone where Merlin said she would have the greatest connection.

Magic is alive.

The stone beneath my feet resonates with energy, and I realize late in the game how much power we'll need to control to reconstruct the veil.

The energy is so primal, so elemental, that it takes my breath away. The sandstone of the Great Pyramid hums beneath me, harmonizing with the melodic chant spilling from Merlin's lips.

Birga trembles in my hand—not with fear, but with anticipation. My spear's unique energy entwines with mine. It zings over my skin and snaps in my cells.

The elemental stones are excited as well.

Their light pulses in sync with Merlin's words, each echoing the celestial element they represent. The steadfast endurance of earth, the volatile passion of fire, the adaptable flow of water, and the untamed freedom of air.

It's a power unlike any I've felt before, an overwhelming rush threatening to sweep me off my feet. The edges of my consciousness blur as the veil between the human and fae realms becomes tangible.

This would be a terrible time to pass out.

I sense Sloan's worried gaze on me and tighten up. Despite the invasive force of magic bombarding me, I steady myself. "S'all good. I've got this."

Gripping Birga tighter, I double my focus and press my fingers against the amulet hanging around my neck.

Then, when Merlin's got the ritual solidly off the ground, I add my voice. The incantation the great oak gave me to recite is the next part to make this happen.

The incantation flows through my mind, the majestic oak's words of magic taking shape on my tongue. I draw a deep breath and focus on my intentions.

"By moonlit eve and shadows deep,
Where realms entwine and secrets keep,
We gather here, both druid and fae,
To heal the veil that lies astray.
From sacred grove to ancient glen,
We seek the realms where spirits blend,
With hearts attuned to nature's sway—"
Crack!

All at once, chaos explodes around us. Figures appear out of thin air, teleporting in from all directions. Loki, Eros, a handful of Unseelie, and others storm the apexes of the three pyramids.

Sloan responds, moving with a fluid grace that always leaves me in awe. The blades of the dual swords he chose for the battle erupt into flames, blazing orange against the ebony sky.

Yeah, baby!

Manx snarls, looking badass in his armor. It's a vicious warning that echoes in the desert night. It's all the warning our attackers get as he lunges at them with extended fangs and claws.

Loki and one of the Unseelie home in on us and rush for the altar. When they hit our shielding, the iridescent blue bubble protecting us glimmers into sight before going invisible again.

Score one for the good guys.

Still, we don't know how long our protective measures will keep them away.

Merlin, Patty, and I keep our focus, continuing the ritual despite the chaos.

We are the conduit of magic.

If we don't do our job, this has all been for nothing.

I restart the great oak's incantation.

"By moonlit eve and shadows deep,
Where realms entwine and secrets keep,
We gather here, both druid and fae,
To heal the veil that lies astray....

As I speak the words, I catch sight of Discord standing off to the side of the melee. The trickster is enjoying the spectacle with a twisted grin.

That fox is messed up.

He garners a disturbing delight from turmoil.

At least he's getting the chaos I promised. Hopefully, that will keep him on our side for a little while longer.

An explosion of golden mist appears, and Dionysus joins us. He locks eyes with Eros fighting against our shielding, and a flash of pure fury lights his face. "Don't you fucking dare."

"You'd really choose her over me?"

"Only if you force me to make that choice. Fiona is my heart. I will defend her to my last breath."

With a determined look, Eros rushes forward, grappling Dionysus. The two of them snap out and are gone.

Where did they go?

I want to scream. I want to track them down. I can't.

Gritting my teeth, I struggle to hold the magic coursing through me and stay connected with the ritual's rhythm. The stone beneath me vibrates with the raw power of the magic we're channeling.

It feels like I might vibrate apart at a cellular level.

There's a physicality to the magic now, and I hope that means Merlin has accessed the veil. Samhain is when the veil is thinnest, and maybe this would've been easier in October, but how many more innocents would've suffered if we waited another seven months?

No. Ostara is a celestial event.

The spring equinox will thin the veil.

This will work.

The words of the incantation continue to fall from my lips, hanging in the air like a prayer offered to the night. When I get to the end of my part, I meet Merlin's gaze, and he shakes his head.

Back at the beginning, I start again.

The great oak gave me these words. The Blind Moon Crescent is warm against my chest, and Birga vibrates in my palms. I give the incantation more volume and voice, projecting my intentions.

I focus harder. I push further. I amp up the magic inside me and call out the incantation again.

When I finish for the second time, Merlin falls silent.

It's done.

I hold my breath, waiting for the surge of magic, the shift in the air…anything to indicate the veil has taken hold.

The silence stretches on, and nothing changes.

The weight of disappointment lands heavily in the pit of my stomach. "Merlin? Patty?"

They mirror my sickening disappointment.

Merlin curses, his brow furrowed in deep consternation. "It didn't work."

CHAPTER TWENTY-TWO

Merlin's words shatter the fragile hope I'd built up around this ritual. But the amulet...and the incantation from the oak...They were signs we were on the right path. How could it not work? Did we do something wrong? Did we forget something?

I scan the violence surrounding the people I love, and the shock of failure hits me hard.

But everyone has given so much.

Well, I can't stay safe in a bubble if this isn't going to work. The least I can do is take out our opponents.

"Keep trying." I pull the pendant chain over my head and hand the silver crescent to Merlin. "I'm leaving Birga lodged in position. I'll buy you more time to figure this out."

When Merlin and Dionysus set up the boundary shield earlier, I ensured it would keep people from getting in, but we could get out if needed.

I need to.

Everything in me says Merlin can do this. If we can keep our enemies from stopping him, he'll figure it out and make it work. I know he will.

Gazing skyward, I scan the dark shadows flying in acrobatic arcs against the night sky. It's too dark to see who's who, but the dragons are on fire tonight.

Or at least *breathing* fire.

Looking good, buddy, I say across my dragon bond. *Any chance you can come get me?*

A warm rush of affection echoes back to me. *On my way.*

"Bestial Strength." My spell is barely audible above the cacophony of battle, but it doesn't matter. It doesn't need to be heard to fill my muscles with power.

Gauging the attacks of Loki, the Unseelie, and two other bad guys, I watch for my opening and choose my exit point from the safety of our shield.

When I find it, I call my armor forward and sprint toward the pyramid's edge. The wind rips at my clothes as I launch myself into the abyss. It's a wild leap of faith, the stone dropping away beneath me, leaving only the cold desert air and a sheer plummet into nothingness.

At that moment, suspended in the darkness, there's a sort of tranquillity, an eerie calm in the storm's heart.

The feeling of freedom is invigorating. It's me and the vast expanse of the night sky, the world narrowing to the rush of wind in my ears, and the thrill of the fall.

I feel Dart before I see him. His massive form swoops up beneath me, his vast wings flapping as he judges his approach.

I know, without a doubt, he'll catch me.

His broad back meets my fall, my body landing gently against his scales. The impact is minimal, the spell absorbing the brunt of the landing. When my boots find purchase, I break into a jog, heading toward my saddle handle on his first spike.

Grasping it, I scan the chaos of the battleground below. "We need to take out the attackers and give Merlin the time he needs to figure out what went wrong."

"Take them out, how? What's your plan?"

"Nothing pretty. Just pluck and crush."

Dart's wings beat the air in rhythmic cadence, propelling us faster. Beside us, Saxa joins our cause.

"Tell your siblings what we're doing. Make sure they only grab the bad guys."

Dart and his siblings are almost three now. While they aren't full-size, the Westerns who live with us in Isilon have grown into formidable warriors.

It's clear the moment Dart sends them my message. The kids, as Patty calls them, roar in a symphony of understanding, and their battle tactics change.

Instead of using their fiery breath to push back attackers, they become bolts of aggression, ripping through the air and plucking attackers off the structures.

Dart's muscles bunch beneath me, and he snatches up a foe, his claws clamping down like iron shackles.

There's a primal satisfaction in the simplicity of it.

Very few warrior races can defend against a dragon onslaught, and we deserve the win.

We're the good guys, dammit.

The frustration of the failed ritual fuels my fight.

These gods, these beings of magical power, are holding our world hostage, polluting it with destruction and division for selfish motives.

Do I feel bad when victims of the dragons' aerial assault are thrown into the air or crushed in draconic grips, only to be discarded like rag dolls plummeting to the unforgiving ground?

Nope, not even a little.

Not even when they're tossed into the air and chomped down or swallowed whole, like a piece of popcorn. Too bad, so sad.

Dart and I weave through the night sky, overseeing the dragon strikes. "Dart, we need to get down there!"

I squint against the wind, my gaze locked on the top of the

next pyramid. It's Da, outnumbered and about to be overwhelmed.

Dart banks hard and swoops low toward the pyramid. I draw a deep breath, release my saddle handle, and launch off his side.

I'm a missile slicing through the wind.

"Diminish Descent." Cold night air rushes past me until the magic of my spell takes hold and slows the downward pull. Tracking my descent, I watch as the worn peak of the pyramid rushes past too early.

I miscalculated. "Shitballs."

My momentum carries me over the plateau atop Menkaure and sends me skidding down the hard stone of its downward slope.

Ass over end, I tumble down the sandstone blocks.

It's a bumpy ride, but thankfully, my armor takes the brunt of the impact. Coming to a stop at last, I stare up at the dragons above as my head stops spinning.

"That was fun." With a grunt, I push myself to my feet, turn my gaze upward, and start a hasty climb to get me back into the heart of the storm.

"Hang in there, Da. I'm coming."

Bursting back onto the summit of Menkaure, I find my father valiantly battling against a group from the fae realm.

When my brothers and I discovered we descended from druids, we were dazzled. When we first saw him battle with a fighting staff, we were flat-out flummoxed.

He's amazeballs.

But even a fantastic fighter can get outnumbered.

I waste no time joining him, grabbing an abandoned sword off the stone plateau as I close the distance. "Hey, oul man."

Da is facing off against three guys with skull tattoos and forked tails. I don't know what they are, but I don't care. That's my daddio.

"Hey, baby girl. What brings ye by?"

I chuckle and take my position as he turns to give me his back. "Can't let you have all the fun."

"Och, no. I suppose not. Ye've always been a bit of a thrill seeker."

"True story."

Our movements synchronize, a father-and-daughter flow that transcends training and skills. We move in harmony born of blood and trust.

In my peripheral vision, I see Dillan and Eva rocking it. "Looking good, D, but your wife is kicking your ass."

Dillan laughs, crosses his arms beside his opponent's ears, and pulls his blades down and to his sides in a swift and brutal slice. The elf drops to the blood-covered stone. "I'm good with that. But is it the woman or the weapon? That scythe is badass."

Dillan's voice is all teasing, and Eva grunts a laugh. "It's the woman. If you want to trade weapons and have me prove it, I'm happy to rise to the challenge."

I duck to avoid a high strike and spin to reposition.

I catch a flash of moonlight glimmering off the sleek ebony mane of Garnet's lion. He's all snarls and fangs as his claws swipe through his opponent's flesh.

He roars, the image of him even more majestic atop an Egyptian pyramid.

Dillan swings back into Da's circle and I'm about to join them when the world grinds to a halt.

Everything stops.

The sounds of battle end so abruptly it's startling.

An Unseelie is locked mid-swing.

The dragons hang unmoving in the sky.

My family is frozen in the silvery moonlight.

It's as if someone hit the pause button on the universe, but I wasn't affected. Straightening, I glance around to see how far this goes.

Nothing moves.

Not a single grain of sand stirs. The wind is gone. Not even the city lights of Cairo twinkle.

"What the what?" I turn a full circle.

We're not in control of this situation.

Not anymore.

The question then becomes…who is?

CHAPTER TWENTY-THREE

For a moment, my mental hamster struggles to catch up. Then I see Dionysus reappear by Merlin and the altar on the other pyramid. He's turning a three-sixty, looking as perplexed as I feel. It's a relief to not be alone in this. *Welcome to the Twilight Zone, Tarzan.*

Dionysus spots me and portals to my side. "We need to go."

Without waiting for a response, he takes my hand and transports us to the ritual altar.

Patty and Merlin look as baffled as I felt a moment ago. Standing with them are Hermes, Zeus, Hel, and a tall, broad-shouldered mountain of a man who gives off the same level of magical buzz as Zeus.

The sight of Hermes' staff gleaming under the moonlight sends a jolt of hope racing through me.

"What's going on?" My gaze shifts from one face to the next.

"This is Odin." Zeus gestures at the man with Hel. "After a long and rather unpleasant discussion with Themis and the Fates, it's clear the pantheons of gods have unduly influenced the mortal world. We are here to rein in the damage."

I blink and look from the two god-kings to the staff of Hermes. "You'll help us with the ritual?"

"Not exactly," Zeus corrects. "We will remove the obstacles and provide what you need, but the efforts must remain your own."

"Fine by me. Yeah, that works."

"Why?" Dionysus scrutinizes his father. "Why now? Why do you care?"

"The veil between worlds is a safeguard. Fiona said the awakening of powers has been rampant and destructive. Families have been torn asunder. Empowered humans have abused their abilities. Communities have become divided and dangerous."

"All true, Father, but that doesn't answer my question. Why do you care?"

"The laws of non-interference are part of our guiding principles. If the members of our pantheons are abusing those laws, whether for personal gain or their amusement, it is our duty to step in."

Dionysus arches a brow. "I don't buy it."

Zeus looks at me. "You asked to use Hermes' staff. It would benefit your goals to perform the ritual with the items needed, would it not?"

Is Zeus genuinely trying to make amends?

"Uh, yes. With the staff, we have a greater chance of success."

He's up to something, Jane. There's no way he's here, doing this out of the goodness of his heart.

Maybe it's not about the veil, so what? Maybe this is him sticking his neck out to do the right thing.

Or maybe you're too good-hearted and caring to realize he's playing you.

I consider that. *Say he has his own reasons, and they extend beyond you and our determination to make the world a better place. Who cares? We've allied with enemies who have the same goal as us before. And Zeus isn't our enemy. Sweetie, I really believe he wants to get to know the man you've become.*

Zeus interrupts our private conversation. "This isn't an open invitation. If I was wrong and you don't wish for our help, we will take our leave."

"No!" I shout with a little too much verve. "Sorry. I mean, no. You aren't wrong. We are honored and incredibly pleased to accept your offer. Aren't we, Tarzan?"

Dionysus sighs and shakes his shoulders, arms, and hands. "Yes. Thank you, Father."

There's a glimmer of smug superiority in Zeus' gaze, but I try not to hold it against him. Baby steps.

Zeus turns to Odin. "If you'll gather your son and anyone who falls under your command, I will do the same."

In the next moment, Hel, Odin, Loki, and half a dozen opponents, both dead and alive, disappear.

Zeus gestures at the altar. "If you please. Do what needs to be done so we can go."

You don't have to tell me twice. I hustle to the altar, and Merlin hands me back the amulet pendant. After slinging it over my head, I pull Birga's spear tip from the crevice and release her. "Hermes? Do you want me to hold the staff in place and leave you out of the ritual altogether, or do you want to hold it yourself?"

"I will hold it," he snaps. It's obvious by the bitter tone of his response he doesn't want to be here and resents having us use his staff.

Tough noogies.

I glance down at the frozen state of things and hold up a finger. "Uh, could I make one more tiny request?"

Zeus' brow arches as he frowns at me. "You push my boundaries, female."

"Yeah, I know. Sorry about that. Still, could I ask that you release my family from your hold and bring them up here to help with the incantation? It can't hurt to have all the druid help we can get, amirite?"

Zeus huffs and flicks his fingers. I might even believe he's annoyed if he didn't have the same dimple that shows up when Dionysus is fighting a smile.

When Da, Dillan, Aiden, Calum, Eva, and Sloan appear around us, they start.

I hold up my palms. "All is well, guys. I don't have time to explain. Anyone who wants to throw in a little extra magical oomph this time around is welcome to do so. Merlin and Patty, are you good to go?"

Merlin widens his eyes at me and nods. "Yes."

"Aye, lass," Patty agrees. "Take it from the top."

Standing next to Hermes, I grip the shaft of his staff. Wait, whoa, that sounded rude even in my head.

Yeah, it did. Dionysus chuckles. *We'll keep that between us. Now, get this done so they go away. I like my family far away on a mountaintop, not here slumming it with us.*

All right, let's do this. Focusing my intention, I call on the power of the amulet, the staff, and the incantation as Merlin and Patty begin again. Da, Sloan, and my brothers form a circle around us with their hands joined.

"By moonlit eve and shadows deep,
Where realms entwine and secrets keep,
We gather here, both druid and fae,
To heal the veil that lies astray.
From sacred grove to ancient glen,
We seek the realms where spirits blend,
With hearts attuned to nature's sway,
We speak the words we need to say.
In light we dance, in dark we thrive,
Where secrets whisper and dreams arrive,
Woven is the tapestry grand,
A bridge of magic, hand in hand.

Light and dark, a balance true,
Both realms divided, old and new,
Let the veil be lifted, oh mystic night,
Conceal the fae's enchanting sight.
Through twilight's mist and starlit gleam,
We beckon the fae, as in a dream,
With sacred reverence, we implore,
Veil the path to the fae's door.
As human memories fade to blank,
With harmony's melody, we offer thanks,
In union divine, we embrace the power,
Raise the veil, this enchanted hour.
By ancient magic, we now decree,
These realms shall thrive, separately,
Mortals and fae may walk side by side,
But fae races will be glamored to hide.
Druids united with our spirits entwined,
The veil between realms shall stretch and bind,
With the words we speak at Ostara's hour.
Raise the veil and block magic's power!

When I open my eyes, I meet Merlin's gaze. He's still speaking his part of the ritual, but I'm encouraged.

The air *thrums* with energy, lifting the hair on my arms. A silvery light coalesces before us, shimmering and twisting like liquid moonlight. It grows brighter and brighter until I have to shield my eyes.

As the last syllable of his incantation falls from his lips, the world holds its breath.

I look from Merlin to Patty to Da and Sloan.

No one is giving anything away.

Then it happens.

The world roars back to life, more vibrant and electric than before. A wave of energy, pure and undiluted, erupts from the ritual site, radiating outward like a supernova. It washes over me, a torrent of unadulterated magic that sends my senses into overdrive.

It's like I've been plunged into a storm of sensations. The scent of the desert, the whisper of the wind, the luminescent glow of the moon—they all intensify tenfold as the world bursts into Technicolor.

The force is so strong that I wonder how we're not being toppled and tumbled off the pyramid's peak.

Zeus' handiwork, no doubt.

The raw power of Hermes' staff pulses in my hand.

Everything settles as the veil between realms solidifies. A shift in the air brings a subtler wave of magic. It's a sensation of balance restored, worlds realigning, and boundaries being set.

"That's good, right?" I ask.

Merlin scans the area with a cautious gaze. "Yeah, girlfriend. I think so."

"It is done," Zeus announces. "The veil is reestablished."

Hermes pulls his staff from my hand and glares at me. "Then our arrangement is at its end."

He's gone before I can utter a word of thanks.

Turning toward Zeus, I stumble on what to say. "*Thank you* seems inadequate for what you've done. You came through for us. We appreciate your help more than I can express."

Zeus meets my gaze. "You said to prove my intentions and make amends with Dionysus that I should do things to make him happy. This was a first attempt."

I nod. "And a massively impressive first attempt it was. Thank you."

He glances at his son and waits expectantly.

I fight the urge to prod or prompt him, but in the end, I don't need to. Being the better man in all things, Dionysus lifts his chin and meets his father's gaze. "Thank you, Father. This was important to not only me but all of humanity. You made the right decision."

Zeus smiles. "I never thought I would hear those words fall from your lips, my boy. It seems there is wisdom in your female's advice. Perhaps she truly does know you better than I."

Yeah, I do. "Thanks again," I add, hoping Zeus will venture back to Olympus before he says too much. "And please thank Hermes, Themis, and the Fates for their parts in making this happen."

Zeus shakes his head, his golden curls swinging freely beneath his laurel crown. "You forget, Fiona. The gods don't influence the lives of men. This was your doing. You and your family."

He casts a curious glance at the gathering of family and friends and snaps out in a burst of golden mist.

When I'm sure he's gone, I throw my arms open and launch myself at Sloan. He catches me, as he always has, and wraps his arms around me. "Ye did good, Mrs. Mackenzie."

"You did good too, Mr. Mackenzie." I give him a celebratory smooch and wriggle for him to put me down so I can hug Patty, Merlin, and Da. "Dionysus and Nikon, can you gather the others so they can join us?"

The Greeks snap out, and a moment later, Garnet, Diesel, Brody, Dan, Anyx, and a few other Moon Called are there to join us.

"What happened?" Diesel asks. "One minute we're in the fight of the century, and the next, it's all over."

I wave away the question. "It's a long story. I'll tell you the whole thing at the debriefing meeting. Tonight, we celebrate. The veil is up, and if the wording of that incantation holds true, we'll be looking at a very different world over the next few days."

"It's really over?" Garnet asks. His natural healing takes hold and seals a long, bloody gash down his left arm. "The veil is up, and it's staying up?"

"Yeah, bossman. It is." I press my luck and snag a hug from

him while he's in a good mood. "If I'm right, your world will go back to being a lot more manageable from now on."

"From your lips to the gods' ears." He kisses my temple before stepping back. "Well done, Lady Druid. You pulled through in the clutch, yet again."

"Nah, it was very much a team effort."

As Team Trouble mills around, relief, triumph, and bewilderment are the emotions floating through the crowd. For me, it's gratitude and affection.

These are my people, and I couldn't be happier to claim them.

Spotting Discord observing from the sidelines, I make my way over to him. "And you," I say, with a teasing smile and a finger wag. "Thank you for not causing more chaos than necessary."

He grins with an impish twinkle in his eye. "See, Red. I told you it would be fun."

"Yeah, I suppose you did." I bend at the plateau's edge and sit with my legs hanging over the stone block. "What's next for you?"

"I'm thinking politics."

I laugh and study him to see if he's serious. He seems to be. "Well, there is certainly enough conflict and drama in politics to keep you entertained. Just try not to kill people. Humans will notice that, and your fun will come to a grinding halt."

"A wise suggestion." He brushes his bushy tail against me and lifts his paw to shake. "Be well, Red. Thanks for making me part of the team."

"Thanks for all your help. We wouldn't be here without your knowledge of the celestial map."

He flashes his teeth in a broad grin. "I know things."

With a flouncy swish of his tail, he stands and trots down the pyramid's stone blocks and disappears as he goes. I've never really understood his powers or what he's capable of.

Maybe I never will.

Sloan sits on one side of me while Bruin and Manx sit on the other. The four of us stare out at Cairo's night skyline. "I'd like to come back here when the fate of the world isn't on our shoulders."

Sloan laces his fingers with mine. "I've been here now, so we can return whenever ye like."

I run my fingers through the thick length of Bruin's fur. "What are our casualties?"

"Nikon took Aiden, Dan, and Thaos to the clinic to be tended to. Nothing vital. They'll be fine by morning."

It's a testament to my exhaustion that I didn't notice my brother was hurt. Well, if he'll be better by morning, I'll catch up with him then.

"What do you say, boys? Should we go home? I'm thinking a long soak in the hot tub and big steaks on the barbecue."

Sloan winks at me and squeezes my hand. "Aye, luv. That sounds perfect."

CHAPTER TWENTY-FOUR

We give the world a couple of days to adjust. The incantation mentioned the memories of magic fading from the minds of men, and by the third day after the ritual, it seems those who didn't know about magic before all of this have forgotten.

The riots have stopped.

The protestors are no longer gathering.

The explosive division and mistrust of two vastly different communities have diffused.

Yay team!

On Monday morning, Sloan, Manx, and I step into the Batcave, and the change in atmosphere is noticeable immediately. Max and Andromeda are in their offices. The phones are quiet, there's nothing on the monitor wall, and Garnet is nowhere in sight.

I knock on the doorframe and lean into Max's office. "Hey, are we doing the Monday meeting?"

Max lifts his focus from his notes and shakes his head. "No, sorry. He sent out a message last night."

I pull out my phone, and yeah, I must've missed that. "Okay, no problem. Is everything all right?"

"Perfectly. Since all is quiet and the chaotic forces will take a few weeks to recalibrate back to the old levels of magic, Garnet flashed Imari and Myra to Disneyland."

"A vacation?"

Andromeda steps out of her office and laughs. "As improbable as it seems, our grumpy lion is taking off his alpha lion hat and exchanging it for Mickey ears."

I snort. "That paints a hilarious image in my head."

"Och, I think it's lovely," Sloan remarks. "Myra and Imari have to share so much of him. It's nice that they're takin' time as a family."

"It is." I take two steps into Max's office and hand him the folder I brought. "I added my full account of the last week into the system yesterday. Here's a copy."

Max slides the folder into a slotted tray on his desk. "Thanks, Fi. I'll take a look and file it for you."

I stroke my fingers over Manx's ear and scrub the side of his neck. "I gotta say, it's freaky quiet here. As much as I love living in Isilon, we are out of the loop on current events. Things are so…still."

Max closes the folder on his desk and stands, sliding his work into his briefcase. "Honestly, it's a welcome change. The reduction of prana seems to have stopped the taint in the air, and the awakenings have ended."

"Och, that's good news," Sloan agrees.

Max pushes in his chair and grabs his jacket. "It is. For now, the fae who fought to be seen have slunk back to their corners and are licking their wounds."

"As they should be," I retort. "I still think Garnet should tear the stuffing out of Malachi for inciting that exposure stunt at Ripley's Aquarium."

"Not that ye want the man to suffer or anythin'." Sloan

chuckles.

I shrug one shoulder. "I admit I have strong negative feelings toward Malachi, but even if I were objective, I'd think he got off too easy."

"Aye, but it's not yer job to worry about that, so let's not take on more than we have to."

Max finishes with his scarf. "Sloan's right. You know there's no love lost between Malachi and me, but if Garnet wants to be the man who polices weasels like him, he can have him."

I suppose. "Still, maybe he could grow a nasty swamp fungus or something."

Max chuckles. "If the universe saw fit to punish him that way, I certainly wouldn't argue. Now, if you don't need me, I have to change hats too. With humanity forgetting about magic and fae powers, I'm back to a full workload as the Deputy Commissioner of the RCMP."

"Yikes, that's a lot."

He slings the strap of his leather bag over his shoulder and prepares to face Toronto in mid-March. "We'll see how things go. Now that I have a full understanding of what makes up the world, I have no problem calling in Garnet or your team if I stumble across an empowered problem."

I hold my fist up for a bump. "We'll come running. Whatever happens, safe home, Max. Keep on keeping on."

"You too, Fi." He meets my knuckles with a bump. "Take care of each other. It's a crazy world."

Sloan extends his hand. "It is. Blessed be, Max. We wish ye well in whatever the universe has in store."

We watch him go, and I scan the empty office. "This will take some getting used to. Do you think it'll last?"

Sloan shrugs. "No idea, luv, but I think Garnet is smart to take advantage of the lull while he can."

"Yeah, I do too."

Andromeda is on the phone, so I blow her a kiss and wave goodbye. "I guess we've got the day off."

We take the pantry portal back to Isilon and step out of the maintenance room in the palace a moment later. After a meeting of the minds with Merlin, Isilon, Emmet, and Brenny, they decided *not* to open a portal from the pub here to Shenanigans.

They have, however, agreed to give this portal a secondary destination, so Liam and Kady can get back to the pub in Toronto if they need to.

Merlin will start working on that later this week. He's more than a little fried after the past year and more recently, our time in Egypt.

"Jane, thank the powers, you're back," Dionysus calls from the Great Room as we exit the portal. "Come in here. I need you."

Sloan and I share a worried gaze and jog to the vast meeting place. I'm familiar with all of Dionysus' moods and tones, and when he says he needs me, he means it.

The moment I see Eros standing with Nikon and Dionysus, my redhead Irish ire—as Nikon calls it—ignites. "Tarzan? What's wrong? What did he do?"

Eros rolls his eyes. "What? That sounded like you think *I'm* the problem."

"I wonder what put that thought into my mind."

He holds up his hands. "Relax, Red. If you must know, I was apologizing to my friends for my recent behavior and asking for their forgiveness."

"Yeah, right. What brought about this big change of heart? You sold us out to Zeus. You petitioned Themis against us."

"Simmer down, Fi." Nikon steps between Eros and me. "I love it when you go all mama bear on our behalf, but it's fine. We're fine."

I blink and meet Nikon's gaze. He looks tired and sad. The Greek pantheon and the battles of the past are wearing him down. "You're not fine. You're hurting. And your Greek brother-in-arms here is responsible for at least part of that."

Nikon chucks my chin and chuckles. "I'm a big boy. Stand down. Dionysus and I already accepted Eros' apology, and we're over it."

I frown and look from Nikon to Dionysus. "Then why is Dionysus upset? Why did he say he needs me?"

"Because I do," Dionysus answers. "As well as coming here to apologize, my father asked Eros to bring the three of us together so he can have a word."

I don't love the sound of that.

"Again? What about this time?"

"I don't know, but three times in one week is enough to give me the runs."

I try not to laugh but fail. "Okay, so he wanted the three of us. Why?"

I point my question at Eros, but he only stands there looking arrogant and stupid.

I don't know what kind of godly ESP they have, but both of them stiffen a moment before the air explodes in a golden mist.

Zeus materializes before us, and on either side of him stand Themis and Atropos.

"Good, you're here," Zeus says.

I search the faces of two goddesses to glean any idea of what this is about. Whatever it is, they don't seem pleased.

Zeus doesn't wait for me to figure it out. "Following our last conversation about the infractions of my people affecting the lives of you and yours, and specifically Hecate's violations, I am righting another wrong."

He looks at Nikon and grows serious. "Nikon of Rhodes. The anguish of losing a wife and a child affected not only one life but three. I offer you another chance."

Atropos sweeps her hand through the air between us and a brunette woman with rich brown eyes and olive skin appears. Her hair is long and hangs in tight curls, and her hand rests protectively against the round of her belly.

Nikon's color drains from his face. "Kallista?"

"Nikon?" She speaks the rest in ancient Greek, but I get the gist. She's disoriented and wondering what's going on.

She's not the only one.

"What's happening here?" I ask.

Zeus meets my gaze, looking surprised. "Isn't it obvious? I'm returning this wife and child to him. Hecate's actions adversely affected the trajectory of this young family. I'm righting that wrong."

Nikon takes two unsteady steps toward his wife. Reaching toward her, he drops to his knees.

Kallista closes the distance between them and kneels. Whatever shock overtook him, Nikon breaks through it and grabs her in a fierce embrace.

He's sobbing.

I'm sobbing.

Hell, even Sloan is streaming tears.

"There is a caveat." Atropos frowns at the scene. "The strings of your wife's tapestry were cut, while those of your daughter's tapestry were never woven. Your child will live her life as if uninterrupted…"

"And my wife?" Nikon asks, his voice thready.

Themis frowns. "Inserting her into a society and a time that are not hers will influence the timeline as surely as removing her did. Once she delivers your daughter, her time will end—"

"She can live here on the island," I blurt before she can take this moment of hope away from him.

When all eyes turn to me, I swipe away my tears. "We made a similar agreement with Mother Nature. My brother was given back to us but lives here in Isilon."

Sloan takes my hand and stands tall beside me. "The island of Emhain Abhlach is apart from the rest of the world. Brendan doesn't affect the timeline yet still gets to live his life with his family."

"Whatever it takes." Nikon stands and lifts Kallista to stand with him. "We'll move here, and Kallista will remain here for as long as we have together."

Zeus grins at Themis. "It seems Lady Earth set a precedent. If she made such an arrangement, you two are worried about nothing. Fiona's solution satisfies your concerns."

I study the expressions of Themis and Atropos.

My heart races as we wait.

"Please, ladies," I plead. "Nikon has suffered long enough because of Hecate. Surely you can feel the anguish and guilt he's suffered all these centuries. He didn't deserve it. That was all Hecate's doing."

Themis looks at her daughter and nods. "Very well. Kallista Tsambikos will live here on the island for whatever time she has left on the living plane."

"And the child?" Dionysus asks. "Their daughter?"

Atropos shrugs. "The child will be born a Greek immortal like her father. She is free to live her life without restriction."

Nikon has Kallista tight to his side and his hand on her belly. "We accept. Thank you."

Zeus nods. "Excellent. Then we leave you to become reacquainted."

"Thank you so much." I rush forward but stop short of hugging them. They don't seem like huggers.

Zeus grins and looks at Dionysus, waiting.

He doesn't have to wait long. Dionysus holds out his hand, and when Zeus reciprocates, they clasp each other's arms near the elbow and lock gazes. "Thank you, Father. For the first time in millennia, I can honestly say I'm proud of you."

Zeus lowers his chin and arches an imperious brow. "Your siblings are proud simply because I am the god of gods."

Tarzan shrugs. "I've never been like them."

Zeus' grin fades. "I realize that now."

The two of them exchange an intense gaze, and I have no doubt they are speaking mind-to-mind. When they ease apart, Zeus winks at me. "Until the next time."

When he snaps out, Themis and Atropos follow.

There's a moment of stunned silence.

Nikon tears his gaze away from the woman in his arms and scans our faces. "Did that just happen?"

"Aye, sham, it did."

I'm the first to hug him and smile at his beautiful wife. "I don't know if you can understand me but welcome to the neighborhood. You and your baby couldn't be more loved and celebrated."

Nikon kisses the top of my head and moves to hug Sloan and Dionysus.

Brendan steps in from the far doorway with Emmet behind him. "It looks like we need to adjust the population sign. We didn't catch all of it, but I take it congratulations are in order."

I pat my eyes with the sleeve of my hoodie and try to stop the waterworks. It's futile. "Damn straight. They need a place to live and to get moved in and settled. I know of a great street with big, beautiful trees and plenty of kids for your daughter to play with."

Nikon runs his fingers through his hair and exhales. "A *daughter*. I'm going to be a father."

"Yeah, you are. And you're going to be amazing."

Dionysus nods. "If you ever need a list of what *not* to do as a father, I've got you covered."

Nikon turns to Kallista, who looks as scared and confused as she did when she first arrived. "Guys, if you'll excuse us. I think I've got some explaining to do."

EPILOGUE

I sit in third position at the head table of the monthly meeting of the Lakeshore Guild of Empowered Ones. Four years ago, my adventure began at a luncheon much like this. That day, I had returned from being held in the dragons' lair and had accidentally siphoned the magic from the city.

I was the pariah of the room back then.

Not much has changed.

During that first summer, I was a mouthy upstart who dared to question the ranking structure, the Guild's commitment, and the man named as Toronto's druid governor.

Because Barghest aren't druids.

I scan the table running perpendicular to where I sit. That first meeting, I sat halfway down the table along the side wall because my level of active power was notable but not mastered.

Nikon sat in the first position looking bored, and in the first position he remains.

Except now, I sit beside him.

Nikon and I are still the bad kids. We still giggle to ourselves and talk over his telepathic link. And we still don't give two shits about the glares and the opinions of the leaders of the other factions.

Haters gotta hate.

Not all the faces around the table remain hostile. Xavier and I found an awkward fondness for one another. Suede and I remain good friends. Zxata, being Myra's brother, is family.

It's been a good run.

Garnet finishes with the agenda topics and opens the floor to any new business.

That's your cue, Red.

It is. I stand and face the gathering of Guild Governors. "Hey, everyone. It's been six months since we reinstated the veil and the world is back to normal. Since my family has moved out of Toronto and I've only been coming back here for work, I'm stepping down as the governor of Toronto's druids."

That catches everyone by surprise, and I'm not sure if the worried looks are a compliment.

"In my place, I've appointed Ciara Doyle, a friend of our family and one of the heirs to the Druid Order in Ireland to take my Guild seat. Ciara lived here for a while with my family and fell in love with the city. She's back, and she's looking forward to picking up the mantle."

"Well, I'm sure I speak for everyone when I say we'll miss you," Zxata says.

I snort. "I'm sure you *don't* but thank you."

"Well, *I'll* miss you," Garnet adds. "You sure livened things up around here, Lady Druid."

I press my fist over my heart. "It's been one of the greatest honors of my life, bossman. If you ever need me, you know where to find me. Otherwise…peace out, party people."

Nikon snaps us back to my Toronto home. Sloan and Ciara await our return. "How did it go, *a ghra*? Are ye all right?"

"I'm good." I smile. "No regrets. If the world crumbles, I'm only a portal away, but unless that happens, I'll be building a life I want more than anything with my family and friends in Isilon."

"Yer sure Tad doesn't mind me livin' in his house across the road?" Ciara asks.

"Nope. He's thrilled." I grab the extra set of keys from the wall safe and hand them over. "He said to make yourself at home, and he'll come and help you move his things into one of the smaller bedrooms once your furniture arrives."

"He's really not coming back?"

I shake my head. "He and Kenzie are happy, and he found his family with the Gagnes. He's right where he wants to be."

Ciara accepts the keys and grins. "Did ye ever imagine we'd get to this place? Me takin' over yer duties fer yer city and makin' a life here and yer lot all movin' off to live in Ireland?"

I laugh. "Never in a million…but here we are. She's a great city. Take good care of her."

Ciara hugs me. "I expect ye to do the same with my isle. If ye need me, call."

"Same." I squeeze her tight and release her to step back. I pull a silver chain with a pentacle and a centurion helmet from my pocket. "Welcome to Team Trouble. Don't let Garnet intimidate you. He's all growls and claws, but he's really a pussycat."

Sloan snorts. "A pussycat who murders people."

I lift a shoulder. "Yeah, true story."

"Tick-tock, Red." Nikon taps his watch. "We've got a baby shower to get to, remember?"

Ciara grins. "Och, Greek. I heard about the arrival of yer baby girl. Congratulations. What did ye name her?"

Nikon beams. "Melina Helene Fiona Tsambikos."

Ciara arches a brow at me. "Ye made the cut."

"I did, but Kallista gets all the credit. Melina is baby perfection. Light brown hair, warm olive skin, and the most beautiful hazel eyes you've ever seen."

Nikon laughs. "I don't think Kallista gets *all* the credit. Half of those genes are mine."

The alarm on my phone goes off, and I end the notification. "Okay, we gotta go, or we'll be late for the baby celebration of the century. Here are my SUV keys. Enjoy the Hellcat. Blah, blah, ya, ya, call us if you need us."

I'm saying the last of that as I hustle toward the pantry. "Let yourself out and lock up. Good luck."

When the three of us step through the other end of the portal and exit the maintenance room in the golden dildo, we snap down to the pub and hear the riotous laughter spilling out into the street before we get to the door.

"Rude. Sounds like they started without us." I release Bruin to join the party.

"Impossible. How can they start without the guest of honor?" Nikon strides forward, and I laugh at the sass in his swagger. Gloriously unburdened Nikon is even more beautiful and lovable than tormented and slightly broody Nikon.

"He's so happy."

Sloan links his elbow with mine and reaches for the door. "Aye, he is. The weight of his wife's death has been lifted, his daughter is here with us, and he finally has the family he's craved his entire life."

My eyes well up and overflow, streaming hot tears down my cheeks. "I'm so happy for him."

Sloan chuckles and pulls out a cotton handkerchief with an embroidered thistle in one corner. "I know ye are, luv. I am too."

We enter Shenanigans II. Liam cuts the music, and my assembled family turns to greet us.

"Oh, man." Jackson rolls his eyes. "Auntie Fi is crying again."

The room erupts in a chorus of laughter.

"Hush now, the lot of ye." Gran rushes over to hug me. "When I was pregnant with yer father, I was a regular weepin' willow fer all nine months. It's perfectly natural. Yer creatin' life, luv."

Da is the next to hug me. "I'm sure it's the hormones, but ye also took a big step today. Ye closed the door on a part of yer life that ye loved."

I shake my head. "Not closed. I told Garnet and Ciara that I'll come if the world falls apart."

Dionysus gasps and frowns at me. "Not in the next four months, two weeks, and three days, you won't. Our baby doesn't want mamma fighting trolls and getting knocked down the side of a mountain."

"*Our* baby?" Sloan chuckles.

Dionysus either doesn't hear him or doesn't care. "Baby Mac wants you to lie in the lounger eating disgusting food groupings while watching rom-coms. Laughter during pregnancy is very good for fetus development."

I laugh. Since Sloan and I announced the arrival of Baby Mac, Dionysus has been tracking the stages of growth and fetal development more than we have.

I finish mopping up my tears and tuck the handkerchief into my pocket for later.

Goddess knows I'll likely need it.

I cast a loving glance over everyone in attendance. Wallace, Gran, Granda, Da, my brothers and their spouses, the monkeys, Liam and Kady, Nikon and his family, Andromeda and Max, Merlin, Patty, Myra and Imari, Dionysus and Jonah, HaiLe and her kids…

I put my fist over my heart yet again. "I am truly blessed. Four years ago, I was blown away when I discovered magic, but the magic we all share has always been with me and is far more powerful."

"Damn skippy." Emmet throws me double finger guns. "Clan Cumhaill for the win."

"Hells yeah," Calum shouts.

"Doesn't get any better," Da adds.

No. It doesn't. "I love you all. Thank you for sticking with me through all the crazy adventures. Thank you for coming to celebrate Baby Mackenzie. And thank you for filling our family with never-ending, unconditional love, acceptance, and a lifetime of laughter."

"Well said, *a ghra*." Sloan kisses the side of my head. "Blessed be, everyone. Slan!"

There's a thunderous round of Irish celebration as Liam turns the music back on. With the Celtic rhythm pulling me into its enthrallment, I sway my hips through the mass of familiar bodies and raise my hands to laugh and point at the baby banner over the bar.

"Welcome to Clan Cumhaill. No apologies. This is us."

ENDNOTE

Thank you for reading *Gods at Odds*, book seven in the Case Files of an Urban Druid series and book twenty-two in the adventures of Fiona Cumhaill and Team Trouble. While the story is fresh in your mind, and as a favor to Michael and me, please click HERE and tell other readers what you thought.

A quick star rating and/or one sentence can mean so much to readers deciding whether to try a book, series, or a new-to-them author.

Thank you.

If you want more adventures with Clan Cumhaill, keep an eye out for the adventures of Emmet and Brenny in book one of the Chronicles of a Hidden City: *Carry On*. It's in the works.

As well, Chronicles of an Urban Elemental has begun. If you want to start on this spin-off series, book one, *Incendio: Flame Born* is on Amazon.

AUTHOR NOTES - AUBURN TEMPEST

WRITTEN JUNE, 2023

And it's a wrap. Twenty-two books featuring Fiona's growth as an Urban Druid. We laughed, we cried, and we fell in love. We fell in love with Clan Cumhaill, the Greeks, and all the characters who needed a family and someone to believe in them.

There are more stories to tell—the reawakening of Isilon, the Dark Weavers, the Crescent Marked kids.

In the meantime, I'm currently working on the Urban Elementals series. Those six books tell the tale of Jules Gagne and her siblings as they discover their destiny. As a Montréal police officer, her elemental powers take hold during the awakenings while the veil is down. If you haven't found them yet, you might be happy to know Fiona, Sloan, Tad, and the gang make appearances in that series as crossover characters. Book one of that series is <u>Incendio: Flame Born.</u>

I've been chatting with the fans on the Facebook page about

Emmet and Brenny having some Cumhaill band-of-brothers adventures. Keep an eye out for book one of the Chronicles of a Hidden City, *Carry On*.

I'm also collaborating with a local writer friend of mine, and we're putting out an Urban Fantasy trilogy about magi in Boston. Those books will be out September/October/November of this year. Book one, *Supernatural Disasters*, is up for preorder on Amazon.

Also, I'm proud to be helping my brother with his first books. Dave has been a fantasy geek and D&D dungeon master since the eighties and has more fantastical ideas than anyone I know. LMBPN signed him on, and I'm helping him find his voice and hone his craft. I'm super proud of him and The Stonecrusher Legacy.

In the meantime, if you want to know what's going on, join us on our Facebook fan page: https://www.facebook.com/groups/167165864237006

Or feel free to drop us a line: UrbanDruid@lmbpn.com

Or follow me on Amazon if you want to be notified of all my Auburn Tempest releases.

Thanks for sticking with me on this incredible journey.

Blessed be,
Auburn Tempest

AUTHOR NOTES - MICHAEL ANDERLE

WRITTEN JUNE 26, 2023

First and foremost, a heartfelt *thank you* for not just reading this one story, but for embarking on the incredible journey of all twenty-two books in this amazing series. You've shared the adventures, the triumphs, and the heartaches of these characters, and I couldn't be more grateful for your continued support and enthusiasm.

A Standing Ovation for Auburn Tempest

I cannot express enough appreciation for the incredible work of Auburn Tempest in bringing this series to life. Her ability to weave her own family dynamics into the narrative has given us a rare opportunity to feel as though we're truly a part of this big, boisterous, and lovable family. Auburn's talent for storytelling has created a world that draws us in and makes us feel connected to each and every character.

That's a hell of a superpower, Auburn!

The Power of Family and Friendship

Throughout this series, we've explored the importance of love, support, and camaraderie among the various characters. These themes resonate deeply with us as readers, as they reflect the very essence of what it means to be human. In our own lives, we rely on the connections we forge with those around us, and it's through these relationships that we find strength, encouragement, and a sense of belonging.

If you don't have it in your personal life, I imagine that could be one of the reasons you are here with us, at book twenty-two. Hell, I have a good family by all accounts, and they aren't like the Cumhaill's.

In the series, we've witnessed the characters grow and evolve, not just as individuals, but as a united family. Their bonds have been tested (a lot. One could imagine Auburn is a bit sadistic), their loyalties challenged, but in the end, their unwavering love and respect for one another has proven to be their greatest strength.

As we bid farewell to this series, I hope that the themes of family and friendship have resonated with you, offering a reminder of the importance of cherishing the relationships we have in our own lives. Just as the characters in the series have leaned on one another through thick and thin, may we all find comfort in the love and support of those closest to us.

Once again, thank you for joining us on this incredible journey, and here's to the power of family, friendship, and the stories that bring us together.

Chat with you in the next book.

Ad Aeternitatem,

Michael Anderle

MORE STORIES with Michael newsletter HERE: https://michael.beehiiv.com/

BOOKS BY AUBURN TEMPEST

Find Me
Amazon, Facebook, <u>Newsletter</u>,
Web page – www.auburntempest.com
Email – AuburnTempestWrites@gmail.com

<u>Auburn Tempest - Urban Fantasy Action/Adventure</u>
Chronicles of an Urban Druid
Book 1 – A Gilded Cage
Book 2 – A Sacred Grove
Book 3 – A Family Oath
Book 4 – A Witch's Revenge
Book 5 – A Broken Vow
Book 6 – A Druid Hexed
Book 7 – An Immortal's Pain
Book 8 – A Shaman's Power
Book 9 – A Fated Bond
Book 10 – A Dragon's Dare
Book 11 – A God's Mistake
Book 12 – A Destiny Unlocked
Book 13 – A United Front

Book 14 – A Culling Tide
Book 15 – A Danger Destroyed

Case Files of an Urban Druid
Book 1 – Mayhem in Montreal
Book 2 – Sorcery in San Francisco
Book 3 – Necromancy in New Orleans
Book 4 – Hazards in the Hidden City
Book 5 – Hexes in Texas
Book 6 – Wendigos in Washington
Book 7 - Gods at Odds

Chronicles of an Urban Elemental
Book 1 – Incendio: Flame Born
Book 2 – Magicae: Power Dawning
Book 3 - Potentia: Bonds Forged
Book 4 - Fidelitas: Trust Realized
Book 5 - Intellectus: Origins Discovered

If you enjoy my writing and read sexy/steamy romance, my pen name for the books I write in Paranormal and Fantasy Romance is JL Madore.

You can find me on Amazon.

BOOKS BY MICHAEL ANDERLE

Sign up for the LMBPN email list to be notified of new releases and special deals!

https://lmbpn.com/email/

For a complete list of books by Michael Anderle, please visit:

www.lmbpn.com/ma-books/

CONNECT WITH THE AUTHORS

Connect with Auburn

Amazon, Facebook, Newsletter

Web page – www.jlmadore.com

Email – AuburnTempestWrites@gmail.com

Connect with Michael Anderle and sign up for his email list here:

Website: http://lmbpn.com

Email List: https://michael.beehiiv.com/

https://www.facebook.com/LMBPNPublishing

https://twitter.com/lmbpn

https://www.instagram.com/lmbpn_publishing/

https://www.bookbub.com/authors/michael-anderle

www.ingramcontent.com/pod-product-compliance
Lightning Source LLC
LaVergne TN
LVHW041905070526
838199LV00051BA/2502